MR. IRRELEVANT

A Novel by:
Jerry Marshall

Published by:
Durban House Publishing Company, Inc.
7502 Greenville Avenue, Suite 500
Dallas, Texas 75231

ISBN
$24.95

Publication Date

Advertising and author tour.

MR. IRRELEVANT

A Novel by:

Jerry Marshall

Introduction

W hen the woman driving that white Cadillac Fleetwood
ignored the stoplight and romped through the intersection at
Brentwood Boulevard and Maryland Avenue, many lives were
changed.

Mine included.

Let me tell you straight and up front: Gambling would be part of
it, along with some broken ribs. And killings. Don't forget the
killings, although even those had twists to them. Mainly, there was
love. Deep, heart-ripping love. Anyway, I'm a sportswriter and
accustomed to writing stories of five to fifty grafs, so I'm definitely
going to be in over my head telling you this story.

Let me first tell you a wonderful idea was conceived in nineteen-
sixty and implemented in nineteen-seventy-six by a man named
Paul Salata. Paul, from Newport Beach, California, had played a little pro football and had made a goodly amount of money after real-

izing he wasn't the greatest pass-catcher to precede Crazy Legs Hirsch and Bob Boyd with the old Los Angeles Rams.

Paul made his money honestly and kept thinking the premium players got all the attention while the marginal players—the grunts, the Corvairs on a Corvette highway—got a lot of nothing. So Paul decided the *last* man selected in the National Football League's annual spring draft of college players would be deemed Mr. Irrelevant and presented the Lowsman Trophy. With the title and the trophy would go a bacchanalian week in Southern California. This would include a parade, a golf tournament, an awards banquet, and, yes, lots of very cold beer and very attractive young women.

Paul's thinking: A player drafted last also would like a trophy. He would deserve a week of revelry every bit as much as that talented guy who had been the most sought-after in the nation.

For the record, Paul Salata's event has raised a tremendous amount of money for charity over the years. He's to be saluted, and his repayment is in presenting the Lowsman Trophy each year to Mr. Irrelevant.

One

We were the only Tenkillers in the McAlester, Oklahoma, phone book and for good reason: We were the only Choctaws in Pittsburgh County who had taken "Tenkiller" as a surname. It's much more Cherokee, but I was told my great-great-grandfather—perhaps add one more great—took that Cherokee name when he headed south from Fort Gibson. Fort Gibson was to Oklahoma's Indian immigrants what Ellis Island later was to New York's Europeans.

Fort Gibson: The terminus of the Trail of Tears, where my ancestor had stumbled across the "finish line".

That ancestor probably was a minor chieftain or something in Mississippi in the days of Peter P. Pinchlynn. I've often wondered if perhaps I'm a descendant of Pinchlynn, the Principal Chief of the Choctaw Republic in the mid-eighteen-sixties.

I'd like to know where I really came from. I've done some homework, and my best guess is my roots are in south-central Mississippi, about eleven miles west of Philadelphia—Philadelphia, where three civil rights activists were murdered in nineteen-sixty-four. There's a Choctaw reservation there, and someday I'll take some vacation time and go down there: head down I-55 beyond Memphis to Lexington, Mississippi, then east to Kosciusko, southeast to State 19 to Philadelphia, then west to Williamsville, and the reservation. Like that. A long trip but worth it to a Choctaw who'd like answers.

But that vacation is a long way off. Meantime, there was Chesty Hake.

* * * * *

I was three years older than Chesty. I graduated from McAlester High four-plus years before his senior season and five years before he graduated. Hake finished at McAlester the same week I graduated from the University of Missouri's School of Journalism and returned to McAlester as sports editor of the *Democrat-News-Capital*. Our paths didn't cross.

I found out from my mom a St. Louis kid was to come play for the Buffaloes, so I kept a loose mental file of his exploits at tiny Blackwater College, because it was less than an hour from Columbia, Missouri. How could I not want to do a sidebar on the first St. Louisan—and first McAlesterite, certainly—to become Mr. Irrelevant?

* * * * *

I parked in a students-only lot adjacent to Blackwater's Donicker Hall and walked into the lobby of the dorm. The first good-sized kid I saw gave me a quick smile when I asked my question.

"Where'll I find Chesty Hake?"

"Oh, that's easy. He's down in The Hole", the kid answered.

"That's our weight room. Go down those stairs over there. He'll be there; he always is."

* * * * *

"No, that's okay, Paul. It's Paul, isn't it?" he asked after lowering the bar full of heavy iron slabs back onto its rack. He reached out his hand. "Today, I'd rather talk than lift, and that's rare for me."

* * * * *

It was somewhat scary, how well Hake and I got along. We had this instant closeness, a warmth I hadn't expected. He suggested we do our half-hour interview at Kotsch & Suda, a takeoff on the Kingston Trio ballad from nineteen-fifty-eight or fifty-nine. Hake explained to me Bobby Kotsch and Kim Suda had been University of Missouri football castoffs who wound up starring at Blackwater and staying to open their spot on the north side of Blackwater. The tables were second-hand-rickety and unmatched, but the pizza was thin-crust and good, the beer was pitchers of Bud at half-price on Thursday nights, and the appetizer specialty was crab *champignon*—stuffed mushrooms—which Hake had taught Kim and Bobby how to make.

A half-hour? Forget it. We ate two large sausage pizzas and two orders of the mushrooms. And we guzzled Bud.

My ten grafs that became twenty-two when Hake was drafted? Hell, I could've written two-hundred this time! The thirty-minute interview over the rickety table became a multi-pitcher evening. We discussed losing relatives in the damndest ways; life for a half-Choctaw kid and for a late-blooming kid; Chesty's scant chance of making the Cobras' regular-season squad; St. Louis as perhaps

America's most ethnocentric big city; David Hake as a shitty role model and absentee big brother; the high incidence of divorce in the sports departments of many metropolitan daily papers; Chesty's *hors d'oeuvres* recipes; early rock 'n' roll; and what the hell, stamp collecting.

We were different, but we had so much in common. A friendship was conceived, carried to term, and born that night.

"Sure, when I went to McAlester High, we had some kids named Deerwater, Pinkwater, Ovalbar," Hake was saying. "That took a little getting used to, I guess. But that's how I knew 'Tenkiller' was Cherokee."

Chesty recited the names of the five Civilized Tribes: Choctaw, Cherokee, Creek, Chickasaw, and Seminole.

"My first brush with small-town America was McAlester," he told me. "Never lived anyplace but good ol' middle-class, middle-America, suburban Brentwood till I moved to Black Mac."

I laughed at the nickname.

"Why'd they call it that, Paul?"

"For the rhyme, I suppose. I mean, the black population always had been minimal, and it's a town that's survived a lot of down periods—black periods. Maybe it's because the sports teams seem to do better when they wear all black uniforms instead of white and gold with black trim."

We laughed, ate, and drank. The next day, I had a terrible time trying to sort out my thoughts. I had to do a two-thousand-word or twenty-five-hundred-word puff piece on Chesty Hake. And I had a terrible hangover. But the beer had been good with the belches to prove it.

* * * * *

By the time I drove the rental car to the Doubletree across from

Weston Stadium the night of the interview, I had some additional ideas: maybe a follow-up piece for *Oklahoma This Month,* a new magazine trying to keep pace with *Texas Monthly.* I was going to write about the Shawnee Hills, molded of deep sandstone, rising gently to the south of McAlester. I thought I would tell about the shallow rivers like the Canadian that seemed tame but actually had powerful big brothers flowing through the sandstone down to sixty feet below the surface, giving us impoundments like the huge Lake Eufaula. Even folks who sing "Oklahoma!" and "The Star-Spangled Banner" before every sports event don't know how Lake Eufaula came to be. Maybe they don't know what an impoundment is.

And then, just before I fell asleep, I thought about what America eats for starters, appetizers by region or interest or ethnic group or income group. I could have some fun with that. Onion rings, French fries, hush puppies vs. tater tots, mini-pizzas, St. Louis' own toasted ravioli, then the more pricey things, most of them involving fish or seafood. Or *pâte.* Or chicken livers wrapped in bacon. What's the name for that? Hell, unlimited potential.

But not in McAlester. Like the little Italian community of Krebs, across Bypass U.S. 69, McAlester eats lamb fries. I, too, loved lamb fries, and I should have mentioned Pete's Place to Chesty. But I fell asleep before I could turn on the bedside lamp and grab the Doubletree note pad.

* * * * *

How about this for inspiration? The next morning, while waiting at the bank of elevators, I looked out the eight-foot windows, across I-70 to Weston Stadium, adjacent to the Chiefs' Arrowhead Stadium. With that vista, I forgot breakfast. I went back to my room and wrote (not the headline, mind you):

**Former Brentwood Star Has Gone
Long Way To Be Cobras' Surprise**
By Paul O. Tenkiller
Staff Writer

How does it feel to be forever known as Mr. Irrelevant, recipient of the Lowsman trophy?

Great, if you're Chesty Hake of Blackwater College and the last guy selected in this year's National Football League draft.

Consider: You're Jud Breden, an offensive tackle from Kutztown State, the next-to-last player taken this year. Your chances: nil. Now, if you're Chesty Hake...

The new Kansas City Cobras are very likely to cut you after rookie weekend, rookie camp or mini-camp. Maybe you'll make it to mini-camp, what with that great first name.

Consider: You're Chesty Hake, a fullback from tiny Blackwater College, and the last player taken in this year's NFL draft. The expansion Cobras are very likely to cut you before you ever knock shoulders with another NFL player. But first, as Mr. Irrelevant, you'll be quoted in *Sports Illustrated, People, The Sporting News,* and *USA Today*. Then you'll be given a red-carpet reception and be toasted and entertained for a week. Included in Irrelevant Week will be a celebrity golf tournament.

Consider: Would you rathe Breden, the next-to-last player plucked in the draft, or Hake? Chesty, a one-time Brentwood High star, is a special guy—merely by one pick.

"I'm very flattered, obviously," he said in response to the special-guy question.

A stocky little fullback from an NAIA school of about seven-hundred enrollment riding one of life's quirky perks. Chesty Hake, five years removed from stardom at Brentwood High, is going to...

* * * * *

My story went on another nineteen-hundred words, and I guess I knew—I guess I kind of figured—I had martyred him. The power of the printed word or whatever. Maybe it was all set there, jumping off the keyboard, slugging words onto page: the killings, that heart-ripping love.

Two

Bobo Lowe checked in at One Stadium Drive. His report carried excitement for the first time in years. He rambled. He had worked as a scout for several NFL teams over a couple of decades, but now he brought warmth to a chilly Kansas City Saturday.

"This Hake kid's got as much want-to as I've ever seen, I tell ya," said Bobo. "This kid, shit, there's some boogaloos in the Hall of Fame never had as much want-to as this Hake kid's got. I say we wait till the final round, then we pounce on his ass. Nobody else'll go after 'im. He ain't gonna cost us nothin'. The commissioner said we get to draft first and last every round, right? So it ain't gonna be bad for our P.R. people to have this year's Mr. Irrelevant."

"Irrelevant" came out as "Rellavin."

"You'll get the papers and the TV's from here and St. Loo, Springfield and St. Joe, Topeka and Wichita. They'll all be in here to take a look at this last kid—the *last* kid. That's always big with them guys, y'know. Hell, Topeka and Wichita and Omaha and Des Moines,

Tulsa—I mean ever'body loves a underdog, don't they? And this little Hake fella is one of them underdogs that's gotta lotta want-to, I tell
ya. He'll fuckin' scare some folks on a football field come trainin'
camp."

Boy Boyajian, the Cobras' scouting director, tried to bring Lowe
back to his senses.

"Yes, we're drafting first and last in every round, Bobo."

"Then let's go ahead and make Hake this year's Mr. Rellavin," the
grizzled scout bellowed.

Boyajian's fatigue showed. He ground a finger into an eye socket.

"All right, damnit, what does this Hake look like? What does he
look like *now*, not what did he look like during the homecoming
game last October? And don't bullshit me."

Dickie (Boy) Boyajian hadn't closed his eyes for more than a few
minutes at a time in twenty-four hours and didn't want any surprises
as the two-day draft neared. Boyajian had been embarrassed in the
past with other teams: selections that should have made a team good
within three or four years went bust. This time, with the expansion
team, he wanted no bullshit from scouts bent on bringing NFL glory
to pet territories: places like Knoxville, Tennessee, and Norman,
Oklahoma, and Tuscaloosa, Alabama. Scouts see this savvy work as
their stepping stones to jobs as scouting directors and assistant general managers.

Those are nice billets. Two or three smart recommendations and
you're a hero. Boyajian's scouting trail had taken him to Grand
Forks, North Dakota, Cedar Falls, Iowa, and Fort Collins, Colorado,
to find players who became solid NFL players. But this day, Boy was
a tired guru.

"Lemme say it again: What does this Hake look like?" Boy bellowed. "We're running out of time! You blow any smoke up my ass
and we're gonna go with the fast-but-bad-hands kid from Jackson

State!"

"Boy, listen to me. Are you listenin'? My guy'll play sixty-one minutes every game. I told you that for—for a good part of a year now. His name's Chesty, and he's—he's funny-lookin', I guess. He five-foot—hell, you've got his stats. And you know it was a new-coach, new-offense situation over at Blackwater. All he got to do was block. But he blocked like a sumbitch: ninety-two, ninety-three percent every single game. I tell ya: He wants to play sixty-one minutes a game. Boy. I say: Draft 'im!"

* * * * *

"With the final selection of this year's National Football League draft, the Kansas City Cobras select Chesty Hake, fullback, Blackwater College."

"Awright!" Bobo Lowe yelled. "We did the right thing, Boy! That little shit may never see a goal line, but I promise you he'll *bend* some people a whole lot bigger than he is."

Bobo knew he shouldn't go on. He shut up.

"And?"

"Okay, he's top-heavy. He's got no ankles and no butt. Thighs like a twelve-year-old's, but they're real strong the whole game. I guess he runs no better'n a four-eight-two forty on a really good day. He's not much taller's five-eight, and he's got skinny wrists with great big arms. Bench presses four-hunnert-twenty pounds as often as he wants, and he scored twenty-eight, I b'lieve, on his ACT tests. The sumbitch listens to marches and patriotic shit in the dressing room before a game. Oh, and his brother was a fag tight end at Mizzou and with the Bears for a while."

Everyone in the draft room, fourteen men, looked at Bobo Lowe. Variously, the faces showed awe, disbelief, dislike, betrayal.

"Oh, and he's selective 'bout his women."

"Thanks, Bobo, you've filled in all the blanks—just a little late, maybe."

Three

The NFL's annual draft of college players is unique. Baseball has two drafts each year, and, frankly, nobody seems to give a damn about them. Most of the selections never are announced. Other major sports conduct drafts, but the impact on the lives of the fans seems minor league by comparison. The NFL's talent bazaar is a capital "D"—the Draft—and the first day of the two-day, nationally televised event is capital "DD": Draft Day. Sports editors of most newspapers plan well in advance that their top story on Draft Day is going to be pro football in April.

So it was that on a lovely, pungent Monday morning in April in St. Louis the early crew in the paper's newsroom crowded around the TV set. The Draft: Everyone even slightly interested knew a quarterback from Stanford—yet *another* quarterback from Stanford—would be the first player selected. The reaction was nonchalance. But there were lots of surprises ahead.

"Everybody knew he'd go number one," said Ben McVey, the

morning copy chief. "If the Forty-niners hadn't taken him, they'd have been shit in the Bay Area. Cincy wouldn't go for him, probably, but the Raiders would've."

"Yeah, I guess you're right, Ben. I guess you're right."

My mind wasn't on McVey. It was on the TV screen. The Bengals would take the full fifteen minutes allowed before making their first choice. Much of that period had me nodding as McVey continued to assess the draft as only a Notre Dame graduate will do.

"Now, if Cincinnati takes the kid from Nebraska, then I see the Raiders going to my Notre Dame guy," McVey said. "Hell, we always…"

Why do they always have to beat on a poor sportswriter? I wondered. Shit, sportswriters never even finish in the money in the one-dollar office pools. Secretaries or Notre Dame graduates usually claim the sixty-four dollars.

The Cincinnati Bengals did take the All-American running back from Nebraska as the second choice, and then the Raiders—denied that Stanford quarterback—made a six-foot-six, three-hundred-pound defensive tackle from Notre Dame their first-round pick.

To escape McVey's whooping, I went to the Sports Department, fired up my computer, and worked some early copy. Young guys on every big paper in the country have to work early slot, I told myself. I punched up the wire service listings of the deaths of celebrated persons, looking for sports figures' names. The only one of any consequence for me was an infielder who played for the St. Louis Browns shortly after World War II. A two-graph item for Sports Shorts on page two, I figured.

"Another of my guys!" came McVey's big voice from thirty feet away. "The cornerback goes to the Dolphins! Hell, we may have *four* go in the first round!"

I tried to concentrate on my screen. My Missouri Tigers, who I had covered for two seasons while in J-School and working for *The Missourian*, would have no one selected this day. You can't lose nine of eleven games and have many players worthy of the NFL draft. But I didn't yell it back to that obnoxious McVey.

Because of the pressures of television, the NFL halts the first day of the draft in time for what those eunuchs in New York call "the news block." In other words, the draft is discontinued at six p.m. on the East Coast, five p.m. in our City Room, three p.m. in the draft rooms of the Chargers and the Forty-niners. The NFL seems comfortable with that, and it allows the Sports Department in St. Louis ample time to do a couple of sidebars and what we call "react" stories. That's the local side of the draft, not what comes down the Associated Press wire from New York, not the syndicates' stuff that has greater appeal for small papers.

The second day of the draft is different. The draftees' schools tend to be Northeastern Oklahoma and Simon Peters instead of Southern Cal and Alabama and – screw you, McVey – Notre Dame. A drafting team is allowed five minutes, not fifteen, to make each decision after the third round.

I again had the early duty in the Sports Department, but at eight-fifteen that Tuesday I noticed I was the only person interested. McVey's Notre Dame blue-chippers all had been claimed.

By mid-afternoon Tuesday, when the commissioner told us the league's brand-new team, the Kansas City Cobras, had selected Chesty Hake; the newsroom became noisy again – all thanks to Chesty and me.

* * * * *

I returned to my desk and told the slot man, Jim Calvin – the assistant sports editor and another Notre Dame alumnus – I'd like to do a sidebar on the selection of Hake, what with his Brentwood back-ground and our McAlester background. Good links, I felt. I explained the St. Louis connection.

"Ten grafs maximum," said Calvin. "I'm tighter than a nun."

"Ten it is," I agreed. "But I bet you'd let me go twenty if it were a Notre Dame story."

"Eight grafs!" Calvin snorted. "Make your calls up to Blackberry or whatever it is. I want – I want your shit from Blackberry right away. And Tenkiller, we're really, really short on space today, so no more than twenty grafs. Hear me?"

* * * * *

I tried Chesty's room number. I tried the third-floor-east number at Donicker Hall on the Blackwater campus. I tried again and again and became more frustrated each time, aware I had been given a ten-graf grace for my story. Still nothing. I tried the athletic department and the coach's office.

Finally, I kowtowed to the deadline clock and wrote around the absent quotes. That was no problem, really. I knew a great deal about the Cobras' final draft pick, thanks to a note from my mom and dad years earlier, telling me a St. Louis kid had moved to McAlester and was quite a player. The two-column headline on my sidebar read:

Ex-Brentwood Star Taken
By Cobras in Final Round
Under my byline were twenty-two grafs. I led with:

> Chesty Hake, a record-setting tailback for the Brentwood Eagles five years ago, was an award-winner in the National Football League draft Tuesday.

He was Mr. Irrelevant.

* * * * *

My twenty-two grafs must have been good. The following day, Jim Calvin, a.k.a. "The Dragon" and "The Pride of South Bend," said "Tenkiller, I'm glad you're in early. Go see Florence and get some money." He cleared a throat that didn't need clearing. "I want you to go to Kansas City and do a good-sized piece on that Lowsman kid – your Mr. Irrelevant. The people upstairs liked the piece you did yesterday, so go see Florence."

"Who upstairs really liked it?"

"Dickinson," he told me too quickly. "He grew up in Brentwood and graduated from Blackwater College. Does that answer all your questions? Wait. It was Wilkinson."

Jay Wilkinson was an assistant managing editor, seldom seen by new people in the newsroom.

"This is what makes my job so damned tough," Calvin lamented. "We're short on people all the time, and now we find a little fat running back at Blackberry College. . . Shit!"

I was jittering.

"Look, Paul," Calvin said, calming down, "that guy upstairs feels a truly perverse love for your Hake kid. Go to Kansas City. Get lots of money from Florence. And spend two or three days with Hake at that college.

"I want you to fall in love with Mr. Irrelevant. Find out what he's all about, how he feels about the distinction. And just think: A couple of three-hundred-pound assholes were taken just ahead of this Hake kid, and only 'bout eighty of these hundreds of kids are ever gonna play in a regular-season game. Really. Think about that. And then consider it an honor Wilkinson wants you to do a good piece on this kid while he's still around. I'll give you six-two-and-one-even he won't be around in September."

"You wanted me to keep that other story to just ten grafs, Jim, and now you want me to be just a three-hundred-dollar-a-day whore?"

"No. But Walter fucking Mitty upstairs sure does," said Calvin. "You gonna fly or drive?"

"Drive, probably. On the way back, I can do something for the Travel Section. How 'bout: 'I-70 Saloons That Don't Serve Notre Dame Fans'?"

Calvin got a pained look.

"Go see Florence. You're wasting my time."

Four

Chesty Hake's father was C. J. Hake, and C. J.'s house always stood out on middle-class Salem Road, Brentwood, Missouri. While most of his neighbors added a third bedroom to their bungalows, C. J. chose to maintain his two-bedroom, full-basement plan. And while most of his neighbors drove Dodges or Buicks, Chesty's dad drove a series of Cadillacs.

But for good reason. C. J. Hake was a general agent for Cadillac Mutual Life Assurance Company, which had a long-standing and wonderfully effective motivation plan for its agents. An agent could own any model of Cadillac for little or nothing, depending upon performance, years with Cadillac Mutual, years attaining Million Dollar Round Table and number of agents recruited.

* * * * *

It was easier for Chesty to call C. J. in McAlester than it was for the senior Hake to call his son in a dorm.

"C. J. Hake."

"Dad, its C. J. Jr."

"Hi, son! What's up?"

"Dad," Chesty said, "I turn twenty-one next month, and I've never had a car. When Sara and I go out, we go in her car – the car her father gave her. So I want to earn a car, and I want to drive a Cadillac. I want to *earn* a Cadillac."

"That's terrific, son!" C. J. said. "I know what you're saying."

"I'm going to St. Louis the day before my birthday, and then I'll take the insurance licensing exams on the twenty-sixth. I'm not going to have any problems with ' em, Dad. Hell, after all those Saturday mornings I went down to the agency with you, I could've passed those exams before I had my first pimple."

"Okay, kid, here's the deal: You get your complexion and your mind clear, go to St. Louis the twenty-fifth, and take the exams the next morning. I'll drive up. We'll go to Statler Cadillac that after-noon and then get a suite at the Ritz-Carlton. We'll celebrate with a couple of big filets and a bottle or two of Merlot. But keep in mind you're not driving. I can afford the car, but I can't afford to let you get a D.W.I."

"I'll pass the exams, Dad, and I've got only one more exam here at school. It's not until the twenty-eighth."

"Chesty, you're making me very happy, and I haven't been happy much lately," the elder Hake admitted. "And you're going to deserve a Caddy."

C. J. hesitated.

"Look, this Mr. Irrelevant thing. You embarrassed by it?"

"With all these interviews and the attention? Are you kidding?" Chesty's voice lowered. "Joke's on them, Dad. Fact is, I'm in. And I'm going to turn a few heads."

"Good boy."

* * * * *

"Find one you want," C. J. told his son. "But use good judgment, for Hake's sake."

They laughed. Chesty had heard his dad use "for Hake's sake" and "for the sake of Hake" for many years when C. J. did business on the phone.

At Statler Cadillac, C. J. dealt with the seventy-year-old general manager, which indicated what kind of deal they struck. While doing the paper work, they mused about how far Cadillacs had come from the days of tail fins.

They agreed to leave the two-year-old burgandy Eldorado for cleanup, and Chesty would pick it up late-morning the next day. C. J. pressed hard on the signature line as he wrote the check.

* * * * *

Just days after Chesty Hake turned twenty-one he got himself into trouble. At the end of his freshman year, he returned to campus driving a slick and sleek Eldorado.

He tried to call Sara but got a busy signal. Within a half-hour, Sara had been recruited by a dozen or more friends and football fans to confront Chesty at Donicker Hall. People needed to know about the Cadillac. Had he opted for an early entry into the National Football League draft at the insistence of an unscrupulous agent? Or had this scholar-athlete taken a dive into the murky, quick-riches pool of drug dealing? The people imploring Sara to answer their questions needed to know. After all, not many Cadillac Eldorados grace a quiet, Christian, grant-in-aid campus like Blackwater College.

"Sara, I promise you: My dad bought it, and I know he got a great deal on it," Chesty told her when finally they were face to face. "The guy at the dealership has been a client of my dad's for something like twenty-five years."

Sara explained the Eldorado on campus. Nothing to be alarmed about. There was no scandal at Blackwater during Finals Week.

But one big, imposing woman wanted to hear the explanation first-hand. Dean of Students Willa Rawlings – an Orson Wells look-alike – summoned Hake to her office just as he was about to head for the dorm's cafeteria.

"Mr. Hake, are you going to be here at Blackwater College for another two or three years?"

"Yes, I think so, Dean Rawlings. I hope so."

She stared at him. "Let me re-phrase my question, Mr. Hake: Do you plan to enter the NFL draft before you've completed your senior season with us?"

"No, but obviously you've heard about my car."

"I have. Not much escapes the dean of students on a small campus. You returned from St. Louis today driving a luxury automobile. Does that seem strange to you?"

"Dean, I can explain."

He did.

* * * * *

"Chesty, I shouldn't tell you this," Dean Rawlings said, "but my husband and I both have Cadillac Mutual policies. Wimmer Hale in your Kansas City agency is my agent – and my brother. He, too, drives a Cadillac."

"So we're okay?"

"We're okay. No infraction. Nothing in your file."

Hake left the dean's office and headed down the creaky, bowed, circa eighteen-ninety-one wooden staircase, then back to Donicker Hall.

* * * * *

Chesty was notified by the State of Missouri that he had passed his licensing exams. The Department of Insurance showed no concern he was only a college sophomore-to-be. The department didn't know Hake had been picking up the business since he was eleven, when his father became a widower and began taking him to his little agency most Saturday mornings.

* * * * *

Hake's junior year was a fairy tale, the best a young man could dream of. He and Sara, whom he dubbed Jumpshot, planned to become engaged, and they talked of marriage with – well, with any-one who would listen to them.

Jumpshot averaged six and a half points, seven rebounds and almost five blocked shots a game. Chesty ranked third in the nation with eighteen-hundred-twelve yards rushing as Blackwater went eleven-one before losing in the quarterfinals of the National Association of Intercollegiate Athletics playoffs. C. J. Hake came for both Parents Weekend and Homecoming, and he seemed to fall in love with Sara Aron Kassel as quickly as Chesty had.

"I had hoped your folks would be here," C. J. said to Sara during Parents Weekend.

Their absence – no, Hy Kassel's absence – made it all the richer a weekend for Chesty.

God, he felt strong! He put on a show for Sara and his dad when he ran for two-hundred-fifty-five yards and four touchdowns in a forty-fourteen rout of Culver-Stockton College.

But the wine of Chesty's junior year turned to vinegar before his senior year began. He knew from the first hour of the first practice of that meltdown August. Camelot no longer was in his ZIP Code. A new coaching staff meant new ways of doing things.

Coach Jon Barton came to Blackwater from tiny Mule Deer Community College in Texas. He brought with him his son, a quarterback who was a sophomore-to-be. Within the first hour of that first practice, nobody missed seeing it: the kid's All-American arm. Blackwater's powerful running game, with Hake as the engine, was going to be Blackwater's showy passing game with Johnny Barton the showpiece. It would be Johnny Barton's arm, not Chesty Hake's legs, that would land Jon Barton a big-time college job a year hence because he could bring with him a quarterback with NFL potential.

Barrel-chested Chesty, who gained more than eighteen-hundred yards as a junior, gained seven on the one carry to open his senior season. On the other hand, he graded out at better than ninety-two percent: effective on thirty-eight of his forty-one blocking assignments. Thank God for Buzzard Baird, back in McAlester his senior year in high school.

"Get this, Chesty, and remember it good. Some are born to be heroes in this game, and some are born to block. You're a blocker, an infantryman in the trenches."

"Got it, Coach."

"And another thing: Running backs are real vulnerable to injury. Blockers can go on for eight, ten seasons. Got it?"

"Got it, Coach Baird!"

* * * * *

Who cared if Hake carried the ball only once in that first game? Or just four times in the Homecoming loss? At least he didn't have to feel mainly responsible when the Blackwater Blazers won six games his senior season, not eleven or twelve.

And not responsible for the downfall of Coach Jon Barton, although Hake could have pointed out to him Johnny the Arm was not Johnny the Academician. Johnny won six games, attended seven classes and cost his father one career.

Meanwhile, Chesty began his upward climb on grit and tenacity, driving that barrel chest and those powerful and curiously skinny thighs of his. Who could have guessed how that trajectory would go, arcing down towards a silenced pistol? A silenced pistol, a pistol with a silencer? Jesus Christ!

Five

Hake told me he cried every night for a month when he learned his father was moving his Cadillac Mutual Life Assurance agency to McAlester. In southeastern Oklahoma? What kind of football could they play down there? Seven-man? Eight-man?

The night C. J. had to break the news to his son, they went to Randazzo's on Brentwood Boulevard and ate steaks. Eating out a night in the middle of the week? Chesty knew something was wrong. Then his father whipped out the Arkansas/Oklahoma AAA highway map and put his finger on McAlester. Chesty told me he refused to cry before they left Randazzo's.

"Eating like this, that kid of yours is gonna be something this fall, Mr. Hake," said Ronnie Carola, the owner, as C. J. silently accepted his change. Chesty already was in the parking lot. "Careful now."

"Yeah. Thanks."

* * * * *

C. J. and Chesty moved into the rented ranch-style home on Carol Drive in mid-July, just about the same time the all-seeing McAlester School Board hired a football coach named Dewey Armstrong Jr. Actually, the board hired the coach and recruited his seventeen-year-old kid quarterback, the pride of White Shoe, Texas, in a single transaction.

So the emphasis suddenly wasn't on the second-best running back in St. Louis; rather, it was on the second-best quarterback out of Texas. There were no battle lines. The McAlester Buffaloes, for two decades a run-run-run team, were going to throw the shit out of the football. And Chesty, if he wanted to play, would have to pass-block. Or be just Hake, the bench-sitting transfer kid from up in St. Louis.

Coach Armstrong planned to make McAlester a one- or two-year stop. He was determined to eventually be a college head coach, and he was convinced the wonderful passing arm of Dewey III would allow him to leapfrog. After all, he would take with him to a prestigious job the kid known to the rest of the players as "Dewey Three Sticks." The Buffs would throw, and Hake would block – or else.

The coach arrived so late in the summer the school board renewed the contracts of all three assistant coaches, including line coach Buzz Baird. Thirteen years later, infantryman-in-the-trenches Hake and Baird continued to exchange Christmas cards. Baird had been a blocking fullback at Northeastern State in Tahlequah, Oklahoma, and his older brother had been an NAIA All-American at Blackwater. Northeastern was a nationally ranked small school virtually every year, rife with running backs. Forget Northeastern. But Blackwater?

* * * * *

Hake was going to walk the mile to the offices of McAlester's school district administration.

"Want me to drive you over? Want me to go with you? I probably should, I guess," C. J. Hake said.

"Naw, Dad, you have plenty to do setting up your office. I'll be all right. I'll call if I need for you to come over."

"Okay. I guess I need to keep in mind you're nineteen years old – not eleven."

Chesty knew all too well why his father had picked age eleven as a reference point. It disturbed the demons, but then they settled. Chesty headed from the east side of McAlester to the north side.

Inside the school building, he should have stopped at OFFICE OF THE PRINCIPAL, but didn't. He walked to the ATHLETIC DEPARTMENT door at the other end of the hallway. A burly, red-faced man was ending a phone conversation.

"Yeah, yeah, I know," Hake heard just before the phone thudded down.

"Coach Armstrong?"

"No, I'm Coach Baird. And you?"

"Coach, I'm Chesty Hake. I'm transferring here from Brentwood, Missouri, for my senior season – my senior year." Chesty was angry with himself over the slip. "I thought I should check in to find out what kind of summer program I should be doing."

Baird liked Chesty and appreciated his discipline; that Chesty had come to the Athletic Department before even stopping at the principal's office to enroll. Baird also told Chesty his "Mr. Touchdown" role was going to end, what with the arrival in McAlester of the two Dewey Armstrongs.

Hake and the hefty line coach spent two hours talking across the counter, with the coach nervously looking up to make certain the door reading ATHLETIC DEPARTMENT remained closed. By the time they concluded their first meeting, Hake knew precisely what he had to do before mid-August – and where he might play his college football.

"It's a fine little school where you probably could play, Hake, judging from what we've heard about you," Buzz Baird told him. "But you've got to do everything you can to improve your game while you're here in McAlester. You gotta widen your scope. You're a one-dimensional player. You gotta learn how to block effectively if you're even gonna play here."

Baird looked nervously at the door again.

"I'll work with you," the coach whispered. "You're a kid who should play, but you already know about the new regime around here, don't you?"

"You mean the new coach and his son?"

Baird nodded

"I don't even know you yet, Chesty, but I like you," the assistant said quietly. "You just show up tomorrow morning, okay?"

"Coach, I'll be there early."

* * * * *

Probably in violation of state high school rules, Baird met Chesty at six-forty-five at Eales Stadium turf those mornings. By the time Buzzard finished with Hake each morning, the kid was stronger, meaner, tougher, more eager and more knowledgeable about the ways of football. He knew how to duck the six-foot-six defensive end's sweeping, menacing forearm, how to dodge the "crab" moves or "spin" moves of a linebacker trying to get to the quarterback, how to make his helmet a veritable arrowhead when a strong safety wanted to mince the sneaking quarterback at the goal line.

The morning before two-a-day practices began, August fourteenth, Chesty and Baird met at Eales Stadium. The time was six-thirty-eight. Hake had on the helmet and undersized shoulder pads Baird suggested he wear for their unofficial summer clinic. Baird wore his customary uniform for collisions: chinos and an undersized black-and-gold BUFFALOES golf shirt. No pads. No helmet.
Baird was that tough.
For three weeks of workouts, Buzzard committed serious violations. But then, nobody but groundskeepers was supposed to be on the Eales Stadium turf those mornings.

"No work today, Chesty," Baird said. "You're as ready as I can get you. You're tight now. You know everything I know about being a fullback – a glamorless fullback." He punched Chesty's upper arm. "Your technique is terrific. Hey, I'll be on your ass every afternoon from now till November fifteenth, but that'll be just to keep you sharp. Wish I had eight others like you. Shit, *I'd* be the next head coach at Oklahoma Tech! It wouldn't be Dewey fucking Armstrong Jr., I promise ya that."

Chesty thought about this. "But when the games start, it's still gonna seem strange pass-blocking, not carrying the ball very often."

"You're time will come, believe me. Meanwhile, let's look at these blockin' schemes I've drawn up here. Then I want you to go home, put on some decent clothes and spend a coupla minutes thinkin', reflectin' on what we've done this summer. And then I'll pick you up about eleven-fifteen and we'll go find some lunch at the Copper Kettle. If I'm in trouble with the State of Oklahoma for workin' with you, then I might as well buy your lunch and make it official.

"Shit-far," Baird went on, pronouncing "fire" as "far." "I'm prob'-ly gonna git farred anyway, but who gives a shit. Let's have a good lunch."

"Thanks, Coach," Hake said. "You ain't gonna git fired – farred. I haven't told anybody but my dad you've been working with me. And I don't really know many of the other players."

* * * * *

Chesty was glad he and Baird got to the Copper Kettle before eleven-thirty, when the rush began. They ate chicken-fried steak and the specialty, a salad of corn, black beans, diced red onion and strips of red bell pepper, with a sweet dressing.

"Miss," Chesty said as the beefy coach was paying the bill, "could I have the recipe for that salad? I like to cook. Always looking for good recipes."

Baird put his wallet back into his pocket and looked at Hake.

That was the same Buzz Baird who, just five months later, would be charged with sexual abuse. Chesty told his dad – emphatically – Coach Baird never, never had done anything to suggest sex abuse or homosexuality. Chesty said he'd certainly be willing to testify to that. He owed Buzzard that.

"No! Absolutely not!" C. J. Hake told his son, speaking louder than he had in years. "You don't owe him anything."

Baird lost his job in McAlester, of course. But he wound up as the offensive line coach at Arkansas Tech in Magnolia. Chesty read about it in the *Democrat-News-Capital.*

And then Chesty went off to Blackwater College in Blackwater, Missouri, a twenty-year-old who was a fine running back and a true technician as a blocking fullback. He later realized he had no regrets, other than he had not testified at Baird's trial. But, hell, on the witness stand, Chesty Hake probably would have told the court the Buzzard had committed a different wrong: making a blocker of him.

Six

If you're huge, quick, strong, fast, disciplined and impervious to pain, you might – *might* – have a chance at being something more than fodder in an NFL training camp. Otherwise, forget it. You're wasting your time. As different as Big Ten Conference ball is from high school competition, the NFL is that much higher again. Only the best of the best of the best – and only the ones with a tremendous pain threshold – make regular-season rosters.

Granted, not many Lowsman Trophy winners have made it into the big-time. But by the same token, there've been a dozen or more Heisman Trophy winners who've fallen by the wayside. For a twenty-two-year-old behemoth to be a first-round draft choice is not a ticket to success in the Ultimate League. So many times I checked The Associated Press wire at about ten or eleven a.m. for NFL transactions, only to learn a first-round pick had left camp, failed his physical or been declared physically unable to perform.

That made Chesty all the more remarkable. If he stood six-three, weighed two-fifteen and ran like the proverbial wind, that would have been one thing. And he didn't come out of a traditional football school like Ohio State, Nebraska or Penn State. This was a plodding kid, soon to turn twenty-four, a guy shorter than five-nine on a good day, coming out of tiny Blackwater College.

Small wonder Hake was a hot media property during the Cobras' first training camp his rookie year. He was a ready-made story for all the other would-be Mr. Irrelevants who read a morning paper or watch the ten-twenty sports segment.

Every kid ever to attend an NFL camp was a hero in a previous life: in college, junior college or high school. But nobody is a hero when he arrives at his first pro camp – even an expansion team's.

And how did the Cobras come about, especially in a "small market" city like K.C., when the Chiefs had been an established club for more than three decades? Money talks, and really big money screams, that's how. W. W. W. Weston, with about a billion of his four billion dollars, fairly screamed at the commissioner and more than three-fourths of the club owners at an emergency meeting in Miami.

W. W. W. had tried in vain to buy the Chiefs. He was sure his native, beloved Kansas City considered him a laughingstock, unable to buy the only thing his life lacked: a pro football team.

So he agreed to build a beautiful domed stadium and, by the way, throw about eight-hundred-million dollars of real estate wealth the owners' way. The Chiefs voted against Weston's application, naturally, but with large money it can be a fuck-you world.

* * * * *

Teams used to have ninety or more players in camp for the first full week in July. Nowadays, it's eighty maximum. Each player gets more work, and – bottom line – the expense for training camp is greatly reduced. Fewer dorm rooms, smaller quantities of food, lessened laundry requirements.

But that first full week: That's when the fun begins. The guessing game begins then, too. Most teams cut to seventy healthy players for the first pre-season game. A week later, for the second exhibition game, most clubs reduce to sixty-five. Then it's sixty for the third and fifty for the fourth – the final – tune-up game. And then a lot of very fine athletes spend a few days looking over their shoulders for "The Turk," the bearer of bad news.

It's one of the best quote weeks of a pro football writer's year.

Chesty Hake was not at all prepared for the frenetic pace required that fateful final week of the exhibition season. But, he thought, at least I haven't been cut – yet. Shit, I'm still here. I'm still here!

An experience that stood out during that anxiety-with-a-capital-A week was a visit from Delaney. He was a bluff, Irish, no-first-name ex-cop now working for the league's security office, and he was accompanied by two foils from the FBI.

Even the dumbest hammerhead of a player stayed awake through *that* meeting. The subjects were spicy: gambling, booze, drugs, prostitutes, AIDS, confidentiality and other matters that could be an embarrassment to or a problem for the team or the league. There were a lot of don't and a few do's. A few historical names were brought up: Paul Hornung and Alex Karras for gambling in the early sixties, a quarterback who was a big-time gambler and pissed away a career *while in prison*, a wide receiver who slit his wife's throat after finding her in the sack with a coach, the quarterback who blew up a TV reporter's car in Phoenix – just to keep the media troops alert. Yeah, Delaney spun a good yarn. But even he might have pissed at a pistol equipped with a silencer.

The foils from the FBI warned Hake and the rest to use good judgment because, each season, billions of dollars are gambled on the NFL, billions of dollars are doled out for illicit drugs and hundreds of pro players make love to women – or men – to whom they are not married. Then there was: "All of this is bad, bad, bad, and you must not do it." Some of the Cobras had heard this spiel by FBI guys a dozen times or more while with other teams. Delaney from league security let the FBI duo have their say.

When they turned the microphone back over to Delaney, he said, "Just don't fuck up, guys."

"Whoa, man, yo' strong!" said aging offensive lineman Ol' Muldrow.

* * * * *

Schenley, Hake's roommate, was a good kid with pro potential. He was the Cobras' choice in the second round of the draft, a nervous guy form Auburn who never gave a college degree a thought after gaining eleven-hundred yards as a fourth-year junior and almost a thousand as a senior. Schenley could memorize his playbook, but his mind wandered easily and often. Usually back to the security he had known in Petal, Mississippi, "poplaysun eight-eight-hunnert," where his papa owned the "Chivvy" dealership and nearby Hattiesburg had just about everything a man would ever need or want. Hattiesburg was a long way from Room Eleven-Seventy-Seven of the Hyatt Regency in San Francisco.

Hake, propped up by two pillows on his bed, sensed his roommate's uneasiness.

"You okay, Schenley?"

"Chesty, I'm skeered," Schenley blurted from his chair at the circular table. "I ain't ne'er been skeered before. Never. Not even at Auburn. Not even when we went over to Tuscaloosa and lost to

Bama my freshman year. But I'm skeered now. I ain't shit in two days, maybe three. Can't even eat nothin'. I'm weak. I'm really skeered, Chesty. What's gonna happen to me tomorra night? If I screw up . . ."

Chesty put down his playbook. He realized how different he was from the handsome, down-home kid sitting across the room from him.

"I wish I could be scared, Schenley," he said, looking at the loose-leaf page of Xs and Os and arrows. "But I can't. I had to quit being scared when I was eleven."

The young man who would be Schenley Chevrolet down in Petal, Mississippi, couldn't possibly understand, wouldn't want to understand. Too dark, too foul, too depraved. Anyway, he wasn't around the next week for an explanation.

Seven

C. J. Hake looked over the patio to the pool, making mental notes as to what needed to be done before the warm weather – swimming weather – arrived in McAlester. He could hear the hooting of a foursome playing the ninth hole at the country club, a few hundred yards south along the ridge from Carol Drive. Hake had joined the club upon moving to McAlester, thinking it would be good business.

He came to realize he had played only three times and needed to make better use of his membership. He had to. When Chesty came back from college in a month, they would play. That way, he wouldn't embarrass himself when he teed it up with Dr. Ruppert or Dr. Stith. And it would be good for Chesty to have a change of pace before he headed off to the Cobras' training camp. Yes, C. J. must play.

The phone jangled in the kitchen.

He knew the caller would be his son – his younger son, his *only* son, really. He realized he and Chesty hadn't talked since the evening

Chesty returned to Blackwater from the Cobras' rookie indoctrination weekend. And here it was, the first of May. Shit.

"Hello there," C. J. said cheerily.

"Hello, Daddy," came David's voice.

That mince.

"David," C. J. replied, hoping his other son, calling from Chicago, wouldn't sense a father's disappointment. "Everything all right up there?"

"Oh, yes, we're fine." The plural pronoun was intentional, a reference to David's longtime lover, Rory Rifkin. "You haven't called me in ages, and I was concerned about down – down there."

"Doing fine, I guess. Keeping busy. New clientele. When you rang, I thought it might be Chesty. Haven't heard from him since his K. C. weekend. Busy, I guess. Finals coming up soon. He's got to make good use of his time."

Silence ran down the wire.

"Daddy, I want to talk to you about my life insurance policy. Have you—"

"Sure, David, I'll be glad to go over it with you," said C. J., irritated by the change of pace. "Come to your brother's graduation on the twenty-ninth of this month, and we can give your situation a good, long look. How does that sound?"

"I don't want—"

"What you don't want doesn't mean shit to me, David!" C. J.'s tension broke free, but he checked that the sliding glass door was closed. "You *need* to be there, David! We'll talk about your policy, but it's very important to me you see your brother graduate. I brought him to *your* graduation, dammit, and he didn't want to be there. He was just a little kid. He's your *brother*, for *chrissake*, and you don't even know him. He's not the football player you were, maybe, but you're going to be there at Blackwater on the twenty-ninth."

"Yes, Daddy," David answered, his voice weak.

Brilliant football prospect but gay. Hard to believe.

C. J.'s plan was to fly from McAlester to Tulsa and on to Kansas City International, where he'd have a small white limousine – a *small* white Cadillac limousine – waiting. He'd meet David and Rory's flight from Chicago. Rory must come, too. David insisted, because he knew some fine antique shops in central Missouri and the Kansas City area. They might stay over.

C. J. wasn't certain the quiet little county seat of Finneal County was ready for a white Cadillac limo, much less the threesome that would arrive in it. His mind raced as he began to hang up. He didn't hang up.

"Sure, David, if you and Rory want to stay over and shop, that's fine. Just rent a car in K. C. when we get back there. I'll have to get back to McAlester for my work. Oh, and David, there won't be any problem with your life insurance situation," C. J. said. "You can tell Rory that."

"Fine. Bye, Daddy."

And then C. J. Hake, the little man with big secrets, began to chuckle. The chuckle grew to a belly laugh. Demons take many forms.

He dialed Brad Quinn, the rental car service on Carl Albert Parkway. Brad himself called back within forty minutes to confirm C. J. had a small white Cadillac limo reserved at Kansas City International Airport for Saturday, May twenty-nine, to be ready by eight-fifteen a.m.

"We stand behind our guarantees, Mr. Hake."

"That's why I called you, Brad."

Demons hidden away in platitudes.

* * * * *

"How far to Blackwater?" David asked repeatedly, looking around the limousine, then at Rory.

"Forever," C. J. Hake said, tapping the accelerator.

David and Rifkin had quit cooing about the fine, fine Martha Washington they bought in Rocheport, and now the three of them were on their way west on I-70.

A car weighing five-thousand pounds, traveling at between eighty-five and ninety-five miles per hour, is a spectacular sight when it bursts through a guardrail. This car, pure white, swan-dived onto a government-funded walking trail, pitched downward but refused to explode until it was ready to bathe in the Missouri River.

* * * * *

EDITOR'S NOTE: Nobody bothered to tell Chesty, dammit! Why not? *Why not?* I'm not asking that rhetorically; I want to know. He went through baccalaureate and graduation ceremonies looking for his father. The hell with David. They never had been close, and David had been an NFL near-hero long before he had learned to mince, long before Chesty would be an NFL joke. Chesty was sure his father would attend the ceremonies. But there was no sign of him. May twenty-ninth: a big day.

You've studied hard and think you knew just about everything there is to know. Then you find out you've gained a diploma and lost both a father and a brother.

But Chesty would be all right. He would not starve. A great football player? No. Emphatically, no. But he knew the address in

Clayton, Missouri – and the phone number, too – of his father's attorney, J. Billy Wingo.

* * * * *

My paper didn't much care about the triple-fatality accident. Virginia Rockefeller Hake had been dead thirteen years, and C. J. Hake had been of a Brentwood stripe. His clientele was not elite Ladue or Clayton or even transient Chesterfield.

So the three-column headline in St. Louis read:

Ex-NFL Star David Hake, Father
Killed in Spectacular Car Crash

Meanwhile, *The Kansas City Register's* treatment was something like:

Father, Brother of Cobras' Hake Killed

And *The Chicago Tribune* put things into a Windy City perspective with a three-column headline:

Ex-Bear Hake Killed in Car Wreck

However, the fatalities didn't leave *The New York Times* as grieved as they did others. The headline on Page Four of the sports section told readers:

David Hake Dead;

Ex-NFL Player

* * * * *

EDITOR'S NOTE: It's strictly
ter of perspective, Chesty should have known. He
shouldn't have been upset. *The New York Times* honestly didn't care about Chesty's dad or brother, and
The Kansas City Register my one-time employer -
–really didn't care much about it because, truth be
told, he hadn't done shit for the Cobras yet.

* * * * *

Here's how the crash story went out of the Associated Press bureau in
Kansas City, with embellishment from stringers in Columbia and K.
C.:

By THE ASSOCIATED PRESS
COLUMBIA, Mo. – Former university of Missouri
tight end David Hake and his father, a one-time
insurance executive in St. Louis, were killed when
their rented limousine went through a guard rail on I-
70 and tumbled into the Missouri River west of here
Saturday.
The Missouri Highway Patrol reported that a passenger in the limousine, Rory Rifkin of Chicago, also
was killed in the crash. The deaths brought to one-
hundred-fifteen the number of fatalities reported on
Missouri roads this year, five below the total at this
time last year.
Highway Patrol spokesman Lt. Wesley Ferrenti said the rented
white Cadillac limousine, driven by the senior Hake, was traveling at
a high rate of speed. Hake and his two passengers reportedly were
going to the graduation from Blackwater College of C. J. (Chesty)
Hake Jr., son of the driver and brother of David Hake. Chesty Hake,

recently drafted by the expansion Kansas City Cobras of the National Football League, was unavailable for comment Saturday night.

The Highway Patrol estimated the limousine was traveling at eighty-five to ninety-five miles per hour when it veered sharply to the right and tore through the guardrail just east of the bridge over the Missouri, approximately ten miles west of Columbia. A driver who had just been passed by the vehicle speculated the senior Hake may have swerved to avoid hitting something on the pavement.

The limousine tumbled over the steep limestone bluff, flipped several times, exploded into flames and came to rest half-submerged in the river. Highway Patrol investigators determined that all three occupants, wearing seat belts, were killed instantly.

> Chester Hake Sr., sixty-two, was a general agent in St. Louis County for Cadillac Mutual Life Assurance Co. before opening an agency for that firm five years ago in McAlester, Okla.
> His wife, Virginia Rockefeller Hake, was murdered thirteen years ago at their Brentwood home. That killing wasn't solved until three years ago.

David Hake, thirty-nine, a former first-round draft choice of the NFL's Chicago Bears, had been an antique dealer in Chicago after a brief pro career. Rifkin, forty-four, was his business partner in a fashionable North Side shop, according to a spokesperson for the Illinois State Police.

> Missouri Highway Patrol investigators said they were trying to determine why the limousine, rented at Kansas City International Airport that morning, was westbound instead of eastbound on I-70 when the crash occurred.
> "He (C. J. Hake) may have missed the Blackwater

Turnoff," said the Highway Patrol's Ferrenti. "That's all I can think of."

Eight

"Chesty, it's obvious ya already know, said Finneal County Sheriff Weeb Houston, fifty-five and hairy-chested. "But it's still ma duty to tell ya."

"Thanks, Sheriff."

Weeb Houston, a former Blackwater football and baseball player, had been more than an hour late in breaking the news to Hake – intentionally.

"I know this hurts you, too," Chesty said. "And you didn't even know my dad."

"Or your brother, son. Or the other fella in the car. But you've spent four years being one of the most prized citizens of Finneal County, Chesty. We never had a single complaint ' bout ya or any trouble at all, and we 'preciate that, believe me. Hotshot football players can be a problem, y'know. Sure, you know. I'd guarantee you've drunk a few beers in these four years at Blackwater. Yeah, I'd guarantee that."

Hake knew the sheriff was having a tough time being the sheriff instead of a fan.

"It's okay, Weeb," Hake said. "My dad – I mean, these things happen. You just hope they won't."

"Thanks for bein' that way, Chesty," said Weeb, perspiring but obviously relieved. "And hey, boy, I talked with Phillip up at Crowell's Pharmacy the other day. Phillip says you're gonna fool people and be real good for them new Cobras. So don't get your dauber down, son – whatever the shit that means."

Chesty managed a smile.

"Oh, and Chesty? One more thing: You make the openin'-day roster, kin ya leave me two tickets at that new stadium in K. C.?"

"Sure, Weeb. No problem."

* * * * *

Barbara's typing and computer knowledge were atrocious, but her numbers weren't.

M   r

CIIIIIIIIIIIIIIIIIIII

IIIIIIIIIIIIIIIIIIIII

IIIIIIIIIIIIIIIIIIIII

Chester J. Hake Jr.
C/o Kansas City Cobras, Inc.
One Stadium Drive
Kansas City, MO 54001
RE: CMLA1821177   INSURED: David R. Hake

Dear Mr. Hake:

Please accept our condolences on the death of David Rockefeller Hake. We are pleased to let you now the settlement of policy CMLA 1821177 has been

approved.   Our check in the amount of
$1,326,003.77 is enclosed. The total amount payable
is $1,326,003.77, which includes interest on the
death proceeds from the date of death to the date 4e
SETTLEMENT AT THE RATE OF/.8888
SETTLEMENT rate of 7.75%.
Sincerely,

Barbara Stppanoa PhickersonBarbara
   Th farBdasbaaa
Fra

* * * * *

The cover letter in the second envelope had been prepared by
someone with reasonable skills. The key numbers were $455,661.11
and $500,000.

Nine

"Look at this, Turk," General Manager Shel Bergman of the Cobras said to the head coach. "This Hake kid is going to be good. He doesn't like repetitive commercials on radio or television, and he doesn't like being cut off in traffic. This kid's gonna be a special teams kinda player, I promise you. I'll betcha next week's paycheck he makes the club."

"I don't see him making it to September tenth," said Head Coach Turk Madigan.

The executive and the coach spent the next hour reviewing the psychological profile of the strange kid they had taken as the last choice – the butt boy, Mr. Irrelevant – of the collegiate draft. The Cobras admitted they had taken a chance in drafting Hake. However, they also knew the selection of a stubby fullback from a nearby school - The little shit should be good for some interesting newspaper copy," as one assistant coach put it – would keep the media people from probing such things as anabolic steroid use, D.W.I.s, paternity suits, spousal abuse, date rape, and the like.

But Hake came to rookie camp and then early training camp certain he was something more than fodder. He came to endure pain, work himself to exhaustion, and make the team. Simple as that.

*   *   *   *   *

Big business goes to extremes to protect itself. The NFL is big business. Just as HUT-HUT follows HUT in a quarterback's cadence, it figures the NFL will protect itself. Therefore, it figures each team will protect itself.

The Kansas City Cobras already had. As a new kid on the block, even Chesty had been put to the test without his knowledge. The league office had a couple of notes about the sexual persuasion of HAKE, DAVID ROCKEFELLER. The HAKE, CHESTER J. (CHESTY) file made mention of his having been held back twice in elementary school, his uprooting to Oklahoma, his transformation from star to grunt both his senior year in high school and his senior year in college, the deaths of his parents and brother (see HAKE, DAVID ROCKEFELLER), the dissolution of his college romance. But Chesty, as a rookie, had a file that was, at this point, still thinner than those of most NFL players.

After all, Chesty never had been in trouble with the law, and the NFL didn't yet know of death benefits totaling more than two-point-two million dollars from three insurance policies. And there would be money coming eventually from David's antique business, in that both he and Rory Rifkin were dead. Ah, but the NFL would find out, and Hake's file would thicken. Very little escaped those people at Four-Ten Park Avenue, ZIP One-Oh-Oh-Two-Two. And what got to Four-Ten Park Avenue soon would cross the desks of at least a couple of people who walked through the new double doors at One

Stadium Drive in Kansas City each workday and most weekends.
No, there aren't many secrets in the NFL.

* * * * *

General Manager Shel Bergman, Scouting Director Boy Boyajian
and Head Coach Turk Madigan had watched hours of tape of their
draft choices, and now they were down to Mr. Irrelevant, Chesty
Hake. Scout Bobo Lowe got the tape from his longtime buddy, Babe
Burda, an assistant coach at Blackwater College. The quality was not
good.

Bergman, exasperated, turned off the VCR and did a thumbnail of
Hake.

"Family man?" Turk asked.

"No, but he'll be twenty-four at kickoff in September, not twenty-
one or twenty-two. He was held back twice – yeah, *twice* – in grade
school. He was that small and that traumatized."

"He was what?"

"Traumatized. He had problems."

"Shit, you get me a little *nudnick* who's five-feet-seven, got
an I.Q. of thirty-six, and you want me to say nice things 'bout 'im
when *The Kansas City Register* does a thing on 'im during training
camp? That's what you want? You're outta your fuckin' mind, Boy.
You too, Shel. Why do you want to embarrass me like this?"

"One-thirty-six, Turk," the general manager said.

"What?"

"Hake was a late bloomer. Boy and I knew that going into the
draft."

Shel talked softly. Good modulation was important when dealing
with coaches. "His profile says he's willing to give up his body to get
the job done, so he's a special-teams kind of player. Oh, and Turk? I

wasn't kidding about that number: one-thirty-six."

"That really is his I.Q.?" the coach asked, incredulous.

Boy chimed in. "Yeah, and just for drill, he scored a twenty-eight on his ACT the first time he took it and a thirteen-thirty on his SAT. You're gonna want to keep this kid. Last round or not. He's had his problems, but who hasn't?"

"What kinda problems?"

"I just told you, Turk. Get a copy of the backgrounder on him. You should've read it two weeks ago, anyway."

Bergman got impatient and stood up.

"Turk, I don't have another hour to spend on this Hake situation. I'm not asking for a starting or second fullback. Just give him a chance to earn a hat." Bergman used "hat" for "helmet." "And Turk, you really haven't heard about Hake's situation, I guess. Shit, his father and his fruit brother got killed on his graduation day."

The coach stared. "How the hell'd that happen?"

"Check the backgrounders we prepare – or even read a newspaper now and then. Back in May, when that limo went into the river off I-70? That was the Hake kid's father and brother and some other strange duck. By the way, the brother was David Hake. Remember him? Played for Chicago some years ago? And Mizzou? Tight end?"

"Oh, yeah," the coach said.

"Gay."

"What?"

"Hake's brother was gay – a legendary fruit, as I hear it," said the general manager. "However, this kid shows no indication of being the type to cop a knob. He and a big, tall woman basketball player were a steady item on campus for four years, the backgrounder says.

"Look, Turk, the kid's a gamer. He gets geared up listening to patriotic music on his Walkman before games. The backgrounder says he likes 'Battle Hymn of the Republic' by the Mormon Tabernacle Choir, and 'This is My Country.' Give him a taste at full-back, but work him hard on special teams. He'll wind up killing somebody, I can almost promise you."

"Ah, shit," Turk said.

Bergman paused.

"He's no family man. And maybe that's good."

Ten

The call to the law offices of Melvin I. Gross & Associates on the twenty-second floor of the Gladstone South Tower forced an immediate fire alarm up there. After all, Hyman Kassel and Mel Gross had been best friends for over forty years, for thirty-nine Florida vacations, for a half-dozen *bar mitzvahs*, for one *bath mitzvah* – that of Sara Aron Kassel – and Hy Kassel hadn't had even one legal problem that couldn't be resolved in those forty years.

Chesty marveled at that when Sara told him of this wonderful efficiency, this wonderful dependability.

Sara told him, and they both had good reason to hate Mel Gross.

* * * * *

"Mel Gross."

"Melvin, it's Hy. Hey." Kassel kept talking, the rhythms of a forty-year association kicking in. "I gotta problem with Sara. She wants to marry this *goy* fucker the Cobras just drafted, the one she's been going with I don't know how long. It's truly driving me – well, he's not us, Mel. He's a football player, of all things!"

"Hy, what should be the problem?" the lawyer asked. "Think it through. It could be the social wedding of the year in Kansas City. As a rookie even, if he makes the club, he'd make four, maybe five times the money he would as a young lawyer with my firm. Cost you a lot of money, though, if she marries him, Hy."

Gross was having fun.

"Bunch for *shekels* for the wedding, I mean. Anyway, what do you want me to do about it?"

Gross knew the purpose of this phone call. He had been expecting it for a year or more; at least since the Hake kid said even a Little All-American wasn't going to sell cars for Hy Kassel.

"Hey, I don't mean to impose, Melvin."

"You're not imposing."

"It's sensitive."

"So talk to me, Hy."

* * * * *

When Melvin Gross called Lake Lotawana that same July day – a day neither Hy nor good wife Lotzey would pick up the phone – and suggested he and Sara get together in his office at nine-thirty Tuesday, she knew it couldn't be I'll-call-you-later. The only thing to know that July Monday was the suite number on the twenty-second floor.

Sara shuddered. She knew what was being said, if only by implication. She knew Chesty's chances of making a career of pro football were minimal at best; they had wrestled face-to-face, eye-to-eye, gesture-to-gesture with that. But they hadn't considered having his slim chance go to zero if his leg were snapped in an alley or a dark parking lot. They hadn't considered the effects of third-degree burns from a car bombing. And they hadn't considered there were people who would say Hake's death at eleven-twenty-nine a.m. was something that happened one minute before a tuna salad on whole wheat was going to be ordered.

Sara knew she must back off. Tears burned, but she had to back off. She was overmatched, she knew – a big, strong young woman but a captive, a slave. Chesty was a powerful, powerful little man but a reject, a pariah.

As I learned much later, Sara grew nauseous in that twenty-second-floor suite as she realized she hated her ersatz Uncle Mel as much as she hated her father. But she was resolute. She wasn't about to get Chesty maimed or killed. She wasn't ever going to let someone say: "He might've made it with the Cobras or some other team if it hadn't been for . . ."

She loved him too much. So she had backed off and forced Chesty to do so as well.

But first, there had been a quick walk on that silver gray carpeting on the twenty-second floor of the Gladstone South Tower. In the well-appointed bathroom, Sara vomited.

At least she wasn't forfeiting her legitimate shot at her father's estate.

"I cleaned up the toilet."

Mel Gross nudged her toward the door. "Forget it."

When Sara got on the elevator, she planned her final call to Chesty. She knew she would go from the sour taste of vomit to the salty taste of tears.

But she'd get even. She'd get even, by God! After all, she knew Goose from her drug-and-sex days at K.U. And Smokey, a longtime employee in the paint shop at her father's dealership, knew "some people" who backed up threats with terminated relationships. Sara would get even with her father for this, money no object.

* * * * *

Good ol' Uncle Mel: The asshole had spent almost a half-hour making it very clear to Sara she was going to become the ex-girl-friend of Chesty Hake.

"Has he, uh, violated you, dear?" Gross asked, being as delicate as a lawyer about to threaten death or maiming can be.

"The answer is 'no,' Uncle Mel, and I hope that's disappointing to you and Daddy, too. I got 'violated' – as you put it – a lot of times when I first got to college. Several, anyway. I want you to look my father in the eye and make sure he knows Chesty and I have *never* made love. *Never!* Because that's the truth. We've talked about it a lot, believe me, but it's never happened. He loves me."

"I understand, Sara, but – but you know your father."

Melvin I. Gross, attorney at law, took a well-planned deep breath. He then went on to explain to Sara that she never again was to see Chesty, would be disowned if she tried to, and never again would be allowed to see her mother. Lotzey Kassel would become a true cap-tive.

"And I certainly would worry about your football player's well-being, Sara," said Gross, pinkie ring catching the sun. "His chances of earning a position with the Cobras could end precipitously. And you know your father."

Before she could plead, Gross told her she should never be respon-sible for Hake's fate. The words were bludgeoned in. She rose to leave.

"He might've made it with the Cobras if it hadn't been for . . ."

* * * * *

Hy Kassel, with Gross's tape recording in hand, started in on his daughter.

"Yes, I'll tell you why I don't like your *goy*. I *can't* like that *goy*. Right? I mean, think about it, Sara: You spent your freshman year flunking out of Kansas by playing basketball and taking drugs and fucking *goyim*, right? Am I right? Did that hurt? Did that hurt me, Sara? And then this stumpy little – *agghh!* He doesn't love you, Sara. He just wants to be able to say: 'I fucked this tall Jew broad from Kansas City.'"

"We've never -"

"That's all," Kassel went on. "He just wants to poke fun at me. He's really no good, Sara. He's not right for you. You can do better. No, you *have* to do better! That's my order!"

Hy Kassel had done his damage. As he reached the door of Sara's bedroom there in the house butting the shoreline at Lake Lotawana, he turned and glowered. Then he slammed the door on his way out.

Sara lay on her side, tears hot.

"Quit saying *goy*," she said to nobody.

* * * * *

When Chesty Hake talked with me, he said he had had no choice but to confront Hy Kassel. He felt the feelings of a hate-crime victim; he was being persecuted because he *wasn't* Jewish! Or was it, in Kassel's eyes, no man was good enough for this towering redhead he'd sired? Chesty had to find out. He chose as his venue the opulent office just off the showroom floor of Hy Kassel Motors.

A salesman in a tan gabardine suit stood between Chesty and the door to Kassel's office – but for only a moment. The door to the

office was ajar – but again, for only a moment. Then it opened nois-
ily. The salesman went through the doorway on the fly, ahead of
Hake. The car deal Kassel was negotiating with an Asian couple fell
apart right there. The salesman looked helplessly, apologetically at
his boss. Then he was guiding the young couple out of the office.

The door slammed. Some waited for a gunshot or at least the
sound of furniture breaking, but the confrontation was limited to loud
voices and lasted two minutes. Anyone listening heard some key
words: "screw," "*goy*," "jackoff," and, interestingly, "love."

When the office door opened, Chesty strode out and Kassel followed closely. After all, it was his dealership.

"You want Sara to have a husband you can control," Chesty said,
turning back. "You want that carrot in front of your used-car salesman. 'Hey, Marvin, you could run this place someday if you let me
rule your marriage.' Well, Hyman, I'm not your Marvin, and I'm not
a car salesman. And I'm not going to convert to your religion."

Chesty wanted to rip into him, no shoulder pads, small or otherwise. Just hit, double him over, and make him puke out his guts the
way Sara had hers in Uncle Mel's john. It was quiet on the showroom
floor as Hake strode out the glass doors. Salesmen returned from the
service garage and paint shop. The sales manager ventured from his
office, which was fist-proof if not bulletproof. Two bookkeepers
compared notes from a balcony perch.

* * * * *

"Kansas City Cobras. May I help you?"

"Yeah, this is Hy Kassel from Hy Kassel Motors. I've been a fan
since the Hank Stram days with the Chiefs, but I wanna stop my season ticket order with you people. Put me through to somebody who
can handle this."

"Yessir," said Shular the Receptionist, never one to roll over. "One moment, please."

Eleven

As an expansion team, the Kansas City Cobras went through a difficult first year. Nothing seemed to go right: the college draft, trades, free-agent acquisitions, cuts, hirings, media relations, the vagaries of the schedule. Behind those big wooden doors at One Stadium Drive, east of K.C. on I-70, there were frequent utterances of "How the hell. . . ?" and "Why us?" and "Jesus bleeping Christ!"

The Cobras were the stepchildren of the NFL. Gonna play the one-and-seven Patriots in the ninth week of the season? Naw, not the Cobras. They get to play the defending Super Bowl champion Bears, thanks to that master plan of the schedule-maker. A banner unfurled at Weston Stadium one Sunday read:

IF YOU LOVE THE COBRAS,
GET A BLIND DATE

* * * * *

Chesty bought ninety-nine-oh-nine Kingsbury Boulevard, Clayton, Missouri 63105 shortly after his rookie season. And shortly after that, it was agreed I would move in. I became a sounding board in his second season.

"Sure, I hate losing," Chesty said, resting his elbows on the breakfast table while I popped him a beer at nine-thirty, six hours after the Cobras had been beaten by a lackluster San Diego team. "But what choice do I have? If I'd gone to a winner last year, I'd be out of football by now, Paulie."

"Yeah, you're right."

"Hell, I could tell you stories about Loose Cannon," Chesty said, referring to the Cobras' quarterback. "In team meetings or even on the sideline during games, he'll use 'okey-dokey' instead of 'yes' or 'right' or even 'yeah.' Just 'okey-dokey.' Can you trust your offense to a guy named Loose who says 'okey-dokey'?"

Hake paused momentarily.

"And how 'bout our backup center, T-A-C-O-B-E-L-L, pronounced Ta-CO-bul, not to be confused with fast food? You see why I like to come home to sanity and spend Mondays in my own house, don't you, Paulie?" Chesty finished the can of Bud.

"Yeah, sure," I said. "But don't you think every team has its cretins? I do. Hell, I see it in my sports department. We've got a guy who had sons playing against each other last year. One kid played center for Cottage Hills High, which, you may recall, has green and gold as its colors. The other was a linebacker for Nixon Academy, which, you may not recall, has purple and white as its colors. So this dumb-shit father showed up for work at the paper that all-important Friday wearing a green golf shirt with a gold logo. And what do you suppose?"

"Purple slacks. Maybe a white logo on the pocket."

"There you go." I added: "He wasn't sent out to cover that game."

Chesty went to the refrigerator for more beers.

* * * * *

He was so regimented I could look at my watch or up at a wall clock and say on a Sunday evening: Chesty'll be here in eight minutes, maybe nine.

A game with a twelve-oh-three kickoff at Weston Stadium could be expected to end between three-twelve and three-seventeen, depending on the score and if the opposing team was a run-oriented or pass-oriented team.

Because Chesty didn't give interviews, he would be one of the first players to complete the painful, smelly regimen of peeling off tape and removing braces, supports and padding. Tape was to be wadded and thrown into one bin, numbered neck collars and lightweight casts into another. Jerseys and pants here, sweatshirts and stockings over here, cups there, jocks in this one, T-shirts and sweat socks over here, numbered, and dentist-fitted appliances in this container for sterilization.

Then, the showers.

A few players shaved before heading for the stadium on game day, but most waited until they had the haven of the media-off-limits shower room to remove the nasty, mean, rough-cut look. Chesty was of the majority who went to the stadium clean-shaven, and one time he explained that preference to me.

"Some game, I'm going to be the 'up' guy on eight punts and have to make seven tackles. Then, in the same game, on punt returns I'm going to have to block on five of them and run one kick back fifty-two yards for a touchdown. On kickoff returns that day, I'm going to stumble into the dressing room too tired to shave. And then I drive back to St. Louis? No, that's why I shave before I go to the ballpark,

Paulie."

We laughed at this pipe dream. This time I got the beers.

Still, I knew within ten minutes when Hake would return from K. C. after a home game. Consider:

With the game over at three-seventeen, he'd pay his respects to players on the visiting team and leave the field at three-twenty-four, be out of his uniform at three-thirty-five, swallow three Tylenol at three-thirty-six, be out of the showers by three-fifty, be dressed and coifed by four-ten, finish talking with the trainers and doctors about bumps, bruises, and any possibly significant injury by four-twenty, be out of the steaminess by four-thirty, pick up a special teams game tape in the front office and exit the players' parking area of the Weston Stadium complex by four-forty-five, meld into the eastbound traffic on I-70 by four-fifty, stop for gas at Warrenton by seven-thirty and put his Jaguar in our garage by eight-fifty.

The first beer was gone by the time our grandfather's clock struck nine.

Which reminds me . . .

DO NOT OPEN

Contents: Remains of Native American

Below the Kriegshauser Brothers Mortuaries logo was stenciled: Property of Kriegshauser Brothers Mortuaries

The reinforced stainless steel container with its Styrofoam lining was home to an iced-down six-pack of Budweiser. Open the phony lock, pull a fresh can, replace a dead soldier, and latch the phony lock. It was as good as the tape recordings case. Interesting contents there, too, I was to find out. Instead of classic folk music, a pistol.

Chesty, fortunately, never got stopped by the Highway Patrol or representatives of any municipalities through which he rolled. Instead, he continued to dash at eighty-plus across I-70. Again and again.

"If I ever get stopped and get asked to open that damned cooler, I'll just tell the cop it's against the law because it contains the remains of an American Indian. I'll explain to him it's a very sensitive thing right now. Then I'll tell him HUT-HUT on my license plates has something to do with a medicine man."

"You shouldn't be driving – day or night – drinking beer," I said, too rigorously. "If I did that and got caught, I'd be a former sports-writer and about seven-hundred bucks lighter."

"Okay, Paul, if I offend you and your heritage, I'll get a different cooler. I'll get one that says COLD BEER on the side. Believe me, the last thing I want to do is offend you."

He called me "Paul" instead of "Paulie," and that's what stung. We didn't discuss it again. And we never discussed the tape record-ings case, the sinister one.

* * * * *

EDITOR'S NOTE: Why did Hake insist upon dri-ving those two-hundred-forty-five miles from Weston Stadium to Kingsbury Boulevard almost every Sunday night during football season? Hell, how could he?

"It keeps my body from tightening up so fast," he once told me. "As soon as you get out of the shower or the whirlpool, your muscles start tightening. A guy who plays on Sunday, goes home, eats, then goes to bed is a zombie on Monday. That's why Turk tells us to come in and get treatment and our paychecks on Monday and come back Tuesday ready to have meetings and practice. It takes that long to recover. But I drink a few beers on the drive back here, have a cou-ple more when I get here and then I seem to have recovered – physi-cally – by the time I get up Monday morning. That's the secret. Hey,

I almost always run or do some lifting, don't I? The drive home is the secret. That's my secret."

* * * * *

My loyalty to Hake gets me upset when I read some guy bench-pressed four-hundred-fifty pounds. Usually, it turns out the young stallion got lucky once, had help getting the weights back on the rack, and went immediately to his school's sports information director or his NFL team's media relations director to tell of his wonderful accomplishment.

Chesty Hake was different. He benched four-fifty every Tuesday, Thursday and Friday during the season, and he did more than just one or two repetitions. He once did twenty-nine reps with two-twenty-five, which is the NFL's pre-draft weight measure. No, not twenty-nine; usually eighteen, twenty, twenty-two, depending upon the player's size.

Nobody in the Cobras' weight room would challenge him for money. No three-hundred-pound lineman would want to do four-eighty, only to have that stumpy little third-string fullback do three or four reps at the same weight – for ten-thousand dollars per.

"No, man, that's a no-win," said an offensive tackle named Big Ocey. "I can't be losin' big money to you. Hell, I'm gonna wait till you' gone home fo' I do my liftin'. I lose money to you tonight, I'm sleepin' ' lone tomorrow night."

Chesty's strength was useful to me. I could tell him we needed to move a davenport and I'd get on one end of it, and he'd say: "No, I'll get it. Just tell me where you want it." Smucker's Raspberry Preserves or Pace Medium Salsa jars opened with a flick.

Since neither of us was a father, we frequently talked about how we would handle that role. Chesty was scared of fatherhood. But it was a way of getting him to talk about Sara.

There was the time he had that critical beer: the ninth, when he should've stopped at eight, or fifth, when he should've quit at four. I asked him what kind of husband he would've been to Sara and what kind of father he would've been to their children.

"Turble, turble hubband," he responded, "turble."

I pressed him about fatherhood and hit a nerve that hadn't been dulled by beer.

"Paulie, you're turble. If Sara an' I'd gotten married, there would-n'ta been any kids. I promise ya. I'm too strong. Or the kids woul-da had a mother dishplen 'em, an' a father – wish his goddamn hands in his pockets."

He paused.

"Outta fear, Paulie."

It was remarkable how Chesty could sober up when he had some-thing   significant   to   say.

"Mrs. Magoo down the street spanks her kid, and the kid cries," said Hake. "That's the desired effect for spanking. Make the kid cry and he'll know whatever he did or said wasn't acceptable. The kid gets sent to his room, and he's allowed to come out an hour later. Whatever. That's not unreasonable punishment. No permanent dam-age done."

I watched him. I didn't want my beer.

I knew some self-recrimination was about to thud into my lap. Could I handle it? Hake was sober. I waited.

"Now, let's take Mr. Chesty Hake. He comes home on Sunday night after doing his job: three hours of frustration and pain on the field and the sideline, and there are a couple of hours of exercise and practice before that. And there might be some kind of physical ther-apy session at the end of the day because Mr. Hake hurts so much.

"Mr. Hake arrives home just in time for one of his kids to throw a temper tantrum. Mr. Hake really doesn't need to hear this shit right now and isn't going to put up with it. Enraged, he decides to spank the kid. But he's two-hundred-twenty-eight pounds of muscle, anxiety, aggression, and frustration. And then the kid suddenly has an arm that makes a strange crunching sound and never will swing normally again. And the kid also has a hip that has to be reattached at St. Louis Children's Hospital.

"Now, Paulie, you still wanna know why that jackoff of a father – *me* – wouldn't want children? He stood. "Goodnight, Paulie."

Twelve

Chesty so much wanted to play running back – and so seldom got the chance – he didn't even mind running a play called Twenty-Three Stick something-or-other in the Cobras' playbook, just so he was in the game. With this play, the designated running back slides out of the backfield after pretending he missed a block, races exactly six yards downfield from the line of scrimmage, then makes a sharp cut across the middle to take the pass.

Late in the Denver game the third week of the season, quarterback Loose Cannon called Hake's number for this precision-timing pass play. Chesty knew he would take a brutal blow to the back. He didn't care.

* * * * *

Uuh . . . uuh . . . uuh . . . uuh . . . uuh . . .
That was his breathing as he sat across from me at the breakfast

76

table Monday. I looked at a man who could do nothing but pretend to read the paper. I wondered: How the hell did this man drive four hours home last night? It wasn't that six-pack hidden in the Native American remains cooler that sustained him.

Huh . . . huh . . . huh . . . huh . . .

The Cobras won, surprisingly, but the blue and orange Denver helmet found Hake's ribs. Two cracked. It was some hit.

Every player on the field heard, and Hake went flat.

Then began the *huh . . . huh . . . huh . . .*

Cracked ribs are like broken toes, he told me; they're taped but not set, and then the hope is the healing process can begin and the injured will stop saying "*huh . . . huh . . . huh . . .*" Chesty played on a couple of the Cobras' special teams the following Sunday. How, I can't tell you.

* * * * *

Chesty Hake's best seasons with the Cobras were his fifth and his sixth, when he was the most effective special-teams player in the National Conference. He excelled on all six special teams: conversion, field goal, punt, punt return, kickoff, and kickoff return. On the punt team, he was the "up" back, the unit's quarterback, and he called the snap cadence in every punting situation in every game those two seasons without a single screw-up. Yet he played for a non-winner and in a small media market, by NFL standards. He was overlooked both years for the Pro Bowl, the NFL's all-star game.

At the conclusion of each of these two seasons, when he learned he had been passed over; he got quiet for a few days. He became impatient with me and was hypercritical of insignificant things. One morning, he was reading a little eight-graf story I had written. His comment: "You misspelled 'expatriate.'"

I hadn't.

Hake's seventh season was a level below. He missed a couple of games with a partially torn biceps, and when he played, he failed to execute as he had in seasons past. He got moody, and frequently the atmosphere was uncomfortable at Ninety-nine-oh-nine Kingsbury Boulevard.

Then came his eighth and final season. There was something very, very different about him from the start, and it took me some time to discover the reason. It blew open my life – several lives. Actually I didn't discover it; it was thrown at me. He didn't tell me until I confronted him after the fourth week of the season.

I was late slot that Sunday, also known as the first of October in some circles. It almost was one a.m. when I got home, and I knew Hake would've been in bed two or three hours by then. I would have to wait until morning to get his slant on the Cobras' lopsided victory over Cincinnati. But I knew from wire service accounts and the accompanying statistics his contribution has been minimal.

At breakfast Monday, Hake's mood was dark. We read the paper in silence that first Monday in October, but as we finished breakfast I could wait no longer. I had to know. I didn't want to share that house with anybody but Chesty. Sorry, no demons welcome.

"Chesty, what's the matter?" I asked as emphatically as I dared. "Why are you so different nowadays? Is it because you're coming down to the end of your career?"

He just stared at me. I took our breakfast dishes and went to the sink to rinse them.

"Whatta ya weigh?"

"Two – two-fourteen. So what."

"This time last year you weighed two-twenty-six or two-twenty-eight. You're scaring me, Ches. What the hell's happened? You say it's not the ribs or any other injury, so what is it?"

He looked past my shoulder at the wall clock, as if he could escape on some time limit, some statute of limitations. He face was tormented for some reason.

"What's goin' on, Ches?"

He gave it to me in one word.

"Sara."

I set the dishes aside.

"Sara is what's going on, Paulie, and I'm having a rough time with it. I'm scared. Not nervous like when I stepped onto a field for the opening kickoff my rookie year." Hake paused. "No, I'm scared like the day I found my mom and dog dead. That kind of scared."

I stood by him at the breakfast table as the sobs came. I was frozen, just frozen.

What should I do, put my hands on his shoulders and try to console him? Tell him I understand when I don't? I didn't do anything. Right then, I couldn't do him any good anyway.

He quieted. The big shoulders stilled.

"Tell me about it."

A long pause gave me time to form another question.

"You've seen her – talked to her, right?"

"No, not yet," he said.

"She called you?"

I knew I had asked the right question.

"When?"

"She's tried seven times now." His eyes were swollen. "So how'd you know?"

"The Trail of Tears, asshole. We got pretty good at sorting out truth from bullshit, we Indians. Anyway, where do you stand?"

"She called me here and at the condo," Chesty said. "She even tried to see me at the stadium. I haven't had – haven't found the guts to talk to her yet. I don't know what to do. She caught me off guard,

I guess. This has been going on for a month now, and she sounds –
she sounds desperate, somehow. I don't understand, obviously. I
really thought that part of my life was over and done with, Paul. I'm
not as much in control as I thought I was – as I need to be."

I could feel my gut tightening.

"What're you gonna do?"

Chesty Hake was an oversized beginning swimmer in deep water.
He needed help, but I certainly wasn't the right guy to offer advice,
much less provide real help. Hell, I had a lousy track record with
women. I stayed clear. The only gambles I made these days were on
pro football games when I was getting information I shouldn't have
had.

But come to think of it, I had gotten lucky at happy hour at Cactus
Otto's not long ago. And then there was the travel editor's desperate
daughter . . . .

"Call her back and go see her," I told him. "You don't have to fuck
her."

"I never fucked her!" he bellowed.

Thirteen

Chesty Hake couldn't have been a better housemate, really. We were so different, and yet we kept finding similarities. We could get scratchy in our relationship, but we had this comfort zone, as athletes call it, when they're gaining six yards at a clip or hitting five-fifty with runners in scoring position. There's probably a word for what Chesty and I had, but I can't come up with it.

Each of us had an answering machine at Ninety-nine-oh-nine, but neither for us ever picked up a phone while it was ringing. That was one of Chesty's house rules. That often infuriated my people at the paper and Chesty's people in Kansas City. But he insisted we both be listed with phone numbers and no addresses in the St. Louis white pages. He was paranoid about that, when I think about it. But the fact remained: It was Chesty's house. I was paying no rent and living a nice life, so I played by his rules. It worked.

"You can fuck anybody you want to, Paulie, including the Veiled Prophet Queen of Love and Beauty and Miss America, but don't do it here at Ninety-nine-oh-nine Kingsbury Boulevard," he told me, when we first arranged I would move from my small, two-bedroom apartment in Brentwood. "This is going to be a private house. I won't fuck anybody here, either. *Nobody* comes here. I've gotta have my – my privacy, but I don't want my house vacant six days a week. Some broad comes here when I'm full of beer and makes a note of my unlisted number, and then I've got problems. Or how ' bout she beats it at three a.m. when she hears me snoring, and with her goes my NAIA Little All-American trophy? Or how ' bout she discovers there's a front-door key on the hook in the hall closet? No, Ninety-nine-oh-nine is off-limits to everyone but you and me."

Fine with me. Hell, I was driving a car seven years old, in part because, until a year before I moved to Kingsbury, my alimony payments had eaten up my savings. Brentshire Way isn't Kingsbury Boulevard.

And he came to me. I insist that to this day. I mean, I was being invited to live in a four-bedroom home in an affluent neighborhood, a property with two-and-a-half bathrooms, two refrigerators, a freezer in the basement, a bunch of TVs and radios and plenty of space in the garage for my Toyota Celica. Why would I complain about his do-it-elsewhere mandate?

Besides, I learned things about an NFL team few outsiders could know. When I called my friend down on Meramec Street in historic South St. Louis, I always got his attention. He liked my money, and I liked his clientele's money. But Chesty Hake never knew I used his information. Never. Swear to God.

It frequently was frustrating, living in that big house, where the owner didn't want to get to know his neighbors and wanted deliveries and meter-readings carefully supervised by me. Any time I thought about suggesting another arrangement, I'd read in my own damned paper a headline announcing the misfortune of a sports star:

**Omar Jones 'Mickey Finned' in
Hotel; World Series Ring Gone**

* * * * *

Chesty and I had a good division of labor. Despite having antiques in the house when I moved in, there was some awful stuff. By the same token, Hake knew Rombauer's *Joy of Cooking* from cover to cover but couldn't decorate a two-foot plastic Christmas tree. And just think: his mother had been a Rockefeller!

I, on the other hand, have a pretty fine eye for interior decorating. Why, I don't know. My parents and other relatives in McAlester knew little about what goes together, what sets off or accents a piece of art or what combines to enhance the look of a room.

Chesty was a very good and creative cook. He liked cookbooks and clipped recipes from the Monday Food Section. One of my assignments was the watering of his herb garden, which boasted basil, coriander, oregano, parsley and four or five other things. Forgive me, but I can't recite them.

The best part of his return each week during the season was that he would prepare a Monday dinner good enough for Julia Child or the late James Beard. Fine, fine eating. And for two of us he always made the recipes for five: three for him, one for me and one for my leftover, be it Wednesday dinner or Thursday breakfast. But he never left enough for two. He wouldn't fix enough of anything that I might be tempted to bring home a mid-week date for dinner.

My mom once told me I should expect to go from one-hundred-thirty pounds to one-fifty or one-sixty as I entered middle age. There was no point in telling her Chesty Hake liked to make one Mexican dip that had twenty-eight ingredients, and we would dip white tortilla chips into it for an hour sometimes, talking with food in our mouths and swilling Bud.

Our mothers wouldn't have approved. But it seemed a fine way to catch up, to solve world problems.

* * * * *

There came the day I weighed in with my fine eye for interior decorating. We should re-do our formal living room in bright yellow wells, white ceiling and black wainscoting.

* * * * *

The atmosphere got quite tense, so I took off on some errands. I could live with his vagaries

* * * * *

I knew I had carte blanche when he told me about his and Terri's slam-bam. I knew he wasn't exaggerating.

"Let's go back to your apartment, Chesty."

"I don't have an apartment."

"Really?"

"No, I have a house."

"Well, then, let's go back to your house. I wanna . . . Never mind. I wanna get out of this car. I want you."

"No, Terri, we don't go to my house. If we're gonna screw our brains out, it'll be at your place, not mine."

"Is there a problem?"

"Yeah. No one – *no one* – comes on my turf."

"Then we'll go come on my turf."

She was one of St. Louis County's assistant prosecuting attorneys,

Chesty told me. Maybe she, more than most, would appreciate where he was coming from.

To some degree, Hake's passion for privacy may have been out-growth of being left alone on "Graduation Day." He also had some trouble telling me about the days and weeks following his dad's death. I don't think he really cared about his brother's death.

David's death was: Now I have to hire a reputable antique dealer on Chicago's North Side. There had to be someone to appraise and to buy and, for an extra cut of the pie, sell to other dealers what he didn't want to take on.

Those are my words, of course, not Chesty's, but they have to be pretty accurate.

Rory Rifkin had no relatives who were eligible claimants to his estate. So Chesty became primary beneficiary of all estates.

Crippled, crotchety D. Jonathan Danner, the sixty-six-year-old antique dealer whom Chesty selected, did a through, conscientious job. He got Chesty out of a situation. Chesty knew as much about antiques as I do air filters on fifty-seven Chevys: nothing. Danner navigated the whole thing.

"I wound up writing Danner a check for a little more than fifty-two-thousand," Chesty told me. "But I didn't care. Shit, he turned around and wrote me one for six-hundred-thousand. I think I've got that number right. He bought all the antiques and took over the lease my brother and Rifkin had, and he made sure there wouldn't be any Illinois probate problems. I came out way ahead."

Chesty paused. I saw him glance over my head at one of my shelves of antique crocks. Something about that shelf of crocks, per-haps, struck him funny.

"Paulie, remind me tomorrow to send Jonathan Danner a dirty greeting card. He loves ' em and I've got the perfect one for him.

Fourteen

When I looked across the big circular breakfast table at Chesty, I saw a face contoured by his trade. The nose, bent left and up, the cartilage probably close to the front of his brain. The left eye, half-closed with that bone over the eyebrow mashed down a quarter-inch. The right jaw rounded and the left jaw square. Not the face of a gourmet cook. One of life's little mysteries.

I wondered aloud to him how he had endured those hundreds, thousands of attacks on his head and face with those forearms, fingers, face masks, knees, cleats, shoulder pads, helmets, fists. Once, over eggs benedict and his marvelous cream sauce, he'd told me.

"Without football, I'd look like a short, wide Robert Redford," he joked. He held up his left hand and extended upward a strangely twisted little finger.

"Redford didn't weigh one-twelve and earn a pinkie like this trying to catch a bullet of a pass. And Redford's eye isn't half-shut like this one," Chesty said. "The reason? He never let a three-hundred-pound defensive tackle put his fist through an old-style face mask."

Chesty poked at his eggs with a fork.

"And my jaw? I look like two different people, don't I? My junior year at Blackwater, I blocked a kid from Baker University with my face. You can't block big, strong guys with your face. Shaving's tough. Sara kept saying: 'You can't play this week, you can't play.' It was NAIA playoffs. I played with these weird patches of bristle on my jaw."

* * * * *

The best way to size up Chesty Hake? Distrusting.

How else could he be after what he went through with Sara and her father, the deaths of his dad and brother, the senior seasons his stardom got yanked? Chesty was terribly distrusting. I felt privileged he trusted me—within bounds—almost from the moment we met. He sure as hell didn't trust anyone else. Maybe that's why I was in his house. And he was so reluctant to talk about Sara or those deaths in his family. He didn't go anywhere with it, but he kept it locked away behind that busted face.

When I think back about it, I felt more triumphant that Chesty and I were confidantes and housemates than I felt, yes, about having screwed the prom queen at McAlester High. And until I moved to Ninety-nine-oh-nine, well, believe, me, Angie Lee Jones was the highlight of my career – high school, college or professionally.

Certainly, Chesty Hake's distrust had its roots in the killings of his mother and dog. But actually, the roots could've been deeper. Chesty knew what he was – Mr. Irrelevant – long before he had to make that fateful phone call and tell his dad what he had found.

* * * * *

As a sportswriter, I never really thought I needed to know that technical football jargon like "two-deep zone," "peel-back blocker," "red-dog," and "seven-step drop." I thought that stuff was bullshit. I preferred to write about young men who were large, strong, and quick; who were limber, agile, and nasty. And who ate pain. I didn't care about the young men who were "effective" in a "two-deep zone." Most of these people, turns out, have common-man problems like diarrhea, hemorrhoids, burned-out bulbs, checkbook balancing, and inability to remember ZIP Codes.

Players who understand football parlance may not understand four-digit subtraction, so they pay agents. Chesty never had an agent. That probably stemmed from his built-in distrust of people. A player's agent likes to have control, and Chesty couldn't have allowed that. And he refused to let pain take control. He'd drive four hours through a November night with an ankle swelling to where it was straining against his running shoe. If the Cobras had won, I'd ask: "How you doin?" I'd get back: "Never better." If the Cobras had lost, the response would be: "Aw, all right. I guess." But never: "I hurt." Maybe I needed to control Chesty. I waited for him to say one Sunday night: "I hurt." But I waited and waited.

* * * * *

Maybe I didn't know a lot about "seven-step drops" and "two-deep zones," but I could tell you about sidelines and dressing rooms. The *noise!* A civilian in the stands or in front of a TV can't appreciate the scary volume of noise that explodes on every play of an NFL game. There's the CLAACK! of helmets and shoulder pads hitting. And, quickly, there's the WHOOSH! of wind from lungs. And then there's the AAAHH! of pain instantly felt, because someone gets injured, to some degree, on every play of every NFL game. Maybe not enough that a guy has to come to the sideline or be helped off the field, but body parts are forced to do things for which they were not intended. AAAHH!

So many times I heard those noises while I stood on a sideline, taking notes. Primal, ugly, frightening. And I'd be scratching away with my pen, reducing it all to print for the city's breakfast tables. ' Pass the bacon, honey?'

And two reactions came quickly to mind the first time I went into a dressing room to do a sidebar story after a game at Soldier Field in Chicago, after the Bears had disgraced the Tampa Bay Buccaneers or somebody: one, damn, it stinks in here; and two, damn, it's hot in here!

Dressing rooms after a game are oppressive. Wads of two-inch-wide adhesive tape don't smell or make a cement block room a steamy ninety-five degrees. People do. Hot showers do. There are few women covering pro football. The reason isn't that they can't understand the game or ask incisive questions or stand to look at men in towel wraps. No, it's that women are too well-schooled, too cultured to venture into rooms that are concrete rain forests, where the humidity is so bad wallpaper can't stick to the walls but jock straps and T-shirts can. Women somehow know better.

You breathe enough Johnson & Johnson high-test analgesic and duck enough wads of Johnson & Johnson tape thrown out of frustration or triumph, even, and eventually you buy some Johnson & Johnson stock.

Perhaps it was the tension of doing a story slugged DRESS, but I gagged the first time I ventured into the home team's quarters at Soldier Field.

* * * * *

If I had been able to do a piece for *Goal Line Weekly* magazine, I would've used that memory of my first time in a pro dressing room. I would've recalled what Hake used to tell me about four types of players. There was the training camp player, the practice player, the game player and the player's player.

"The player's player prepares for Sunday by taking home tapes for review, takes the chance of getting hurt because of his intensity during practice during the week, gets his ankles taped when the trainers first begin their work early Sunday, then goes from the hotel to the stadium on the first of the team's two buses if it's a road game, checks the dampness of the field and the bare spots, checks the crown down the center of the field. And the player's player always checks the height of the grass if it's natural. If it's synthetic turf, he checks the hardness and the seams."

He paused, making sure his mental checklist had been completed.

"I've gotta be a player's player, or I'm gone, Paulie," he said. "If I'm good only in August, I'll never see September. If I'm good only on Wednesday, I'm on waivers Friday. Gone."

* * * * *

Chesty Hake should go down in NFL history as of the best of the special-teams guys. There may or may not have been outstanding special-teamers before the nineteen-seventies; I can't say. But then came a handful. Some of them: Mickey Zofko of the Lions, Hank Bauer of the Chargers, Tim Kearney when the Cardinals were in St. Louis, Steve Tasker of Buffalo, Ron Wolfley.

As Wolfley once described his job: "You're either a star or you chase kicks. I chase kicks."

And that was Chesty during his eight seasons with the Cobras. Zofko, Tasker and Bill Bates for Dallas all scored more touchdowns than did Hake – if each scored just one. I'd have to look it up.

* * * * *

"Up! Go!" Hake screamed as he and his teammates streamed downfield for a kill.

Fifteen

By his second year in the pros, Chesty Hake reached two conclusions that would change his life: He knew nothing about furnishing that condo in Lee's Summit or our house in Clayton, but he would do both – poorly, or course. And he no longer needed to drive an aging Cadillac Eldorado in memory of his late father.

That's when Damon Thibodeaux, a tall third-year linebacker out of seldom-seen Louisiana Baptist, came to Chesty with an offer he couldn't turn down.

"I don't want to sell my Jaguar to you, Hake. But, mon, you are the only feller in this whole dressing room that can 'preciate it," said the Cajun. "I ain't gonna give you any back-ass Cajun shit. I'm just gonna sell you my car."

"Wrong guy, Tibby. Not interested. I don't need a car. I've got the one my dad gave me."

"No, little mon, your daddy didn't give you no car," Thibodeaux said, raising his voice. "You got it 'cause you were the last Caddy mon in the family. Evabody can know dat. You should have *my* car."

"Why do you want me to buy your car, Tibby?"

"Why? ' Cause the car for you it is! With the ladies, an All-Pro you will be! With my Jaguar! You'll break records, little mon!"

The twelve-cylinder Jag coupe was beautiful. The odometer showed only thirty-one-hundred miles, and the car had been kept well – washed and waxed, checked weekly under the hood, a gleaming extension of a *nouveau riche* athlete's ego.

That fine automobile also was the contact point in Liberty, Missouri, for a drug ring out of a Louisiana bayou. Tibby was one of five brothers and cousins who had shown their faith and commitment by purchasing the same model of the same luxury car with the same special deep gold paint job in five different regions two years ago. Oh, and the same oversized console between the front seats.

But that was two years ago. Now Tibby knew he was going to prison. Everyone in the Cobras' dressing room knew why. Two cousins had elected to save their dark souls with confessions, and Tibby knew his days were numbered. His time with the Cobras were numbered, and his indebtedness to his family's illicit business back in Bredeaux, Louisiana, was monumental. But that's how it can go in the illegal drug business.

Tibby didn't want to be killed in prison. He knew, if he died behind bars, it would be an ugly, horrific death, the kind that makes headlines. So Tibby, for once, determined he didn't want to be in the headlines and would rectify his family debt problems before he got the official word from the NFL and the Cobras that he no longer would be on the payroll.

How to come up with something in the neighborhood of seventy-thousand dollars? Well, one way was to discount some of the drugs Tibby had so cleverly stashed in his apartment in Liberty. Another way was to sell his gold Jag, and that way he wouldn't have to go to prison a pauper. If he had some money, he'd be safe from the rest of the Bredeaux Gang. Yes, he could pay off those pesky debts.

So the Jag was identical to the ones purchased by brothers Dorman and Delmar and cousins Ray and Royal two years ago. Sell it, Tibby! Dorman was one who could have him erased in just about any penitentiary in the U.S. Dorman was that mean and that well-known.

"With this vehicle, you'll break records," the tall linebacker told Hake. "You'll break my records, so help me."

"Tibby, I don't have any money, and I don't want your car," Chesty argued. "I can't help you."

"Hake, you are deserving of something good. I want to be good to you. You've played good, and I want to be good to you. Gimme forty-thousand bucks for this beautiful car, and it's yours."

Chesty was reasonably certain he was about to buy a car.

"Forget it, jackoff," he muttered. "I don't want your car. And I don't know what you're going to do with it, Tibby. You've got a big problem."

"No problem."

"Tibby, I don't want to buy your drugs, and I don't know anybody who can help you now. Tell you what: I'll give you thirty-thousand dollars for your car – today, now, tonight."

Tibby grunted, then said: "I paid seventy-three-thou, motherfucker, so give me forty for it. I gotta have forty, at least."

"No, Thibodeaux, you gotta have thirty – and a title transfer. Otherwise, your relatives in the swamp are gonna read in *The Times-Picayune* in New Orleans tomorrow or the day after that you've been suspended by the league for a third substance abuse offense – and you have no legitimate income, and a court says you're going to prison for dealing with intent to distribute. That's really gonna piss off those Cajun relatives of yours. Cut your losses, Tibby. Sell me that car right now for about twenty-five-thousand in cash. Your cousins and your brothers really insist upon cash, don't they?"

"Twenty-five-thousand? Thirty, you said."

"Twenty-five, Tibby, and, in about ten seconds, you're going to have only twenty."

The five-second standoff cost Thibodeaux a thousand dollars a second. Chesty didn't open his mouth until he had mentally clicked off five seconds.

"Now it's twenty-thousand, and you're going to have to placate those relatives somehow," said Hake. "Twenty-thousand, and that'll include the Missouri title and a definition of the word 'placate.'"

"Aw, thirty-thousand, you said."

"Twenty, Tib, or I'll call Area Code Five-oh-four and tell those relatives of yours I've just paid you ninety-three-thousand dollars for the drugs. And Tib, if there isn't a title or a title search agreement in the glove box or the console, I'm gonna call Area Code Five-oh-four anyway."

Thibodeaux didn't want to die.

So a seventy-three-thousand-dollar car sold for twenty-thousand, including a bonus in the specially designed console.

Ninety minutes after Tibby had backed down, he met Hake in the Marriott near Weston Stadium. It was the lobby, and Hake was aware others were going to witness the transaction. That was fine with him. Should anything happen, should Chesty be accosted, he at least would be able to recognize and identify several witnesses if needed for prosecution. If Tibby's relatives down south happened to read something picked up by The Associated Press from *The Register*, something that appealed to the national editor of *The Times-Picayune*, for instance, Tibby would lose fingers and toes and perhaps an eye if those Cajun relatives thought he had screwed them. Then they'd kill him. His body would be left somewhere that the night creatures could pick it clean.

Only his NFL medical and dental records would be of help in identifying the corpse – if there were one. Tibby didn't want it to come down to that disgusting prospect.

* * * * *

"Trivia question," Hake said aloud as he left I-471 and wheeled onto I-70 westbound for Weston Stadium. "What do I have in common with a bunch of people named Thibodeaux in Bredeaux, Louisiana?"

At the west side of Weston, he sprang open the cover of the oversized console. His old Eldorado never had been without a comb, a bottle of Binaca and a vial of Polo. This console, however, was equipped much differently. It contained a small, compact seven-point-six-five-millimeter pistol, German-made, with a stubby silencer, a full clip and a spare clip.

Chesty shivered.

He slammed the console. Obviously, the gun was Thibodeaux's, and Hake needed to get rid of it.

Chesty operated within the law. With that in mind, he knew whom to call. Becky Shular, receptionist extraordinaire, would know how to reach Tibby even if his time with the Cobras was over.

"Shular, give me Tibby's home number, please," Chesty said as he entered through the wooden doors.

"Don't have it, Chesty," she responded, smiling. "I really don't. Tibby was like you: no home number available, it says. Sorry."

So he had a handgun with a silencer, not the type of weapon or accessory a young professional football player wants to have discovered in his car on, say, that fateful night he gets nailed for a D.W.I. in Clayton, Des Peres, Ballwin or even Grain Valley.

A weapon with a silencer possessed by a man with a powerful

body, a temper, and no license to carry. Terrific.

* * * * *

"Hey, man, answer me a question: Why ya got dem HUT-HUT plates on ya Jag?" Vincie Simpson, the Chiefs' prized rookie corner-back, asked that afternoon.

"Why do you ask?"

"Cause, man, ya ain't the type."

"No, probably not," Chesty replied absently. "You're probably right about that."

"But man, ya always so – so serious and so private, an' den you go put dem vandy plates on dat vee-cul o' yours. What is it?"

"Vanity, not vandy, Vincie," Hake answered. "The plates were a gift from – from a friend. From a long time ago, Vincie. About the time you were accidentally getting black Kiwi on the pantlegs of guys just off cruisers and carriers at Norfolk, Virginia. Sailors in dress whites: good, clean sport, weren't they?"

"So?"

"So?"

"Shit, man, long 'go and far 'way" Simpson said, dismissing Hake's jab. "But man, I'd really like to know 'bout yo' HUT-HUTs. Yo' a dead give 'way, man. Oughta get rid of 'em. I mean, if you wanna be private, man."

"You want those, don't you, Vincie? Oh, yes, you do. You'd love 'em, you jackoff. As soon as I'd turn 'em in to the state, you'd apply for 'em. You damned well would. Well, forget it, Vincie. They're mine."

Chesty's voice had risen, he realized. But the HUT-HUT plates were all he had left of his and Sara's love.

97

Sixteen

In researching a second in-depth piece on Chesty Hake, I came across some information I buried. There definitely were some aspects of the story that didn't need to be brought out, didn't lend themselves to even out a story of a hundred or two hundred grafs.

"He used to eat his lunch in the john," a former Brentwood High classmate told me, half-snitching and half-trying for a laugh. "Hell yeah, he'd sit on the can with the door locked and his feet propped up so nobody'd see him, and he'd eat his sandwich or whatever. His pants were up, of course; we knew that. He wasn't pooping or anything. One day, we got Gary Royal – about six-foot-six, I suppose — to leap above the door of the commode and check on Chesty. He was called Chet back then, in the eighth grade, I guess. He was sitting on the john, eating a PB&J and reading a book about the early days of rock 'n' roll.

"Gary Royal told everybody what he'd seen, and almost everybody at Brentwood knew about Chesty – even before we started call-

ing him Chesty. He was just so shy back then, he couldn't force himself to walk into the cafeteria. I kinda felt sorry for him. And then
he started to grow, and he grew some more, and then he quit eating
his lunch in the can. I guess – well, you already know. You know
about his mom being murdered, don't you?"

I didn't need to do anything more than nod.

"When Chet – Chesty – got good, everybody just kinda forgot he
had eaten his PB&J in a second-floor commode. Pretty soon, he got
so strong and so good that nobody ever thought about saying: 'Hey,
you used to eat your lunch on the john, shy boy!' Chesty would've
kicked ass."

No, I didn't pursue that aspect of his adolescence in my follow-up
piece. And I didn't pursue the murder of his mother. And as for the
pistol with the silencer, well, that still was in the future.

By November of his sophmore year, Chesty strode into that basement cafeteria each school day and ordered double portions. He sat
at just about any table he wanted. Nobody – *nobody*, not even juniors
and seniors – dared mention that second-floor boys' room.

Something else I omitted from my second piece on Hake: As a pro,
he always liked to say the second-smartest thing he did to prepare for
a game was to study all that videotape. He reviewed punt team, punt-
return team, kickoff and kickoff-return teams, field goal team.

There were so few special/special people – Mickey Zofko of
Detroit comes to mind – people who didn't mind being called "head-
hunters" or "Kamikazes." They knew what they did best, and they
knew they were the best at what they did.

Usually, none of them really was very good at his assigned position, be it wide receiver or running back or strong safety or whatever. But each of these specialists – Hake included – was very, very
good at bolting downfield, knocking a blocker on his butt, thwarting
a less-minded tackler, completing a block suitable for the post-season

film. Oh, and the tackles! For a special-teamer, there's nothing more rewarding that the tackles – "crunches," as they were called.

But the smartest thing Chesty did preparing for a game – be it Brentwood, McAlester, Blackwater or the Cobras – was to know the names of his adversaries. He wanted to know the *first* names of the players with whom he had to deal: Derrick Watson, Western Alabama, fifth of six sons, majoring in general studies; Tyrone Simpson, Ohio State, six-foot-seven and three-oh-five, son of a cop killed in the line of duty during a drug bust.

And he wanted to know the names of the officials with whom he would deal each Sunday afternoon or Monday night as a pro, such as line judge Dub Lattinville, number twenty-five, age forty-four, graduate of Portland State, an insurance company vice president, second year in the NFL. And Dave Arneson, umpire, number eighty-eight, age fifty-one, graduate of Michigan Harbor, college professor, ninth year as an NFL official. And the spotlight guy, the referee, Gene Wirth, number fifteen, age fifty-seven, podiatrist from East Hampton, New York, Misty and Bill teenagers and twenty-one-year-old Heather at Vassar. Hake filed all that in his mental helmet.

* * * * *

"My inspiration?" he repeated as we let the interview wind down to serious Budweiser time. "Jim Otis, I think. He played fullback for the Cardinals – the St. Louis Cardinals – in the seventies after kicking around with the Chiefs and New Orleans, then set club records for carries and yards rushing. Just hard work and perseverance. He took his work very seriously, but he was no animal. He did a lot of civic work and wanted to be part of the St. Louis community even after he retired. I liked that.

"Otis was a plugger, and that's the way I see myself. He'd been cut by New Orleans and the Chiefs before he found a home with the Cardinals. He was about five-eleven and two-fifteen – small for a fullback even then. And he wasn't even the best back at Ohio State his senior year. They had three great athletes: Rex Kern as the quarterback and Bruce Jankowski and Leo Hayden as halfbacks. And they had Otis plodder, at fullback.

"Guess who succeeded in the NFL?"

Seventeen

In Chesty Hake's second season, shortly after the Great Jaguar Purchase, came the Great J.O. Flap. For that, he could've been waived, suspended or at least fined. He survived with a fine.

When I had a pen and notepad or a tape recorder as my armament, he would fire back with well-thought-out salvos. He appreciated a good battle, of course. I got one good story using this approach and eventually would get a second one. And I could've had more, from different angles, had I pressed him.

But Chesty hated encounters with young men and young women bearing microphones. He thought of them as SIJOs: Self-Important Jackoffs. He put up with them through his first season, but after that his confidence grew and his patience dwindled.

After a post-game Sunday flap that reached St. Louis TV, I asked him immediately upon his arrival home: "Why did you call that television guy a jackoff?"

"Aw, shuddup."

I answered in kind, knowing it was going to be a good, good conversation, none of which ever could appear in print.

I wondered how many people from the media already had tried to get Hake's unlisted phone number. We could hear his dummy phone – with the answering machine on automatic – ring several times.

"Paulie, they were running tape. I'm trying to get dressed to come home. I'm just out of the shower, my hair's wet, and I'm thirsty. This hair-sprayed reporter has me look at a little monitor while he says: 'And here's a great goal-line tackle by you, Chesty.' It was his statement, and it wasn't close to correct. I don't play defense. He wanted me to comment on one of those non-questions, and I'd have been lying if I had. I've played one down of defense in the NFL. Why then did he have to shove a mike in my face and make me watch his monitor?"

"But why did you have to call him a jackoff on live TV?"

"I guess I'll hear about that Tuesday – and a long time after that."

"Yep," I assured him, adding: "unless they release you."

"Hey, Paulie, what you see on TV are microphones actually holding overpaid jackoffs. That's just the way it is. And the next time somebody says to me: 'Chesty, between you and I . . .' I might strangle him. No college should ever graduate someone who says shit like 'between you and I.'"

* * * * *

General Manager Sheldon Bergman intercepted him as he came off the practice field Tuesday afternoon.

"You know, of course, what you have to do, Chesty," said the G.M.

"Yeah, Shel. You have the number?"

"Call the number Becky Shular has for you. Ask for Mr. Coe, the station G.M. Just make your apology sincere, and make sure it won't happen again. Then tomorrow, we'll announce you've been fined an undisclosed amount."

Chesty didn't ask the size of the fine. He showered and got the number of KMOB-TV from Becky at the receptionist's desk. The call was quick and relatively painless.

* * * * *

A Foamcore sign materialized over Hake's locker:

RADIO/TV OFF-LIMITS
'JACKOFF' USED HERE

For the remainder of Chesty's football career, no electronic media type ventured close to his locker. Nobody seemed to want to interview him after practice.

The headline in the paper read:

Hake's Fine for TV Obscenity 'Considerable'

The story speculated Chesty had been fined twenty-five-thousand. The following Tuesday, when he picked up his Sunday game check, he noted it was light a thousand. He dismissed the letter from NFL Headquarters at Four-ten Park Avenue with a tsk-tsk. But privately.

That was Chesty: a man perversely superior, along with distrusting. After all, he had won the Lowsman Trophy.

No wonder, either, that Chesty continued to use "jackoff!" as a proper noun. My thinking was that this superiority was getting in the way of his inferiority. After all, only a couple of dozen young men had been just as talented to be Mr. Irrelevant.

Hake's tough-nut persona was of part his need to defend himself. This had to come from his elfin size as a child, the murders of his mom and his dog, the need to have lunch while in a locked commode. More and more nowadays, I wonder: What if my mom had been savaged and ravaged, my dog skinned, and I spent my childhood under-

104

weight and half a head shorter than any other boy in my grade school class? What would be showing up in my personality now, two decades later?

Hake's way of alienating much of the Kansas City media came back to haunt both of us. Even a fast-rising fellow with whom I graduated from the University for Missouri School for Journalism arched his back in print. Media types would try to club Hake. For instance:

HAKE ISN'T JAKE

By

Hank Mather

> Ever hear of a professional athlete who wouldn't talk
> to his roommate?

We have.

Paul Tenkiller, a former classmate and co-worker of ours and now working for the daily in St. Louis, has just that situation. He recently began sharing a pricey home in the suburb of Clayton with Chesty Hake, the second-string (make it third-string) fullback and special-teams whiz of the Cobras. They don't see much of each other during the season, of course, and they don't even discuss football when they're together.

> Seems strange, doesn't it? A lot of us would
> love to have that kind of built-in information bank
> for stories, but not Tenkiller. He told me last week
> his relationship – hetero, he assured me – would end
> immediately if he wrote anything significant about
> the reclusive Hake or told co-workers or bosses at his
> paper what he really knows.

We've known Paul for years. He doesn't need to tell us anything about Chesty Hake, and he also doesn't need to tell his paper anything. But his paper probably would like to see an "insider" piece now and then. Paul is willing to endure the slings and the arrows to preserve his promise of silence to Hake.

Keep in mind, please: Hake, as a second-year player, is on somewhat thin ice. He called a local television type of guy a masturbator and then told him, off-mike, to fornicate in a humanly impossible way. He has given no radio or TV interviews since and has had precious little to say to us print people.

So pro football and the media "guests" don't darken the Hake-Tenkiller doorstep in St. Louis. We figure it's fortunate Paul and Chesty have common interests: stamp collecting, beer-drinking, tall women. Sorry Paul.

On other subjects that delight a columnist . . .

* * * * *

Hell, yes, I was furious when a copy of Mather's crap was placed in front of me by Jim Calvin.

EDITOR'S NOTE: What Mather didn't know was Chesty and I almost always talked by phone on Friday nights during the season. He wanted to know how well I had mowed or raked the back lawn. Had I cleaned the gutters as promised? Had the trash haulers bitched about the overfilled cans? Had I gotten some butterfly pork chops? Were we out of minced garlic? Anything else he should know about? I found out whether or not Dallas really should be favored by five points over the Cobras. How bad was the injury situation? Ol' Muldrew okay this week? What kinds of cleats were the Cobras likely to wear if the synthetic turf proved to be spongy by Sunday morning? Are you taping those two bad fingers together, Ches? Which hand is it?

And Mather thought we didn't communicate!

* * * * *

When I think about it, Chesty was very, very good for me. Aside from my casual buddies from work – "Let's have a beer at The Missouri Grill if we ever get out of here" types – I really had no close friends in St. Louis. My circle of friends changed drastically after my wife, Sandy, left me. I no longer met interesting, high-visibility people at cocktail parties or fund-raising functions. My acquaintances went back to being the guys from the paper who wanted to have a beer when we got off work at midnight or eleven a.m. or whenever. I still loved her, for whatever that was worth. Where did I go wrong? Was it me? Or could it have been the crazy working hours?

Perhaps I groped for a friendship when Chesty came along – a meaningful friendship. I don't know. I wasn't that introspective back then. I used to use a line with women: "I really don't know myself that well." Sometimes it worked. But dammit, Hank Mather, Chesty suggested the rooming arrangement, I didn't need pricey Clayton.

Although Hake and I both had answering machines, I often wondered whether or not my ex-wife Sandy ever tried to get in touch with me but hung up before the fourth ring. Until she became "Sandi" and married the lawyer who was en route to becoming a St. Louis County Councilman, I made certain the alimony check was on time if not early each month. That was my way of proving I still loved her and still wanted her respect.

And I did love her. A deep, heart-ripping love.

What would Sandy give me for Christmas this year? Better yet, what would Sandi give me?

There was an irony in the Clayton home arrangement, but I never told Hake. Sandy's use of the English language had been dreadful, but the conflicts I had with her were not the between-you-and-I stuff.

However, after our divorce, any woman I heard use that phrase suddenly became less interesting.

Chesty and I had that in common. He wouldn't have been a fan of Sandy's – or Sandi's.

* * * * *

Hake told me one day about his junior year in high school, his year as a true hero: eighteen-hundred yards rushing, all-everything, runner-up to the Metro Player of the Year in St. Louis. None for it sounded boastful, but eventually he wanted to talk the conversation away from his exploits. Without saying so, he insisted upon talking about the music of the nineteen-fifties and nineteen-sixties.

"All I ever listened to was the stuff from the fifties and the midsixties," he told me. "That's what interested me. I think I listened to enough of that wonderful yet awful stuff and read enough about it that, right now, I'm an expert. That's all I have in the way of tapes in my car. I've got Bill Haley, the Five Satins, Gale Garnett, Ivory Joe Hunter, Dion and the Belmonts, Dion without the Belmonts, the Crystals, the Shirelles, the Orlons, Martha & The Vandellas, Frankie Laine, and Mathis and Andy Williams and — hell, I used to be able to tell you who were the disc jockeys on WLS-Chicago and WWL in New Orleans and the old WIL here in the early, glory days of rock 'n' roll. And I used to memorize lyrics, too. How's this:

Chesty sang the first couple of bars of "We'll Sing In The Sunshine," but obviously not as well as Gale Garnett had sung it in September of nineteen-sixty-four.

"You know who that was?" Hake asked.

"No, but you've got a nice baritone."

"Gale Garnett, and that was the title. That was back when a lot of country music became pop. City kids didn't even know there were country charts. It goes back to the mid-fifties. Think about it: 'A White Sport Coat and a Pink Carnation' was the biggest thing Marty Robbins ever had, but the teenagers in Newark and New Orleans didn't realize it was a country-western hit first. And how 'bout one I've got on about four or five of my driving tapes, Jack Scott's 'My True Love'? Country as could be, but a big hit on the pop charts in fifty-seven."

He sang the dramatic finishing measures.

"Nice."

"Hey, I still sing. I don't need a bar of Dial to come up with some nice notes. And once upon a time . . ." He broke into "Once Upon a Time."

"Matt Monro did it better."

"Good! Hey, I didn't think you knew singers." He paused. "Paulie, I'm going to tell you something about music I couldn't tell the Cobras' P.R. guy my rookie year. Not even on that form we filled out: you know, favorite music, most inspiring NFL player, what I plan to do after retiring, off-season interests."

He was serious now.

"I had all that success my junior season. But at Brentwood, in the spring, I was in *a capella* choir for some reason. Our choir director, Mr. Boriyev, told me I was going to sing the baritone solo of 'Graduation Day' for the senior class.

"I said, 'yeah, right,' or something like that. Boriyev was a big sumbitch with a big bass voice and a really big set of eyebrows. He stared me down. And then he told me, as a Mizzou graduate, he could make sure I never would play football at Missouri. So I made a deal with Mr. Boriyev, and I went ahead and sang the solo for the class ahead of us on the third of June. I remember the date."

I was glad to have the john-lunches anecdote documented.

"So how did 'Graduation Day' go?" I asked.

"I was Robert fucking Goulet, if you must know. Well, Goulet's a little better, but I was very good."

"Goodnight, Chesty."

I lay awake that night listening to my kind of music: the Statler Brothers' "Class of '57." The lyrics scared me when they said Paul sold life insurance and part-time real estate.

* * * * *

In the first, fateful story I did on Chesty Hake when he was drafted by the Cobras as Mr. Irrelevant, we determined that we: one, had lived in McAlester, Oklahoma; two, were stamp collectors; three, had an unabashed fondness for Budweiser; and four, shared an interest in music that was off the mainstream. I tried to be competitive when it came to musical trivia of the fifties and sixties, but he barely had to flex his memory muscles to whip me.

"Chesty, what did Angelo D'Aleo, Freddie Milano and Carlo Mastrangelo have in common?"

"Too easy," he said, looking sheepish, as if he were about to come up with an outrageous bluff. "They were the Belmonts of Dion and the Belmonts, nineteen-fifty-eight to nineteen-sixty."

"Son of a bitch! How can you keep all that stuff in your head?"

"I used to study it."

I guess, deep down, it bothered me. Along with quizzing on being out of fresh garlic, and Sandy and Sandi. Lots of things nibbling at me. And the pistol? When that came on the scene the velocity of our lives picked up and we got to the killings. Chuck Rio's sax and Tequila didn't mean shit.

Eighteen

If Chesty Hake were here, he'd agree that our line-up was good. I could handle his insistence on privacy, and he never seemed to have any trouble dealing with me being stuck in my ways. To me, scrambled eggs and buttered toast are a challenge. Hake could do his famous garlic-*jalepeno* spread or what he called his hurry-up hollandaise sauce for eggs benedict as easily as a grilled cheese sandwich.

On the other hand, he couldn't decorate a two-car garage. He had no sense of color, symmetry, or proportion. He couldn't hang a picture straight with a carpenter's level. I used to chide him about his artistic shortcomings, since I had to live with all the furniture in our home. But he had inherited many fine to very-fine to near-mint antiques. They came from his mother's side. Rockefeller, not Hake.

Stacked, piled and rolled up in the basement when I moved in were eye-opening things: fine old boxes, delicate gate-leg tables, vases by Steuben and Tiffany, two small paintings by A. A.

Rockefeller, a spectacular children's china cabinet in English walnut, the finest Martha Washington I had ever seen, a mahogany bookcase I couldn't identify, Oriental rugs of marvelous quality.

We hauled to the trash area most of the stopgap furniture within a week after I moved in. But he'd still say a dresser with a good Formica top was a helluva lot more functional than a two-hundred-fifteen-year-old Elijah Benton. A Bud can's not good for Elijah's old maple. But he went along.

Given access to pieces I never could afford and seldom let myself admire in galleries, I decorated our – Chesty's – house the way it should've been decorated. I was proud, and he was mystified.

"How much is that box worth?" he asked as I stacked and stood back, re-stacked and stood back again for another look. He was pointing to a sewing box, black with pearl inlay, from the ship of Captain Reuben Rockefeller Smith, out of Mobile, Alabama, about eighteen-oh-eight.

"Somewhere between forty-five-hundred and twenty-thousand, I imagine."

"You're shittin' me!"

"Nope. Your mother liked small and delicate things and things with a Rockefeller connection. See Captain Reuben Rockefeller Smith's name sewn into the satin here in the lining of the lid? Things like this nowadays don't have small price tags. I'm going to bring you out of the Formica Age. This is a William & Mary side table. It's cherry, so I'd say it's from somewhere like upstate or western New York, and it probably goes back beyond seventeen-fifty. A nice piece."

"Lemme guess: ten thousand bucks."

"Try fourteen to twenty-five-thousand."

Chesty stared.

"Paul, you really know about this stuff, don't you?"

"Well, I took a course at Mizzou just as an elective," I told him. "I know just enough to be dangerous, I suppose. What I know for sure is, I'll never be able to afford any of it. That's why it's fun to play. This is an Easter egg hunt for me, a damned Easter egg hunt."

"The stuff may be valuable, but it's old."

"And beautiful."

The late gay brother had a clear monopoly on good taste.

A year or so later, I still asked myself the question: What happened to the contents of the gay brother's antique shop in Chicago? Knowing Chesty's taste, I suspected some treasures went in the finest garage sale in the history of Rush Street. No matter that intermediary D. Jonathan Danner might've taken a cut of the proceeds for his efforts. It wasn't Chesty's way to worry about such things. After all, the deal had been fifty-two-thousand-dollars paid out and six-hundred-thousand received. Why quarrel? And when I looked happily at what I'd accomplished on Kingsbury Boulevard, I wondered where all those beautiful things had been displayed or stored during Hake's two-bedroom childhood on Salem Road.

"Beauty needs to be shown," I said. "And, by the way, that cheap-ass breakfast table is going. We're going to have a good, big, circular butcher-block table – with four big chairs, not flimsy ones like these. And I'm going to pay for the whole damned thing."

I did. As it turned out, that was twenty-seven-hundred dollars well spent. Over the years, Chesty and I ate many a fine meal, drank many a Bud and solved many a world problem – some of our own, too – across from each other at that maple table. And I got information about player injuries, salaries, illnesses, psychological kinks, and sexual preferences for which some gamblers and some publications would've paid the price of dozens of butcher blocks.

It was across that table Chesty Hake and I firmed up a bond few men could hope to enjoy, I suppose. But what a shame he insisted

only two of those four chairs ever be occupied. That rule again. NO
BROADS.

* * * * *

I knew as a teenager I never would be rich. At the same time, I
vowed I'd never be poor, either. It was the Tenkiller way.

My father had kept secret a nice leather-covered box, perhaps
fourteen inches by nine, and, at the top of the domed lid, it stood
about eight inches. I never dared to explore it. Even in my childhood, Dad or Mom made it clear: Nobody was to touch that box.
That was *Dad's*.

But the day before they drove me down to the Holiday Inn on
Bypass U.S. 69 where Mom worked – to catch the Greyhound for
central Missouri – Dad brought out his box. He didn't make a production of it, other than to backhand from the curved lid some invis-
ible dust. That was Dad's idea of a production.

"Son, I want you to look at this picture," he said, handing me a yel-
lowed black-and-white. "Look at it for a full minute."

I didn't understand, but I looked. I was eighteen, and I think my
fear was I was about to be subjected to some mysterious Choctaw
rite.

"Have you looked at it for a full minute?"

"Yes, Dad. Why?"

"Because, Paul, now I know you will be a success. You will have
it better than your mom and I have had it. You will have it better than
your ancestors had it. See, Paul, this is a picture of a home without a
kitchen sink, without a flush toilet, without a garage or a carport,
without fertilizer to make that front yard grow green. This was a *tenk*
house – our family's home long ago – in Mississippi. We didn't want
to leave it, we Folsoms."

Folsom: Our family name back then.

"But we had no choice. Our ancestors were herded – *herded* – here to Oklahoma, and maybe thirty to forty percent of our people died on the Trail of Tears. But those of them who reached Oklahoma, it was a pretty good life. Took generations, though.

"And while we're thankful for what we have and who we are, when you get on that Greyhound tomorrow, you keep I mind this picture of our Mississippi *tenk* house. And, Paul, you're to take our family one step further."

* * * * *

"That's all he really needed to say," I told Chesty across the breakfast table. "When I got to my room in Lewis Hall and started unpacking, something amazing happened: I found that picture of a Choctaw *tenk* house near Philadelphia, Mississippi, right there in my shaving kit. He knew when he put me on the damned bus I wouldn't embarrass him or the rest of the family – the remnants of the family. He had talked about 'one step further' and made certain of it with that old photo."

Until the eve of my departure for college, my dad never talked much about the Tenkiller background. Or the Folsom heritage. He said he was a Native American, not an American Indian. It wasn't that he was ashamed of his heritage. Certainly not, or he wouldn't have kept that old photo of the family *tenk*. He was much more concerned about the future – my future – than he was about the trail his grandparents or great-grandparents had trekked.

My dad once talked about changing our name from Tenkiller to Johnson – Johnston, perhaps – or Patrillo, which was my mom's maiden name. Yeah, we need more Indian kids named Johnston and Patrillo.

Dad got outvoted by my mom, who didn't want a handsome man with red skin to have to live as a Patrillo. Then there was my dad's ugly older brother, Horace, a strange guy who kept up with the tribal stuff. If Dad had changed our name from Tenkiller to Johnston or Patrillo, Uncle Horace would've slit his throat – in the daytime, with me watching, I think. Uncle Horace was that nasty and that proud of the Tenkiller name.

* * * * *

Anyway, every time I was frightened by Chesty Hake's power or anger, I'd be intrigued by his zeal and intensity, and I'd think about Dad and Uncle Horace. Wonder how Uncle Horace would've done playing football. Defense, of course. Definitely defense.

* * * * *

Chesty had stored dozens of gorgeous boxes after his dad died. There was cherry, mahogany, oak, English walnut. This was a miraculous, inadvertent treasure trove. Something must've told him: keep 'em. This was surprising because, during his rookie season, he lived at the Hyatt Regency in Kansas City.

But when he bought the house on Kingsbury, it ended up a strange mix: a few nice things and a truckload of *schlock*. Contemporary Formica was the theme. But he found room for a fine mahogany dining table, circa eighteen-eighteen. And the one fine contribution from the Hake side: a chest from Lansing, Michigan, documented eighteen-fifty-nine. Chesty's great-great-something-or-other had created it out of eight woods. It was made during his cabinetmaker apprenticeship so he would earn enough to pay for medical school at Michigan State. Papers in a drawer documented this.

By contrast, I came from the Tenkillers and the Pinks, the Folsoms and the Pinchlynns, probably, and my people trekked and trucked and travailed. Carrying your belongings on your back certainly isn't earning a degree in interior decorating.

Yet I was able to make our house – I call it *our* house – very impressive. Antiques – seventeen-ten to eighteen-eighty-seven – made it look good. I admit that.

"There are more boxes," Chesty told me one day.

"What do you mean?"

"In a storage locker. There's a lot more stuff."

"Jesus Christ."

"It's a locker over on Page," he said.

* * * * *

I dare say HUT-HUT was the first twelve-cylinder Jag ever to put four tires on the property of Hannigan's Perfect Climate Storage Service, right next to Hannigan's Tire & Muffler Service. Chesty unlocked the heavy door and swung it open.

"Good God Almighty!"

I looked round and round, dizzily. This was the real Easter egg hunt. All around me were antiques that numbed the senses. The furniture, the accessories. Stacked and stored in plastic bags and large plastic wrapping were dozens of small wooden, silver, brass, copper, crystal, and, yes, gold boxes. Some were bejeweled. I couldn't concentrate, there were so many of them. My only clear thought was: Thank God someone knew how to wrap these things properly. Thank God!

"See why the basement was so cluttered?" he asked.

I just stared around me. King Solomon's Mines on Page Avenue, Overland, Missouri. I knew my first stop Monday morning, before heading downtown to the paper, would be The Library Ltd. book-store. I had to have more reference books on antiques before I could truly appreciate what I was seeing in Space Ten-C at Hannigan's Perfect Climate Storage Service.

"Chesty, what's in here?"

My eyes had hit upon something different. Carefully, I held up for inspection a fourteen-by-eighteen painting – also wrapped in clear plastic. I looked at the lower-left and lower right. There was no numerical designation to tell me this was a print. There was only the artist's all-caps name, lower-left.

LOCK CORTLAND

Lock Cortland! Lock Cortland lived his entire life in Canadaigua, a tiny community on a seven-hundred-sixty-foot-high "peak" at the northern tip of Canadaigua Lake, one of the picturesque Finger Lakes in western New York. He preceded Rockwell and came to be con-sidered the Rockwell of western New York.

The stark difference between them was that Cortland wanted no part of commercialization. He worked on his own schedule and wor-ried relatives and townspeople when he would be gone from his little studio for weeks at a time. The idea of having his work on the cover of the *Saturday Evening Post* would've angered the frail, rumpled Cortland.

He was little-traveled. He painted no kitchen scene east of Syracuse, no snot-nosed kid west of Ashtabula, Ohio, no dusty ball-field south of Cooks Run, Pennsylvania, no perspiring grandpa or energetic grandson north of the Lake Ontario shore at Shadigee, New York. While Lock Cortland wasn't well-traveled, he was immensely well-disciplined with his brushes. His wonderfully folksy style, his accurate, focused depictions of Americana from nineteen-thirteen to nineteen-thirty-five belied he was forty-four, and he died two years later, in nineteen-thirty-seven.

Ironically, a Rockwell expert at Pawtuckaway College in New Hampshire wrote in an academic journal twenty years after Cortland's death that Rockwell never had heard of Cortland until the guy died. But others had. His works, when he was willing to part with them, brought nice prices early in his career. Cortland fanciers saw themselves and their simple lives captured in his work.

Then, when Rockwell gained fame for his wonderful *Saturday Evening Post* covers, knowledgeable art people found they were willing to pay dear prices for Cortland's work done even ten or twelve years earlier. The styles of Rockwell and Cortland were unique but uncommonly similar in their homeyness, as if the two artists had studied long and exclusively under the same teacher.

Amazing how I had recalled all that from an art appreciation course at Mizzou!

I held up a Cortland.

"What's the problem, Paulie?" Chesty asked. He stood at the door, letting in the Page Avenue air.

"Don't you understand?" I yelled at him, waving the plastic-covered painting.

"Obviously not. So tell me."

I quieted down.

"Chesty, just what do you think this is?"

"A man sweating while he's mowing his lawn with a hand lawn-mower," Hake said.

I shoved the wrapped painting at him.

"Hake, this is a Cortland – a Lock Cortland!"

"An original? He did that?'

"Yes! Why do you think I'm – I'm shaking like this?"

"I thought you just liked storage lockers."

"Cut the shit, Chesty. Look. Your mother had three – count 'em, *three* – Cortlands. Look at these other two. They're a little smaller, maybe, but I promise you they're special. Fuck the *Saturday Evening Post* and its Rockwells. Just look at these. They're originals, Chesty, *originals!* A man sitting at a cluttered desk. You've never seen that, and neither have I. And a woman sitting in front of a pile of socks needing darning while the kettle's whistling. Your mom – or someone, at least – had the good sense to wrap these really well in plastic."

"Shit!" Chesty muttered.

"I know, I know."

"So who's Lock Cortland?"

Three Cortland paintings, that furniture, and all those wonderful small boxes in one storage vault at Hannigan's. But the paintings puzzled me.

"How could she have gotten these, Chesty? I mean – "

"Dunno, Paulie. Keep in mind I really didn't get to know my mother very well. We never – never had the opportunity to discuss the finer things. Hell, I was an adult before I understood the significance of my mom's maiden name. Rockefeller didn't mean anything to me. And I don't think I ever told anybody in school my mom's family had come to St. Louis from New York. I knew almost nothing about my grandparents – on either side. Keep that in mind before you bitch at me or give me your Trail of Tears saga."

Hake stopped to figure which way our conversation should go. He handed me the largest of the three Cortlands and gestured toward the other two at the rear of Hannigan's Space Ten-C.

"Look, Paul, these are just three paintings by somebody I've never heard of. And these things over here are just a bunch of boxes made by guys in seventeen-fifty and seventeen-ninety or whatever. To me, these things aren't even as important as how the Cowboys and Broncos will handle punt returns on a given Sunday.

"It's just me, Paulie. If Dallas has a guy named Cortland and he's L-Four or L-Five some Sunday, I'm gonna knock the shit out of him on the opening kickoff and then go looking for the return man. It's just me. I'm R-Five, Chesty, nothing more."

Now you know. As much as I cared about Chesty Hake, I had to admit he'd prefer some guy designated L-Four than to go to Phillips-Selkirk's or Norton's with me to determine the value of the three previously unknown Lock Cortlands.

I ached when he slammed and locked that heavy metal door that Saturday afternoon at Hannigan's Perfect Climate Storage Service.

But I was inspired. On our way back to Kingsbury Boulevard, I insisted we stop at Hepburn's Hardware to buy tung oil, lemon oil, four-oh steel wool, Regg's Finest Silver Polish, Porter's Friend for polishing brass and other metals, and light oak Brie Wax. As I say, I was inspired. Hake must have had five hundred bucks in his wallet, but he let me pay the bill at Hepburn's. I didn't mind.

Nineteen

I had come to really enjoy our home. There are a lot of things you can do with a four-bedroom house with nice crown molding and well-done chair rail, oversized doors and wide entries. The handsome staircase with its newel cap would have a special meaning as our lives tumbled.

I took measurements of the rooms and the lawn and then inventoried the marvelous antiques and things Chesty had brought back from his dad's rental home in Oklahoma, by way of Hannigan's and by way of Brentwood and by way of Albany, New York. While I worked on a yellow pad some mornings, I wondered how Chesty, his mom, his dad and his older brother had maneuvered all that wonderful stuff in their matchbox bungalow in Brentwood. Perhaps it was a good thing David was long gone for most of Chesty's childhood. Otherwise, nice things like a circular dark mahogany dining table, circa eighteen-eighteen, and a proud, beautifully restored Martha Washington, circa eighteen-fifty-seven, would've taken a horrible beating.

And then I'd think back to my own Formica childhood on South Sixth Street in McAlester, where a nice piece of wood was something in the front hallway – the front hallway of a home my mother cleaned Tuesday and Fridays, her days off from the Holiday Inn on the Bypass.

"Paul Boy, the Pearsons have a breakfront that goes from here to Anadarko," she would tell me twenty years earlier. That piqued my interest. I guess that's why I took that three-hour elective course in interior decorating and the one in art appreciation. I can't think of any other reason.

* * * * *

"I'll cut the tag off this table," Chesty volunteered.

"No!" I yelled. "You can't cut off that tag."

He froze, then asked why he shouldn't snip it.

The piece was my favorite among all of Virginia Rockefeller Hake's things: a small maple table, about twenty-two by thirty-four, with a heavy cord wrapped around the narrow side to keep a three-by-five India buff card attached to it.

I had not been a good high school golfer and had been an inadequate collegiate golfer, but Chesty had to be among the world's strongest true duffers. I asked him to read aloud the card, and even he appreciated the forty-eight words inked onto it. It read:

> Believed owned by Baltus Roll, a rich farmer whose Dutch ancestors probably settled near what is now Springfield, New Jersey, site of Baltusrol Golf Club, often the venue for the United Stated Open tournament. In eighteen-thirty-one, Roll was dragged from his home and murdered in a robbery attempt.

123

Hake slowly looked up from the yellowish card. He stared down at the table, then back up at me. I told him: "Now, if I can fall in love with this table, think how an Arnold Palmer of a Jack Nicklaus or a Hale Irwin or even a rich hacker from a rich country club might prize it, Ches."

"Holy shit! Holy shit!"

Touchdown.

* * * * *

Hake was a chef so talented I often wondered: Why the hell can't I do that? His response, any time I asked, was: "And I can't decorate a half-bath, Paulie. It evens out, I guess." We liked the way we complemented each other. I couldn't make a decent grilled cheese sandwich, and he couldn't buy a decent throw rug for in front of a toilet.

Never could I pry from him the secret of his culinary knowledge. He frequently bought cookbooks, but it takes a helluva more than _Betty Crocker's New Picture Cookbook_ or _The Silver Palate_ or _Crème de Colorado Cookbook_ or whatever to know your way around the kitchen the way he did. His big appetite aside, we had wonderful food when he was around. He'd make the telltale "serves eight" or "serves four to six." Even after he'd headed back to Kansas City in the pre-dawn Tuesdays, I'd know I'd have fine leftovers for lunch or supper – or even breakfast – depending upon my schedule at the paper the next couple of days.

One Monday night, we had Hake's memorable Cuban pork roast. He'd told me a week earlier he was going to prepare it, and I had to handle the marinade Sunday twenty-four or thirty-six hours in advance, between plays of the Cobras' game at Seattle. What if I missed Chesty's only NFL touchdown because I was nurturing a three-pound boneless pork shoulder?

I didn't. He didn't score, of course, but our Cuban pork roast did. I claimed minimal credit, as would the guy kicking the extra point after a ninety-eight-yard touchdown drive.

* * * *

EDITOR'S NOTE: Professional ball has its perks. That's indisputable. Hake wasn't a star, but he got his freebies. For instance, he had a half-dozen of those tall, cylindrical wastebaskets – white, with the Cobras' oft-copied, yellow and black logo.

Together, we had a dozen Cobras golf shirts – ten extra-extra-large and a couple of large – yellow and white or white on yellow. The same with running suits, T-shirts, gym shorts, hooded sweatshirts, stocking caps.

But the price was right. And just for the record, I didn't have a Cobras helmet phone in my bedroom.

There had been some speculation in the Sports Department. No, my phone was a plain white instrument with nothing-fancier that "re-dial" – and that answering machine, of course. Screen everything. Keep people out.

Twenty

Just when I thought Chesty Hake was going to open up and really talk about Sara Kassel, that psychological barrier went up. I was so curious to hear about six-foot Sara, his strange woman, his only woman. I thought he would tell me things I needed to know if I were going to avoid stepping on myself when the subject came up. I had, after all, made a fool of myself a couple of times in the past.

And then Hake wanted to go back two decades, back to the deaths of his mother and his dog. I tried to think of something – _anything_ – other than a cramped dining room splattered with blood, an underdeveloped boy cowering under that black circular table, trying not to look at his mother's nude body. I knew I'd lose it if somebody didn't say something. And yet the joke was on me, see, because I didn't know what was coming, this love and murder thing.

"It's all over now, Ches," I told him. "All that has been over for a long time. It's over."

I added up the years. I knew he had had some therapy. I hadn't.

Who needed it more?

What should I have done? Or said? What? In this conversation, he had mentioned his mother just once. How many times the dog? How many times had he spelled P-H-Y-D-E-A-U-X, the dog's name for me?

"Yeah, you're right, Paulie." Hake sounded okay, but it was eating at him. The shrink hadn't got to it in his childhood, hadn't cauterized it, burned it out. "When we get right down to it, I'd rather hit somebody from Denver or Dallas. I can't kill that jackoff who killed my mom and my dog."

Across our – _my_ – big maple breakfast table, I got my thoughts in order. I had to measure my response.

He squirmed, and I was glad.

"Clean hits or dirty hits?"

Hake knew what I was asking.

"Paulie, there's no comparison," he told me, emphasizing "Paulie" as my across-the-table name. "Clean hits. _Clean_ hits! I'd much rather have a good, clean hit on somebody than showboat and get oohs and aahs and headlines."

I didn't interrupt. He had more.

"I'd rather see my helmet get buried in some shoulder pads on kick-return and knock the other guy flat. That's better than going for the knees, seeing those knees cave in. I've never been that way, Paulie. I've never had a coach teach me that way.

"Knock the shit out of the other guy? Fine. Cheap-shot the other guy? No. But if you sit over there and ask me if I get a thrill out of knocking the shit out of somebody, the answer is: hell, yes!"

Chesty breathed deep, then paused. I knew why. I knew that pause. I had scribbled it in two notebooks, after all.

"Oh, it's not orgasmic or anything like that, but it's strong, really strong. That's why I've come to love playing on special teams.

That's why I've gotten to be pretty good on special teams."

I watched those gray-blue eyes. God, this hulk of a man was so committed to pro football! Yet, Hake never was selected for the Pro Bowl Game. He never had a chance of being All-Pro. And, sadly, he never even scored a touchdown in his eight years with the Cobras. Hake was a grunt, a true grunt. He was the prototypical grunt and lover of the game.

Twenty-One

Chesty bought the deep gold Jaguar coupe the year we got together, and his admission about the silencer-equipped pistol obviously bothered him.

"Do you know anything about guns, Chesty?"

"A little, I suppose. My dad – after my mom died – bought a gun. Every once in a while, we'd drive out to a firing range beyond Warrenton, maybe fifty miles, and spend an hour or so working on marksmanship and gun safety. I'm no Daniel Boone, but I got to be a pretty good shot. Dad really wanted me to be, I could tell. Because I was small and frail, I guess. He made sure I knew the gun – a lightweight semi-automatic – was on a shelf in his bedroom closet and it had a full clip. He had lost his wife to a murderer and his elder son to a lifestyle he couldn't handle. All he had left was me – and his insurance agency.

"It was important to Dad I learn to shoot," Chesty said. "On the way back in from Warren County those Saturday afternoons, we'd stop somewhere on the highway and have what I considered a great lunch: fried chicken at Big Boy's or something like that. While we ate, he'd praise me for my gun handling."

"Not a bad memory," I said.

"Once I asked Dad over lunch: 'Was David a good shot?' What a mistake! Dad immediately was ready to pay the bill and haul ass. By the time we got to the car, the sky was overcast, but I remember him putting on his sunglasses anyway. As we pulled out of the parking lot, I knew he was crying."

There was a question I had to ask Hake.

"Do you still shoot?"

"No, but it would be fun to see if I still can hit a beer can."

"Don't bother, Chesty. Not now, at least. I saw too much of guns when I was growing up, and I had to hear lots of stories of guns and generations past. That pistol in your car: Get rid of it."

* * * * *

The gun issue wasn't discussed much for five seasons. I suppose I should've said "five years," but my life had become one in which time was measured in seasons rather than calendar years. My year – Chesty Hake's year – began in July and ended in December. Then we had seasons: the off-season, the college draft season in late April, the mini-camp season in May, the training camp season from mid-July to mid-August, the pre-season season from mid-August to early September, then the _real_ season from early September until the end of December.

Warped, perhaps, but that was the way the year cycled for a pro football player and those around him. Wives, children, girlfriends, fiancées, live-ins, parents and drinking buddies: They all had to understand the player's calendar. I sometimes wondered what kind of quality of life there could be to a player's marriage. Good earnings don't always go with good marriages.

But the allegiance I owed Chesty was not what a wife owes her husband, or vice versa. I could walk out. There probably would have been some tugs, some resentment, but the split never would see a divorce court docket or warped kids.

* * * * *

C. J. Hake wasn't that old, fifty-four, when he rented that big, nineteen-sixties home up on Carol Drive, but age overtook him quickly and settled like a vulture. Chesty's dad, as I learned, went from middle-aged to elderly in no time at all. Chesty was in college much of those five years, but he probably knew what was happening to his dad.

* * * * *

"Dad really was a nice guy," he told me across the breakfast table. "I respected him, and I loved him for the right reasons, I think. He made me keep my napkin and my left hand in my lap at the dinner table because he had been brought up that way in an orphanage and because my mother made that a priority very early. My dad was the guy I depended upon when I really needed someone. David was long gone, into his gay lifestyle, so dad felt he had to be both father and big brother.

"I think our closeness was as good for him during that rough time as it was for me. I mean, I ate lunch sitting on a school john in the seventh and eighth grades. But maybe Dad did, too, or maybe his problems poked out in other ways. But he could relate, too, y'know? Until we moved to Oklahoma, I probably was the thing that kept my dad going.

"And yes, Paulie. I got teased about eating my triple-decker peanut-butter-and-jelly sandwich and my Fritos on a second-floor commode. A lot of the kids didn't know about Mom and Phydeaux, or they wouldn't have been so vicious. But I had only one way to go. I had to build my body. I had to become a success somehow, at something. If I hadn't achieved – well, I probably would've been a teenage suicide. I simply had to achieve; I _had_ to. I couldn't spend my life sitting on the john with a peanut-butter-and-jelly sandwich."

All I could do was nod.

"I don't think my dad committed suicide – or murder," Chesty said. "I can never believe that. I think something awful happened, but my dad – no."

For the record: No, C. J. hadn't killed anybody. Yet.

I wasn't about to bring up the subject of Chesty's gay brother and his brother's companion-business partner, Rory Rifkin, just because they were dead, too. A quick thought popped to mind, though: Should I explain to him both my parents died fairly young, and I could understand what he had gone through when his dad sent that car a hundred feet off a bluff into the Missouri River?

"A hundred feet?"

"Well, maybe ninety."

"And your brother's death?"

The tension got me by the throat. I seemed able to feel Chesty's powerful hands. But it was a matter of indignation and defense, not anger. Tension dissipated. Chesty's facial muscles slackened. Those big muscles that made his neck bulge finally settled down. Shut up, Paul. Just shut up.

* * * * *

We lived together enough years that I felt comfort in having his trust and respect. But I also say I hated and feared his strength. I once asked about his never wanting children for fear he might turn violent.

"Sara and I talked about it," he told me. "I just knew we never would be having any kids. She knew, too."

* * * * *

EDITOR'S NOTE: Each game tape was to Chesty what an *etude* is to a pianist who's very good but not yet an artist. He would watch, forward, reverse, watch again, often scribbling herky-jerky notes on a yellow legal pad, reminders of what he'd seen.

My previous paragraph contained a terrible analogy. Chesty's brutish fingers with the dislocated pinky on the piano keys. No, please. He may have known about early rock 'n' roll, but he sure as hell couldn't have banged it out on a keyboard. Tapes in the car, singing favorite phrases, and no pistol. Play it that way.

* * * * *

"Paulie, come watch this with me," Chesty said while I cleaned up after dinner. It was ninety minutes until "Monday Night Football." "You need to watch this."

I sat in my customary seat at the breakfast table and watched as he pored over his playbook and notes on his legal pad.

Checking. Checking again. It probably was no more than a minute or a minute and a half, but it seemed a half-hour. Finally, he pushed away the loose-leaf binder, pulled the yellow pad to him and said: "You gotta watch this."

He flickled on the VCR, and I watched a Cobras-Jets kickoff. Hell, I knew so little of the inner workings of pro football that my concentration might as well have been on the ladderback woodpecker at our backyard feeder.

"Just watch this for a minute," Hake said. He was puffing, and his brow was moist. "I wanna show you what can happen."

I watched. I watched a tape of a stout young man in jersey Number 33 go flying down the field. I wasn't impressed by replay after replay, and perhaps that's the reason Chesty and I had that wonderful relationship from the beginning.

"See what I've been doing wrong?" he fairly yelled, leaning toward me. "Now I can handle it when they do that to me! I'll be all right, Paulie!"

"All right about what?"

"Look, if I don't do my homework, I'm screwed. I'm the worst athlete on the field every Sunday, and I've got to make them believe I'm good, I belong. There are some guys in K.C. tonight – teammates, and maybe some of the Chiefs – getting drunk, getting laid, getting weird on drugs, getting arrested and maybe even getting shot or stabbed. And that's okay – for them. They all have superior athletic ability. They'll be back Sunday afternoon, good as they're expected to be. My situation's different. I have to work very hard every day just to make certain I can get that Sunday afternoon. Sunday afternoon means _everything_ to me. I can't piss away a Sunday in September or December."

Chesty ran a finger over his legal pad.

"I don't have enough of those Sundays."

I said nothing.

* * * * *

I had a game I much preferred to raking leaves in October. When

I was a kid in McAlester, a true game of skill – no videotape, no scoreboard, no press box – involved hunkering in a dusty parking lot and lagging pennies against a cinder block foundation. Closest to the wall wins. Hit the wall and forfeit the penny. Now, that had appeal! I used to fantasize about lagging for quarters, but my contemporaries and I seldom had enough nickels and dimes, much less quarters, to make much of a game at those stakes. Pennies it was. Old Man Pinkwater, at his tacky, moldy, out-of-date variety store on South Seventh, often asked why we kids would buy something insignificant on the way home from school and ask for our change in pennies.

No, I never needed a VCR or a yellow pad or a playbook. But a lot of times, I'd inspect the dusty area behind Pinkwater's Five and Dime and maybe smooth it a little. Chesty probably never spent a nickel at Pinkwater's, but it would've been fun to take him around back, point to where the dust met the cinder blocks and tell him: "Look at this! Here's where I won thirty-seven cents from Joey Pond. It was a Thursday. Thursdays were my days."

* * * * *

Since nobody could come to his house, Chesty insisted I save "some lunch money," as he put it, for a motel room, should the urge possess me and the opportunity present itself.

"And really, if you're not working, I think you should watch our game against the Falcons," he once told me. "Sitting in a sports bar with your hand in you lap while you drink beer, you have very little risk of contracting anything heartbreaking."

"Stick it, Ches," I said.

When I think back, Hake suggested I watch the Cobras' game not to see him be a hero, but rather for me to know, if he got hurt enough, he wouldn't be home at nine-thirty or up to enjoy one of his omelets at seven-thirty Monday morning. After all, driving cross-state with a kidney bruise, a hip pointer or a shoulder separation, maybe even one of those nasty stretched ligaments, is difficult.

I often wondered how Chesty held on to see the I-170 exit heading south off I-70, then the Delmar exit. I remember there were times he barely could make it up the steps to our back stoop. And even after more beer, sometimes he never would've gotten to bed if I hadn't helped him up the stairs to his bedroom.

Sometimes he'd limp in, tell me he was "never better" because the Cobras had won, tell me he'd feel worse if it weren't for the driving and the beer he'd already downed, and then he'd riff a Four Freshman falsetto with 'Day by Day . . .'"

But even with a six-pack in his belly and pain through much of his body, Hake would sleep Sunday night through. I'd hear him moan as he changed positions in his sleep, while his knees didn't want him to. It amazed me to see him already at the breakfast table by the time I came down at seven or seven-fifteen on a Monday morning. Sometimes he still had pain in his eyes from negotiating the fifteen carpeted stairs, but he would do his damnedest to be convivial.

"We won, Paulie, but — "

"I saw it. It wasn't what you'd call a classic victory."

"You're right," he'd concede. "Actually, it was uglier than – than that girl I screwed at the Holiday Drive-Inn. Anyway, we're tied with Denver."

"Right."

Before plopping down, he went and inventoried the refrigerator.

"Question, Ches: Why didn't they put you in with a minute and a half to play? At least you don't fumble."

"I damned near missed my block on that thirty-three-dive-dragon. I barely got a piece of the guy, and I had the key block. If I'd missed him, and he'd gotten Rayfield in the backfield, I'd still be in Kansas

City watching tape with Harry S Truman."

It was an oblique reference to the late president, the man whose name adorned the adjacent sports complex of football and baseball stadium.

"I wouldn't have let myself come home."

* * * * *

The last couple of weeks, I found myself saying to myself: Something's wrong, something's different. What? There was a gap between us across the kitchen table.

Twenty-Two

I was doing a story on the alarming number of serious knee injuries suffered by NFL players. One of the people I interviewed was Dr. Jim Cohen, a Barnes-Jewish Hospital orthopedic surgeon who had operated on several Cardinals baseball players and some of the Blues hockey players. He told me why Chesty moaned in his sleep.

"Only two species of mammals have knees unsuited to football," Cohen told me. "One of those has chosen to play and suffer the consequences."

"What's the other?"

"The elephant. The St. Louis Zoo once asked me to rearrange my surgery schedule in order to work on an eleven-thousand-pound bull elephant with a ligament problem. Think about it: Eleven thousand pounds – or at least a good portion of it – coming down on that joint. The big guy was in serious pain. The irony of this is that a kid with an anterior cruciate ligament tear – my scheduled surgery that morning – wasn't much better a football player than the big bull elephant might have been – with some coaching, of course."

So now I knew why Hake moaned or cried out in his sleep. Ligaments. Oh, and that cartilage. I'd lie awake, listening through the night. Some mornings, when I was trying to edit copy on early slot, I'd think about Chesty's night noises. Obviously, he thought it was worth it and didn't know how they bothered me.

What would my life be right now had I not done that first story on Mr. Irrelevant? I asked myself that frequently when I had early slot, when there'd be nobody around the Sports Department to break into my reverie or bitch at me.

* * * * *

Football's a fine game, I suppose, but I got very twitchy about it each autumn. When Chesty came home in September, he would be energized, even if the Cobras had lost. Then, in October, when the Cobras had a losing record and Hake had cuts, bruises, pulls, and strains, living in the same house with him would become more diffi-cult. Oh, he'd still greet me with "never better" after a victory. And he'd continue to do his homework in October and continue to drink his beer.

By November, Hake was run down. His pace was slower, and the sloped left eyelid was more sloped. He still did his homework on the VCR, but he took an extra hour on a Monday night.

During the second half of the season, November and December, he washed down a lot of Extra-Strength Tylenol with Budweiser. And he still groaned in his sleep.

The first year we lived together, I thought he was having bad dreams. But then I realized his knees, hips, ankles, shoulders, ribs, forearms, and elbows were taking so much punishment that he was experiencing out-and-out pain every time he rolled from one position to another. I could hear him cry out, and I couldn't sleep worth a damn, even through a closed door.

* * * * *

Quiet, ordinary Salem Road never was the same after the death of Virginia Rockefeller Hake. Some neighbors sold out. Others wasted little time putting on a deck or adding that saleable third bedroom. A few blamed the tragedy on C. J. Hake because he was a showoff, driving those Cadillacs all the time.

One day, out of curiosity, I drove east a half-mile from where I had had my apartment. I just wanted to see what Chesty had described to me.

Up a step hill off Manchester Road, there was a nice "starter home" compound dating back to World War II. A few of the decks and third-bedroom additions dated back to the sixties, but most were newer. I looked up a greened terrace to what had been Chesty's boyhood home, Twenty-six-oh-seven, and shuddered – and I'm a Choctaw. I couldn't imagine a refined woman, a respected neighbor, a valued resident on a quiet street like this one, viciously murdered in that white-brick bungalow.

When I turned around in the Bedford Drive _cul-de-sac_ and headed south toward Manchester Road, I averted my eyes from Twenty-six-oh-seven. I wanted to get away.

Then when I made a right turn onto Manchester, I had to ask myself: What's my hurry? I didn't share in Chesty's childhood horror. I'd seen what I needed to see. But it stayed with me, that malignant mantle. Chesty wore it all the time.

* * * * *

I felt true Choctaw guilt on Friday. I did something I shouldn't have done. I went through Chesty's closets and drawers. I never thought of a rich man, a borderline celebrity, as having so few clothes. I thought about the last time I had seen him. Captain Plain: khaki shorts, white running shoes, white golf shirt with a small yellow helmet logo, cotton anklets, fashionless haircut. Mr. Irrelevant and Captain Plain all in one.

Few clothes fitted Hake. His closet had a half dozen white button-down shirts and a half dozen blue ones. Twenty-inch neck, thirty-three-inch sleeve. There were some dress slacks, jeans and a few pairs of what Mom used to call "play pants." There were some golf shirts bearing "Kansas City Cobras" or just "Cobras" in script. One tux. Three suits: blue, charcoal, and tan. Maybe a half dozen sport-coats.

The coat that caught my eye was the vicuna from J.B. Simpson Clothiers, definitely one step up from camel hair. Chesty had given me a gift certificate for a matching one – a forty-long, not a fifty-two-short – for my birthday one year. A thousand bucks! I never went in for my fitting.

That's why I quickly, shamefully, closed that closet door.

141

Twenty-Three

An art dealer in St. Louis' Central West End, Trevor Baque, had a daughter who was a pretty fair high school swimmer and diver. She had developed something of a national reputation, so I did a story on her – what we call a "puff piece," all flattering data and planned quotes, nothing about her drug bust or abortion, with a photo that took longer to get right than I took to write the story.

Trevor Baque, as expected, was pleased. He also was willing to custom mat and frame the three Lock Cortlands for me about a week later. He also was willing to keep his mouth shut. Trevor didn't want a follow-up story done on daughter Julia, explaining why she had dropped out of the University of Miami the spring semester of her freshman year. By the same token, I didn't want all of St. Louis to know the three previously unknown Lock Cortlands had turned up in a storage locker. Trevor and I thought that was a fair exchange.

Baque and I had a significant chat after I wrote him a significant check for the matting and framing. He turned out to be a trivia freak, too, and I told him the owner of the Cortlands was an expert on rock 'n' roll.

With the Beatles' "Penny Lane" in the background, Baque armed me for my next duel with Chesty.

* * * * *

"These are wonderful, I suppose," Hake said as we hung the Cortlands that night.

"Yeah, they are. But I'll tell you what: You're gonna pay me back for the framing and matting if you can't answer my next trivia question. I'm gonna give you a good one. And since you won't be back until two weeks from now, you've got plenty of time to work on it. If you get it right, I hand you a hundred-dollar bill and eat the tab for these Cortlands. If you don't get it, you pay for the matting and framing. That fair?"

His response was a scowl.

"Hell, you're not gonna stump me when I've got two weeks to think about it, Paulie. I spent a lot of hours on the can, memorizing this stuff. But it can't be any later than nineteen-sixty-five."

"Right. And let's up the ante. Forget the hundred-bagger. If you don't get it right, you bring down to the paper a yellow and white Cobras golf shirt for every member of the Sports Department – sized to fit. We've got a couple of XXLs. How's that for a bet, jackoff?"

"Two questions: How many shirts total, and do I have to do an interview while I'm down there?"

"You're afraid of this one," I told him. "What does the number of shirts matter? The Cobras are going to pay for them anyway."

"No."

"Chesty, you don't give a shit how many shirts. You're just not so sure you're as good at rock 'n' roll trivia as you should be, that's all."

"Okay, you're on," Hake muttered. "And *I'm* paying for the shirts. Now, how many are we talking about?"

"Thirty-five yellow and thirty-five white, and you'll have a list of all the sizes. If somehow you answer my question, I hand you five hundred-dollar bills."

I could see a slight smile.

"I want your money."

"Those Cortlands look good grouped on that wall, don't they?"

"I want your money, jackoff."

* * * * *

"Getcha a beer?" I asked, taunting, as I left the breakfast table.

"Gimme two more minutes, and I'll have the answer," Hake said, smarting.

"You've had two weeks."

"Where's my beer?"

As I returned to the breakfast room, I knew I had him, and that felt awfully good.

"Let's see, most of the guys will be large or extra-large golf shirts, and the women will want..."

I handed Hake his beer.

My question for Hake, before a week of practice and a nice, tidy, no-injury eleven-point victory over the Chargers at Weston Stadium had been:

> What singer's wife was the inspiration for a hit tune
> by Jan & Dean in nineteen-sixty-three?

Even before Chesty got home at nine-thirty-four, I knew I was going to be a hero in the Sports Department. Then some guilt dug in. What if he had neglected his studious ways, forsaken his dedication? What if he had been more intent on figuring out the answer than doing his homework? And worse, perhaps all along, he knew the answer. He'd hidden that small smile. No, he didn't have the answer!

Linda McCartney, wife of Paul McCartney.

* * * * *

"How many shirts did you bring?" I asked, watching him trundle in from the back stoop, through the kitchen and toward the big staircase.

"Two. And they fit me fine."

* * * * *

As he had been taught, Hake was reluctant to discuss the inner workings of the Cobras. Face to face, he didn't want to talk about injuries, personalities, or problems that might affect the outcome on a given Sunday afternoon. Nothing solid.

When it came to rock 'n' roll trivia, however, he thought he was special. Just as no one would bench press with him for money, no one would challenge him at pre-nineteen-sixty-six music, either. "I tell them I don't know shit about music or movies after sixty-five, and then I let them try to stump me for a hundred bucks. What the hell. Most of 'em won't even try. Some wouldn't know rock 'n' roll from 'Rock of Ages.' I try to encourage them. If anybody wins the hundred by stumping me, I get to ask him a question. If he gets that right, I give him a thousand.

"I let Ol' Muldrow stump me one day and gave him a hundred. Then when he asked me a Whitney Houston question in return, I grabbed my hundred back and explained to him she wasn't born until August of sixty-three. See what I mean?"

"Yeah, but I got you with the Linda McCartney question."

"Actually, that was damned good. How'd you come up with it?"

"Lock Cortland."

"Cortland? Hell, he died in nineteen-thirty-something, you told me."

"Believe me, Cortland helped. And when you get home Sunday, I'll have a complete list of the shirt sizes you need to get. Then, the following Monday, we can go down to the paper together and give out the shirts. I'll help you carry them. Seventy-two shirts will be unwieldy, I know."

"No interview, right?"

"No interview. Oh, the managing editor said to tell you he's a large, unless they're cut skimpy."

"Okay."

"Would you have known this one? What vocalist was No. One on the charts for three weeks and died in a plane crash in eighty-five?"

"Too easy. That was Kyu Sakamoto, who had 'Sukiyaki' in sixty-three. That was good but not as good as your Linda McCartney."

I stared at the Cortland paintings.

"Thanks for the shirts."

Hake went to the refrigerator for beer. We talked about the game and our schedules, and then he ambled off to bed.

Twenty-Four

I didn't want to hear any more about Virginia Rockefeller Hake or the dog. But Sara? A different story. Chesty believed she was alive, maybe married, maybe not. And he needed her. He didn't need me.

The subject of Sara came up while we drank a bunch of Bud.

I told him he should've bought a condo in Clayton, not a four-bedroom house, if he wanted to maintain St. Louis roots. He should've maintained his privacy and mixed his lovely Nathaniel Niere tables with his Never-Mar tables. No one ever would've known. No, Chesty didn't need me. I wasn't the person who was going to make his life complete.

Suddenly, he wanted to tell me things—significant things.

"This is the first time you've really talked about her."

He rubbed that grisly, slanting eyebrow.

"Nothing to talk about. All I've got left from my time with Sara are my HUT-HUT license plates. Not even memories."

I thought about it. I'd never talked about my ex-wife, and yet I still loved her. And I had memories. Memories of what killed the marriage, what it was like to be married to a stranger—a social and political climber.

So why should I have expected Hake to talk? Perhaps he really didn't care about my situation, which would've been natural enough. Perhaps he didn't consider it any of his damned business what I had to say.

Instead of talking about Sara or my ex-wife, Hake suddenly wanted to talk about non-threatening but still important subjects. We would sit face-to-face across the big maple table. Stamps I couldn't afford, like the ninety-cent dark blue Washington, No. Sixty-two in the Scott's U.S. Catalog. Why he preferred stone-ground to wheat crackers or tortilla chips with his garlic-*jalapeño* cheese dip. When Dion sang with the Belmonts and when he sang with the Wanderers. Why athletes say "y'know", "I mean", and "This may sound like a cliché, but..." and why I mow the boundary of our lawn and then work my way into smaller and smaller rectangles.

* * * * *

After I'd finish the lawn, I'd yell "Beer time!" Chesty never left me dry. A Bud would be on the breakfast table by the time the mower had been tucked into the back of the garage. Of course, the routine ended about mid-July. For the hottest of the Midwest's heat, mid-July to the end of August, Chesty Hake had a prior commitment in Liberty, Missouri.

But one June day, when he returned from working out and I returned from my time with the Toro, we sat across from each other and swigged. This seemed a good time to again try "Operation Sara." Why was I so insistent?

"You're actually afraid to talk about Sara, aren't you?"

It came out almost as one long word.

"Tell you what, Paul. On your next day off, drive to K.C. and check out Sara for yourself if you're so damned interested. Or maybe get your boss to send you over to William Jewell College to do a couple of Cobras training camp stories. Between the morning and afternoon practices, you'd have plenty of time to find Sara. Somebody at her asshole father's dealership would help you, I'm sure."

Chesty got out of his chair, big torso over the table.

"I'll be back."

I thought he was going to work out at Shaw Park for another sixty or ninety minutes. Instead, he headed upstairs. When he came down, he had four college yearbooks and a stack of photos in a couple of rubber bands. He sat.

"Beer."

I went to the kitchen.

The yearbooks told me what I thought they would. Chesty Hake was the biggest little man on campus. Here he was, diving for a touchdown, reaching high for a pass, holding a football high after scoring, receiving a trophy, shaking hands with any number of people in photos that should've been credited "Photo by Joe Pose." And here Chesty was wearing his letter jacket at a Friday night pep rally and bonfire, signaling "touchdown" after putting the ball in the end zone. Nothing I didn't expect from his junior year.

Then I met Sara.

She wasn't beautiful. Statuesque, yes. Her basketball picture showed muscular thighs, a muscular, athletic butt, and a thin waist. The other two photos were her class picture, showing her eyes to be quite large and sparkly, and her lips to be full; her yearbook staff picture, showing several members pointing at a layout and Sara's index finger much longer than anyone else's.

An action shot of her on the basketball court had been cropped so poorly, the lower calves were gone, as was the top of the ponytailed head. She, like Chesty, was No. Thirty-three. She had broad shoulders.

Number Thirty-three? Same as Hake? Coincidence? Probably. And I wasn't about to ask and risk ruining this breakthrough with Chesty.

"And then we have these," Chesty said.

The four-by-six and six-by-four snapshots told much. There was Hake, the stout, squarish, somber man in his black robe, with the mortarboard at an ill-advised angle, delicately holding the large hand of a tall, proud redhead.

She was almost a half-foot taller than he, and I could tell her eyes were bright green and her hair was a long and lovely vermilion. As promised, her nose was prominent and her lips were – oh, what the hell, lush. I had kinda hoped her hair would be orange or auburn, so it wouldn't have been perfect. But it was vermilion: perfect. She looked like a taller, better-built, lesser-groomed Streisand—and I'm a guy who has fantasized about Streisand.

Her shoulders were wide and square, like a swimmer's, and her breasts were proud and high, if not particularly large. The photos had been poorly cropped. Her calves were left to my imagination.

I put the best photo of Chesty in his graduation robe and mortarboard on the top of the stack.

"You look professorial," I told him, handing them back.

"Screw yourself."

"No, Chesty, you look like a dean's list kinda guy—with good taste in women."

I didn't know what reaction that would bring. He pointed at my beer can.

"Want another?"

"No, Mr. Dean's List. Think about it."

"No, thanks."

Twenty-Five

Chesty Hake loved his stamps. I'd guess his collection of American stamps from eighteen-forty-seven to the present had to be among the best in the Midwest. He had worked on it for years, refined it, upgraded it, added to it with judicious purchases and done smart bidding at silent auctions. He knew it was worth more than a quarter-million dollars, but nobody else was to know that. He made that clear to me. Hell, even the luxury-item rider on his homeowner's insurance policy didn't reflect the value of his collection. That was asking for trouble, he thought. I thought the opposite.

He worked on his stamps for an hour or two most Mondays when he was home from Kansas City, more during the off-season. He found the discipline—identifying, cataloging, sorting, confirming watermarks, mounting recent additions, measuring perforations of the borders—very therapeutic. It took his mind off the aches and pains to which he was subjected. I'd watch those powerful hands, that twisted pinkie finger, as he worked his stamp tongs.

He thrived on the no-contact competition of the silent auctions at Chaim Salinsky's stamp shop. They were weeklong, ending at eight-fifty-eight each Monday night. Hake would stop by briefly during the day Mondays, then go back in the evening before "Monday Night Football" on TV usually, if there was something he thought was worth a bid. If he had the winning bid, he would pay for it the following Monday. That was his arrangement with Salinsky and the elderly dealer's niece, Raiza. Hake seldom bid, but always seemed to want me to spend.

"Bid, Paulie, bid," he whispered to me one evening as we surveyed the glassine envelopes on the beaverboard wall. "Bid on this No. Sixty-one. You're never going to see it go this cheap again. They've got twenty-six-hundred bid. Go three big."

"Can't afford that, Chesty," I whispered back. "If I pay three thousand for that thing, I won't be able to sleep nights. Besides, it's going to go for more than three-thousand. It's too good."

I poked around Chaim Salinsky's small, cramped shop to make certain my words weren't going to any ears but Hake's.

"Got car payments, y'know."

"Put in a bid, or I'm going to."

"No."

He didn't but...

"Hey, Paulie, this is for next week's auction. You've got time to change your mind."

* * * * *

"Mr. Salinsky, this is Chesty Hake."

"Ah, Mr. Hake. I got your message, and it said I was to call collect. The young lady who took my call seemed to know what for I was calling," the stamp dealer explained, putting a "k" on the end of "young" and "calling".

"Mr. Salinsky, you have a very fine No. Sixty-one red-orange Franklin in your silent auction this week," Chesty said into the lobby phone, making eye contact with the Cobras' receptionist, Becky Shular. "I want it. I want to pay exactly two-thousand dollars more than the highest bid as of, say, five o'clock Friday. At five-oh-one, put my bidding number, seventy-eight, on the sheet and add two-thousand. Then put the stamp in your vault."

"But—"

"But nothing! I want the red-orange Franklin. Put it in your vault Friday afternoon, and I will come by to get it Monday afternoon."

You don't push men like Salinsky. He was a Russian immigrant who had been in business for himself much longer than Chesty had been alive.

"Bring cash Saturday or it goes to the highest bidder."

Becky Shular pretended to be busy at her desk.

"It's two-thousand extra, you little jackoff, so you come out an additional two-hundred ahead. I'll bring cash next Monday, not Saturday," Hake said, then lowered his voice for effect. "You don't seem to understand, Salinsky. I've got a football game to play here in Kansas City Sunday. Now, you'd better have that Franklin in a nice, fresh glassine envelope for me when I get there Monday. I'll be there about one-thirty, so do yourself a favor. Don't screw up. I'm a nasty bastard, Salinsky. A lot of people will tell you that."

Becky looked up, but she didn't smile. She wasn't for sale.

* * * * *

Chaim Salinsky, not Chesty Hake, admitted to me nine thousand-dollar bills and a five-hundred changed hands at one-thirty-four the following Monday afternoon. So he had a small glassine envelope containing a red-orange treasure, printed in eighteen-sixty-one and wonderfully preserved. That treasure looked so nice in my collection. It went well with other Christmas gifts from Chesty over the years, none of which catalogued at less than about five thousand dollars.

That first Christmas, I protested his extravagance. He was ready for me.

"Paulie, I don't spend one cent of my salary on stamps," he said calmly. "I always make sure there are performance clauses in my contract from year to year. Shit, the people in management know my situation. They know I'm not going to be a problem child when it comes to contract negotiations. I've never had an agent; never will. The fact that I'm a millionaire may keep me in the NFL longer than I deserve to be. Who knows? I'll work for the minimum. But that aside, those performance bonuses let me do my stamp collecting. And they let me help you with yours. Okay?"

"I'd never buy this stamp."

"I know," he said, obviously angry and a little hurt. "Look, if I give you a five-thousand-dollar stamp for Christmas—maybe a nine-thousand-dollar stamp—it's because you're my friend and because I can afford it. If I were a clerk some place, you'd be down to a box of cigars."

"I didn't mean to hurt you," I told him.

"Then believe me when I tell you these stamps are free—compliments of the Kansas City Cobras. Hell, I make extra money if I carry five times a game—eighty times a season. I make several thousand dollars extra if I've played in all sixteen games the previous season, if I score three or more touchdowns in a season—forget that shit—or if I grade eighty-percent or better in blocking for the season, or if I'm in on twenty-five percent of the special-teams tackles, or if I make the Pro Bowl Game or the All-Pro team. I have plenty of money to buy stamps."

"Two McAlester guys."

Hake smiled.

"There you go."

Twenty-Six

Although I was the third man off the bench for the McAlester Buffaloes basketball team by my senior year, Hake easily would've been able to beat me playing one-on-one. He was quicker, stronger, younger, had better stamina, and he had leaping ability that was amazing for a bulky five-foot-nine going on five-eight.

But there was one sport in which I came out on top: golf. I had been the last man on the McAlester golf team, seldom breaking ninety. Then, as a lark, I tried out for the University of Missouri golf team in my freshman year. A walk-on!

While the Stan Utley types were dazzling with sixty-sevens and sixty-sixes on the A.L. Gustin course in Columbia, I counted ninety-five—maybe ninety-four—and didn't bother to turn in my scorecard. Drink a beer, put your golf bag in your shoulder, and hope someone will give you a ride to your dorm, Tenkiller. But I was in there.

Much of golf is go-for-the-throat. I never saw Chesty throw a club or break one, but he wanted to. By the time we'd get to the sixth hole at Ruth Park, a nine-hole course less than a mile from our house, he'd be snorting. That didn't produce good golf. If we played five bucks a hole or a bingo-bango-bongo for three, I knew I was going to have beer money.

Chesty hit the holy shit out of the ball. We once had an elderly playing partner at Ruth Park who marveled at the length, not the accuracy, of Hake's drives. He asked Chesty: "You're hitting an Innacle, aren't you?"

"An Innacle? No, it's a Pinnacle," Chesty replied, checking the brand name. "See?"

"No sir, it's an Innacle," the old man insisted. "On the last tee, you knocked the pee right out of it."

* * * * *

Then there was the celebrity tournament in Pensacola, Florida. Chesty seldom accepted invitations to play in such celebrity events in Kansas City or St. Louis. However, he agreed to play in a tournament in Florida's Panhandle because it was sponsored by a friend of Chesty's late father.

He wished he hadn't accepted.

Upon his return, he told me he was having the time of his life and playing decently, too. His team—two wealthy drunks, a prominent Florida amateur and Hake—were in fifth place after the first two days of the three-day tourney. Then a minor sportscaster from a network station was in the same course-to-hotel courtesy car with the attractive, mid-forties society matron driver, an angular pro basketball player and Chesty.

A bad mix.

Chesty was sitting left rear in the Lincoln, occasionally catching the reflected glance of the driver. He admitted, later, he was much more interested in talking with her and making certain she would feel his breath on her neck if he leaned forward to speak. But the TV guy got in the way.

"Hake, tell me about your gay brother. Was he good?"

The sportscaster leered over the back of the front seat.

Kristin, the blonde driver, saw trouble coming. The big Lincoln came to a skidding halt on a steep shoulder, a nice, soft ditch. A sign no more than twenty yards away read:

Country Club Shores

PRIVATE

"What the hell do you care about my brother?" Chesty asked. "You gay?"

"Guys, I've got my door open," Kristin announced. "We kin get out this way."

Hake stepped onto the pavement. When the reporter got out, Chesty leveled him. It was ballet. Such a clunky, trained athlete. The blow carried a lot of memories and drove in hard on a lot of frustration. So what if Chesty hadn't been as gifted an athlete as David had been! So what!

"Mr. Hake, that man just went all the way over the hood."

Chesty touched her hand and could feel it shaking.

"I'm sorry, Kristin. I didn't mean for you to get upset, and I'll make it up to you, okay?"

"Okay."

"Let me take you to dinner tonight."

"Okay, I guess."

"Lobster thermidor and filets."

"Okay."

* * * * *

Hake and the rest of his foursome—no, the rest of his gang—shot a best-ball seventy-three the following morning at the lengthy, arduous Santa Rosa Shores Country Club, leaving them many shots back of the winning foursome.

* * * * *

"I couldn't hit it worth a damn yesterday," Chesty was saying at the breakfast table. "And the day before, I busted the chops of some smart-ass Florida sportscaster."

"What the hell happened?"

"He was TV. He started in on me about David. He wouldn't let up, Paulie."

"You need to loosen up," I told him. "Don't beat up somebody because your brother happened to be gay."

I knew immediately I had said the wrong thing, and something occurred to me while he stalked off to the shower. I wondered what had become of that pistol of his.

A couple of times, I prowled through the interior of his car: the console, the glove box, under the front seats, in the trunk. The gun was gone, or at least I couldn't find it. It lingered in my mind, though, that he still had it. If it had been in a drawer or on a closet shelf, that was better than having it somewhere in a flashy car that could be stopped by police or even stolen.

I snooped through Chesty's bedroom and couldn't find it. But it worried me. I needed to find that gun, but I should've been worried about other things, like Chesty's slow decline and his obsessive nature.

Twenty-Seven

It was a classroom in Blue Springs.

The little redheaded girl's hand was waving.

"Young lady, what's your name?"

"Me? My name's Ginny, Mr. Chesty."

She reminded him of what his mother—and Sara, come to think of it—must have been like at the same age: gangly and redheaded. Smiling. Engaging.

"Ginny, do you have a question or something you would like to say to me?"

"Yes, Mr. Chesty. My question is: Do you do drugs?"

"Ginny, I'm really glad you asked that question. I've got the right answer for you. I'm very proud to tell you I've never done drugs. *Never*! There are about sixteen-hundred players in the National Football League who are better than I am, but the reason I still can play is I don't do drugs. And I work hard. Ginny, I do homework almost every night. At my age! My homework is on videotape, and I watch movies you can't rent. But I look at those videos again and again, and I take notes. You know why?" Hake paused. "Anybody?"

"'Cause you wanna score?" a kid in the back of the classroom asked.

"That's part of it," Hake responded. "I want to *succeed*. I figure, if I can't be the best, then I'd better work harder than anybody else. That's why I watch tapes almost every night. Kids, hard work is the thing we can use to succeed."

The kids clapped. The teacher came to his side, smiling. He pressed an envelope into her hand. Inside were two tickets to Sunday's game.

As Hake was about to leave, the teacher told the kids to give him a standing ovation. Hake said: "You kids must think I'm going to score a touchdown Sunday. Well, I'm probably not going to. But I'll think I have if I've convinced you guys to stay away from three things: drugs, alcohol, and guns.

"Think of it this way: If you make an 'F', that's a ten-yard loss. Make a 'D', that's a five-yard loss. Make a 'C', you were stopped for no gain. If you make a 'B', that's a first down, and let's hear a cheer. And now, an 'A'—an '*A*'—that's a touchdown, and the fans are going wild! And four of those on your report card? Hey, kids, you're an All-American in my book. Now, go do it!"

As always, Hake's eyes got wet. That's why he didn't do much public speaking. He let the teacher follow him from the classroom.

"Chesty?"

"Miss Stanley, did it go okay?"

"You were sensational," she answered. "And thanks for the tickets. I've never let myself afford a Chiefs or Cobras game. I think I'll take Ginny—unless her parents are big fans of the Chiefs and won't let me."

"Take Ginny. By the way, I hate speaking in front of adults, but I enjoy working with kids."

"Do you have any—any kids, I mean?"

"No," he said quietly. "I've never been married. Considering my situation—pro football—I've never thought it would be fair to *any* woman.

"Miss Stanley, that's a debate for another time, maybe. But would you let me talk to Ginny for a moment? I won't say anything about the tickets, of course. But I just—I just want to talk with her for a moment."

"Sure, Mr. Hake—Chesty."

Ginny came reluctantly into the hallway, perhaps frightened at being singled out. He went to his knees, grunting slightly. He stayed at her height, viewing the world through her eyes. He didn't touch her.

"Ginny, I just want you to know I think you're going to be a hard worker all your life. You're going to work hard and be so successful that pro football players will come to hear *you* give speeches."

Green eyes watched him, searching for truth.

"Do you mean that?"

"Of course I do, and I'll tell you why," said Hake. "The two neatest ladies I ever knew looked very much like you when they were nine. One was my mom, who was a true lady and died—died quite some time ago. The other was my old girlfriend, my fiancée' from long ago, who had hair just like yours. I have a feeling my mom—her name was Ginny, too, believe it or not—and my girlfriend, Sara, would be happy knowing I have a crush on you."

The little girl was speechless until Hake reached the front entrance of Camilla K. Case Elementary, Blue Springs, Missouri. Then she let loose.

"Do a touchdown, Mr. Chesty!"

* * * * *

Laurie Stanley's voice filled the room. In Chesty's bedroom at his Lee's Summit condo, the answering machine scratched a little.

"I want you to know you had a telling effect on my class. My one difficult child was good all week, and Ginny and I loved the game. Yes, it was a first for each of us."

* * * * *

"You leave yourself wide open, Chesty," she said over her beer.

"I suppose so, but I don't care. There's nothing more here that you can know. Let's not get into it."

Laurie Stanley sipped her beer, letting the silence trail out. Finally, a man with some sensitivity.

"Why the fixation with Ginny?" she asked. "I was trying not to listen in the hallway. Your mother? Was that it?"

Then it was Hake's turn to pause.

"You don't let up, do you?"

"Not if there's still a chance."

"Okay, Laurie, I'll make it bright and brief."

She waited.

"Ginny looks like my mother's early pictures," Hake told her. "My mom was tall and gangly and had that same wonderful red hair. And from what I learned about her, she was very much in need of answers to her questions when she was a child. She must've asked questions the way Ginny did the other day. And by the way, how come I was assigned your class?"

"I simply told the woman in the Cobras' marketing department you specialized in grade school talks."

Hake felt better.

He told her of his one love, Sara (no last name), and that their rela-

163

tionship had been incomplete, then forbidden.

* * * * *

"Why do you play football?"

"That's the best and the worst question I've ever been asked," Chesty said, lightening up, reaching across the booth to take Laurie's hand. "I *have* to play; I absolutely *have* to. I don't need to. I don't need to make big money. I can't play much longer, but for now, I have to play. I'm probably the worst guy in the NFL, talent-wise, but I don't care. I'm lucky I get to do what I want to do for now."

Chesty looked at his hand covering hers.

"Laurie, I don't have a choice but to be a team player. I'm one player who never can be a star. I'm not made that way. I play for the team, or I don't even get to play. That's a fact of life.

"Hell, I'd like to be six-foot-two and run the forty in four and a half seconds. But I'm not, and I can't."

"I like you all right," she said, covering his hand with hers.

* * * * *

Laurie and Chesty made love in her bed, seven stories up in an apartment overlooking Hy Kassel's automobile dealership. At three-oh-six a.m., when Hake painfully trundled from the bed to the bathroom, he looked down from the sliding glass door in the living room. He considered opening the door, going out onto the balcony and hurling his spent condom down onto Hy Kassel's roof. He didn't.

* * * * *

"Chesty? Mr. Chesty? I think I know why you're such a good football player," Laurie Stanley said, childlike, curling deeper into his shoulder. "You carry a lot of anger, and when you make that anger motivate you, you are very, very good."

"Bullshit." Then, in a soft voice, he added: "Bad read, Laurie. I'm not angry."

"It's not a bad read."

"Bullshit."

"Tell me more about Sara. Why did your love come apart?" Laurie tilted her face up.

"Why do you need to know about Sara?" he countered. "Why does everybody want to know about her?"

Laurie could feel the tension in his muscles.

"I want to know. I think I *deserve* to know. A woman wants to know how tough her competition is."

The silence was long.

"You have to let me go slowly."

Laurie waited. Somewhere, a car horn sounded, telling life to get out of the way.

"Ginny was my mother, and the psychiatrist kept telling me someone would replace her," Hake began. "I was eleven when she was killed. I was a different person then, believe me. Anyway, the replacement probably was Sara. Maybe not. Who knows? I'm not a shrink, and some of those people are dumb as shit.

"My dad was a good guy, very bright, and I'm pretty sure he loved my mother," Hake said. "He was an insurance agent and a stamp collector, but he'd never spend big money to improve his collection. He didn't show his love for Mom."

Her fingertips moved lightly across his back.

"We lived in this little white bungalow in St. Louis County, and Mom always thought we should move to a better area with bigger homes. His insurance agency was only three blocks from home, and he always used that—the convenience—as an excuse for not moving. And he would talk about being a product of the Depression, which translated into: 'We can't overspend by ten cents this year, much less ten thousand dollars."

"And Sara?"

"I don't know if you're ready," Hake said.

"Try me."

Hake dug his hand into the pillow. Laurie's bedside radio was on low, drifting. Look at me.

The song was grand but wasn't one that made Mathis' elite list.

"I was a wimpy little nothing at eleven. I came home from school for lunch one day and found a situation that put me into a couple of years of therapy. I was twenty when I finished high school, Laurie. And I'm probably not straight about it to this day. I've told only one other person—voluntarily about it."

"Sara?"

"No, no. Shit, she couldn't have handled that."

"Who then?"

"Paulie. Paul Tenkiller, my housemate in St. Louis," he told her. "I thought—I hoped—he could handle the whole thing."

Her fingers ran his spine.

"If you can tell it once, you can tell it again."

"Okay," he said, making the word almost a warning. "I came home for lunch most days if the weather wasn't too bad because I was afraid to be around other kids in the cafeteria or on the playground at lunchtime. I was such a little, insecure shit.

"That day, I opened the front door, and the first thing I saw was my dog, this cute, cuddly Llaso apso named Phydeaux—dead. She had been *skinned*. There was a lot of blood. And when I looked for my mom, I found her naked, bleeding, with her neck over one of the supports under the dining table. She was in a kneeling position. She had been strangled and anally raped."

Laurie went rigid in his arms. But she wouldn't let go. Chesty gave her that. He shelved the stuff about his father's death and his brother's death. It was over, anyway.

Twenty-Eight

They came at Chesty one year, perhaps because he had a helluva lot of unearned money. What they quickly determined was that Hake and I shared living quarters—in quotes: "shared living quarters." That sent up a warning flag.

My interview with Bob Haberstroh of NFL Security was as enjoyable as a barium enema.

"Mr. Tenkiller, you've been a sportswriter out here in Kansas City quite some time, haven't you?"

"Mr. Haberstroh, I was a sportswriter *'out there'* in Kansas City, briefly, some years ago. I've been a sportswriter *'out here'* in St. Louis for quite some time, if that's what you mean."

"Yes. Yes of course," said the fat little man from Four-Ten Park Avenue. "Now, let me ask you another question, Mr. Tenkiller: How long would you estimate you and Chesty Hake have been—been, ah…"

I stared at him.

"You dumb bastard. What's the commissioner's private number? I'm calling him."

"Why, I can't tell you that. I won't tell you."

I dialed Hake's private line in Lee's Summit. Haberstroh started to get up from the living room sofa.

I waved him down.

"Hello?"

"Chesty, this is Paul. Haberstroh from the NFL is here, beating on me about our relationship. You wanna talk with him?"

"Those jackoffs!" he snapped. "They're after me, obviously. Apparently they'll do whatever it takes. So keep your fucking mouth shut, okay?"

"Sure, Ches."

"Let me talk with Haberstroh."

I signaled to the heavy-set man in the dark suit. He came to the phone.

"Bob Haberstroh here."

"Fuck yourself, you jackoff!"

Haberstroh stared at the dead phone, then at me.

"Football players," he said.

I just smiled.

* * * * *

Haberstroh must've known he screwed up. "Out here" in Kansas City, "out here" in St. Louis. How different those two cities are! In terms of metropolitan area, St. Louis is much older and has almost twice the population. Kansas City covers almost twice the square miles. Within the city limits of K.C. there is farmland, which you certainly won't find in constricted St. Louis. Kansas City has many beautiful fountains, those famed barbecue restaurants, and the

Country Club Plaza. St. Louis is renowned for its zoo, Italian restaurants and the Gateway Arch. Kansas City drivers seem to like to signal when changing lanes, while St. Louis motorists are notorious for the rolling "St. Louis stop" at intersections.

And Haberstroh came a thousand miles from New York, on the NFL's expense account, only to confuse the two Missouri cities? Chesty was right in calling him a jackoff.

* * * * *

When Four-ten Park Avenue called, Hake was uncharacteristically frightened. His presence was required within two weeks in the office of the commissioner. The meeting would be with Donn Donnelly, the NFL's chief of security and the boss of Robert Haberstroh. The phone message reed two-oh-five that Monday afternoon, six hours before the kickoff of a ten-point loss to the hated Raiders on "Monday Night Football."

Yes, the league knew exactly where to find Chesty when the order went out.

It was the middle of the night when he came barging into my bedroom. He didn't have to wake me.

"You didn't do anything, and I didn't either, Paulie," he said, after driving from Weston Stadium to Kingsbury Boulevard in less than three and half-hours. "Sorry to wake you, but we should talk."

It occurred to me he never had trespassed into my bedroom. Not that it mattered, really.

"The commissioner's office has sent for me. It's Haberstroh's boss: the top cop. You said you made it clear to Haberstroh our relationship is straight. I don't get it. I don't gamble, and I don't do drugs. Hell, I don't even sell my autograph."

Chesty paused.

170

"Other than my – our – problem with Haberstroh, I can't think of any reason why they want me to come answer 'some questions.' That thing with the TV reporter was a long time ago, my second season. I can't figure this out."

"Want me to come with you?"

"No, no. I appreciate that, but it's probably not a good idea. They'll always think there's the risk you might do a first-person story that could change the look of the NFL or something. I just don't know why they want to talk to me in New York, that's all."

"Chesty, if you think it's gambling, I'll sign a letter vouching for you. No matter what my paper's likely to say about it. Shit, you're no gambler. You don't have the *time* to be a gambler. Evidently, big-time gamblers really have to work at it. Well, anyway, if that's why they're dragging your ass to New York, I'll vouch for you. I know you're not gambling."

* * * * *

He dialed the private number of security chief Donn Donnelly at NFL headquarters, and he didn't have to go through a secretary. The chief of security came on the line too quickly, as if he had been waiting for Hake's call.

"Yes – yessir," Chesty told the receiver. "Yessir. I don't have a set schedule, but I usually drive to St. Louis on Sunday night and spend Monday here during the season. What time? Well, unless I'm hurt and need some treatment, I get to St. Louis by nine-thirty or nine-forty-five."

He listened.

"No, normally, that's not a problem," Hake told New York on that Tuesday morning. " I don't need a lot of sleep. On Tuesdays, I usually get up at about five-fifteen and get on the road for K.C. by six for eleven o'clock meetings at the stadium."

He listened.

"Mr. Donnelly, can you tell me anything about this?" He finally asked.

"No, I can't. Not right now, not on the phone. I wish I could, but we'll do so much better across the conference table from each other," Donnelly said, with what sounded to Chesty like a practiced tone.

Hake ventured a guess – a wild one – as to why he was being summoned.

The response was stammered. His guess had been good.

"Well, Mr. Donnelly, at least now I know what kind of shit to expect from you," he told the phone. "I won't have any answers, but at least I'll understand the questions."

"What is it, Ches?" I asked.

"I can't tell you, Paul. Believe me, I'd tell you if I could. Let's just say I've got a problem I didn't know I had."

Was it my gambling? Is my betrayal of Chesty about to come out? Oh, shit: I must've said that to myself a dozen times.

"When do you get back?"

"Thursday of Friday. I'm going to miss some practices. I've never missed a practice. Donnelly said the league would call Turk for me, and he said don't bring any paperwork to New York."

He looked at me.

"I definitely don't understand this, Paulie. If there really is a story here, you'll get it before the league gives it to *The New York Times*. I promise you that."

Not my betting. Thank God!

* * * * *

Hake wore his oldest suit, a dark gray glen plaid, and a burgundy print tie for his first session in the Park Avenue offices. He was underdressed, quality-wise, but he remembered a Cobras linebacker had been instructed by his attorney before some sort of civil proceeding to wear brown slacks, a brown-and-gold striped tie and a short-sleeved white shirt. Hake had none of these. What he forgot was that the kid got six months, an eleven-thousand-dollar fine, plus court costs.

* * * * *

Here's what was handed out by the NFL and went to every wire service in the universe:

> Chesty Hake, running back, Kansas City Cobras, as of this date, has been placed on the Disqualified List by the National Football League, pending further review.
>
> His disqualification is not to suggest the Leag conducting an investigation into the possibility of substance abuse, turpitude, gambling, or criminal activities.
>
> The reason for Chesty Hake's disqualification not be made public by the National Football League. Media speculation for this disqualification will not be appreciated.
>
> Bottom line: Leave this alone, people. You know all you need to know in good time.

Jim Golden

V i c e President/ M e d i a Relations

National Football League

* * * * *

Speculation in newsrooms across the country was rife that night. What's being covered up? Why disqualification, when the Cobras could have been given an extra injured reserve? He's never even been slapped on the wrist. No, this was something different, something particularly sensitive, pundits concluded. But why Hake, hardly your glamour player?

Many radio and television stations read Golden's advisory/release with a light touch, and many papers ran it in its entirety in their "mail" editions, "city" editions and "lifts" – the papers that go onto lawns pre-dawn and into vending machines at rush hour.

* * * * *

Oh, the Kansas City media were having a wonderful time speculating as to why blue-collar Chesty Hake had been placed on the never-before-used Disqualified List. It wasn't a suspension, which is punishment, and it wasn't Injured Reserve. So?

Gambling? Drug use or drug dealing? Association with a known underworld figure? Psychiatric? Guys on the special teams: You have to wonder. Or had he called another radio or TV interviewer "jackoff" once too often into a live microphone? None of those made any sense. Any would be suspension or Injured Reserve, not disqualification.

The Cobras and the league were saying nothing. It had to be something pretty sensitive.

I wondered if the Cobras' hierarchy, General Manager Sheldon Bergman in particular, even knew the situation. My bet would've been he'd been left as dumb as the rest of us.

Personally, I liked the way the league handled things. I couldn't say that to my boss or the people on our staff, of course, considering my situation. I was the natural guy to get the exclusive on Hake. And, after all, I'm the guy who had to be prodded to do a second first-person piece on Hake when the paper's big guns learned we were housemates. I could've wound up being the perpetual early slot – not enviable duty – the lonely fart who, early each morning, pulls and sorts the wire copy and advisories so things have at least a fifty-fifty chance of going smoothly in the department when the bulk of the staff arrives. Drawing early slot was preferable to being in the backfield, answering phones to settle barroom trivia fights. Early slot also was better than facing a Guild grievance hearing.

But I didn't know anything, and the sports guys in K.C. were being made to suffer, too.

I thought about Chesty's faults and vagaries and idiosyncrasies, but I couldn't come up with anything the NFL would find sensitive. Not a thing. I was certain he wasn't a gambler. If he knew any gamblers other than me, I would've been very much surprised. He didn't speak the language, use that lexicon. He drank his beer at home, at Krueger's occasionally, on I-70 eastbound, or at the Missouri Grill when forced into it. He had a similar routine in suburban K.C., I'm sure. He drank beer in little places where his tip, not his autograph, was appreciated.

Drugs? No! Women? No again. He laid what came his way but never pursued. Anyway, the league doesn't make a production of that unless rape or sodomy charges are filed.

I opened a Bud and fired up a Healthy Choice Beef Sirloin Tips Dinner in the microwave, then sat at the breakfast table and thought back to what he had told me about his phone conversation with the league's head of security.

By the time I heard BEEP-BEEP-BEEP announced from the microwave, something had crept into my mind. As I ate, I became certain I knew why Hake was the NFL's conundrum.

The gun.

That seven-point-six-five-millimeter accessory Hake bought when he paid cash for his gorgeous gold Jaguar.

The gun had been used in the commission of a serious crime. That had to be it. Tread lightly here, I told myself. Who really knows? So I waited.

I went through the garage and let my Beef Sirloin Tips Dinner grow cold. Hake had taken a cab to the airport for his flight to New York, so I took my time prowling through HUT-HUT. I went through the oversized console, the glove compartment, looked under each front seat, reaching in front to back and back to front – twice. Nothing but tape cassettes that hadn't been replaced in those mini-suitcase storage cases. No wonder he was so good with his rock 'n' roll knowledge.

How 'bout the trunk? Locked, of course.

I ran back inside, up to Chesty's bedroom, only to realize he would have his keys with him in New York. But there were a half dozen keys in a lovely little pewter box on his dresser. Two of them had cat heads – Jaguar heads.

I opened the trunk, knowing I desperately needed to uncover that German pistol. For that, I really didn't like myself very much. But my self-esteem popped right back. There were four more cases of tapes, a first aid kit, and a nice, compact little tool kit.

And no gun.

I replaced the Jaguar keys in his pewter box and got out of there.

My Healthy Choice entrée was colder than Kelsey's balls. Why did Chesty get dragged to New York? Where's the damned pistol?

* * * * *

Never let it be said the University of Missouri's School of Journalism doesn't turn out resourceful graduates. Our staff always had six, eight, even ten of us, and the Cobras "beat" writer in Topeka, Kansas, knew it would be good to call our department, trying to get a line on the Chesty Hake disqualification. It had been two days since the league and the Cobras had announced this procedural move, and Wayne Overby's bosses in Kansas were pushing. Bob Marek, part of our J-School coterie, was the late man that night.

He was very busy.

"Sports . . . Marek."

After a pause: "Weasel! How are ya? Still in Topeka?" Another pause. Then my name went on the griddle.

"The guy you want to talk to is Paul Tenkiller," said Marek, looking at me. "Remember him from J-School? Well, he's the guy for you, 'cause he actually *lives* with Hake."

There was a pause that bothered me.

"Yeah, really," Marek responded. "But he told me and told Jim Calvin he doesn't know anything, either. Hey, that's what he says."

Marek nodded for me to pick up the phone at my spot on the rim, the horseshoe of desks topped with computer terminals.

I tried to be friendly, candid, and professional during my two-minute conversation with Overby. I assured him I knew no more than he did about Hake. No, the Associated Press story written after the dual Kansas City/New York news conference didn't lack any information I had. No, I was not being pressured for "inside stuff" I couldn't provide. No, Hake hadn't returned, and I didn't know where he was staying in New York. Finally, I said I doubted the Cobras were stiffing the media when they said they had no additional information.

"Believe me, I wish I could give you more," I told him. "Next time we both know we're going to be in Columbia for a Mizzou game, let's get together at the Heidelberg and see if we still know how to dribble beer."

Bob Marek eyed me with obvious suspicion as I hung up.

"Tenkiller, I didn't like you in J-School, and I don't think much of you now. If I ever find out you've held back anything – *anything* – about this Hake bullshit, I'm gonna kick your Indian ass."

"No, you won't. And, no, I haven't," I told him. "Don't ever get tough with me, Marek. Just do your job, and I'll do mine."

The sports copy desk got quiet for some time.

Word spread. The phones in the Sports Department and my home phone rang numerous times in the next couple of days and nights, each caller wanting to pick my brain. I gave each the same answers I had given Overby. But one New York writer tried a different tack.

"Considering your situation, Tenkiller, do you know of any gay writer-player relationships in sports?"

"No."

He didn't quote me.

Twenty-Nine

"You don't need to put your 'game face' on for this," the big man said from behind his desk. "I'll tell you up front you're probably going to be here until Saturday. We had thought it would be Thursday or Friday, but it may even be Monday. On the other hand, I can tell you you're in no trouble with the league right now. I want to make that clear. All we – all *I* – want to do is clear up some details. The integrity of the league is so important, you know."

Hake told me later he saw this as a set-up. Three or four extra days? Security chief Donn Donnelly was smooth, smooth.

"Then why am I here, Mr. Donnelly? I've got work to do," Hake told him, his voice probably a little louder, his emphasis probably a little stronger than it should have been. "We play Denver Sunday, and that's a divisional game for us."

"I'll get you back to Kansas City as quickly as possible, Hake," the former FBI official said firmly. "We'll try to tie up everything in four days. It may be five. But understand you'll miss the Denver game and perhaps the next one as well. We'll see.

"But do yourself a favor. Keep in mind that, while you're in New York, you're not to contact anyone – *anyone*. We're going to discuss some highly sensitive matters. Neither the commissioner nor I would want to see these matters in *The New York Times* or on WJAK-TV. This, you will see, is in your best interests. It's for that reason we've imposed one of our rare news blackouts."

Hake shivered at this.

Donnelly hunkered over his desk at him.

"I'm going to ask you a great many questions, Hake. I know it'll get tedious for you, just as it will for me. But it'll go faster and easier if you'll just answer my questions. I'm going to put a premium on honest answers."

Hake focused on the plum-colored wall covering. He knew he had to control every response. No sneering, no shouting. Be as smooth as Donnelly, if possible. No flare-ups like "jackoff."

In the following four and a half hours that first day, Chesty answered questions, recalled key conversations, recalled numerous documents that held his late father's signature and his late brother's signature – but didn't bear the signature of his late brother's companion.

That, obviously, was one of the NFL's concerns. Hake wondered only momentarily how the league had obtained Cadillac Mutual Life documents. Was he suspected of killing his dad and his brother? Then he got focused again.

"Mr. Hake, you're a licensed agent in Missouri for the Cadillac Mutual Life Insurance Company?"

"Assurance. You can see it there in front of you. It's 'Assurance,' not 'Insurance.' It's Cadillac Mutual Life Assurance Company."

Chesty picked up on Donnelly's switch to "Mr. Hake." He also realized right then this quick-hit conversation was going to take on the scope of a full-scale trial.

"Yes, I'm licensed in Missouri, and I'm an agent with Cadillac Mutual, Mr. Donnelly. I have been since the day I turned twenty-one and passed my state licensing exams."

"How much insurance do you write?"

"I write a few policies for friends and teammates, but I can't devote much time to the business during the football season. I've written policies on six, maybe seven teammates in the past two or three years, and I wrote a couple of the married guys from Blackwater College.

"I'm a football player, Mr. Donnelly. I belong on Stadium Boulevard right now."

* * * * *

They blocked Chesty's phone, and all he could get was the concierge's desk. His room service dinner was the double veal chop with a large spinach salad with bacon and crumbled egg, to be washed down with six cans of Budweiser. The chop was superb, the salad was fine, and the Bud was tasty and had the effect Chesty hoped it would have. His day had been a long one.

The split of *sauvignon blanc* went uncorked.

He didn't stay up to see whether or not his situation had made the eleven-twenty-two sports block on TV. Out. Gone. Snoring over dirty plates.

* * * * *

He sat across from Donn Donnelly at eight-twenty-five.

"Chesty, we need to talk about the deaths of your father and brother," Donnelly said, his voice flat.

Hake huddled down.

"There was an accident. You know that."

"Yes."

"It was my graduation day," Hake said. "They didn't tell me about it until after the ceremony. I kept looking around for my dad."

"Ummm."

"Do you know something I don't, Mr. Donnelly?"

"What do you think, Chesty? You've had time to think about this. Could they have been murdered?"

Hake was numb.

"I dunno. No. I really don't think so. Why would anyone murder my dad?"

Graduation, caps and gowns, speeches. Murder.

"Or why would anyone murder your brother?"

Plum-colored wallpaper.

"I don't know that, either. He and his friend were fine together, I think. They didn't give anybody any shit, as far as I know."

Donnelly riffled through a file folder. Scratchy paper sounds.

"C'mon, dammit, where are you going with this? I mean, if you've got something to tell me, it's important to me, y'know? I came into considerable money – as you obviously know – and if there's been a murder, I need to know about it. I need to talk with the people at Cadillac Mutual."

"I've already talked with people at Cadillac Mutual. Just answer my questions. You may get back to Kansas City sooner. Keep that in mind. Also keep in mind that nobody really cares you were once Mr. Irrelevant. To me – right now – what you tell me is relevant. Keep that in mind."

It lasted three more days.

Hake was asked about his father's move to McAlester, their social lives in McAlester, the never-to-be-forgotten "jackoff" quote on TV, his relationships with Laurie Stanley and with me, his demand for privacy, the therapy he underwent as a kid, his willingness to be less than a star, his reaction when Sheriff Weeb Houston notified him his dad and brother had perished, his drinking habits, and, yes, his relationship with the Kassel family.

In four days, there was no mention of HUT-HUT or the pistol.

* * * * *

At twelve-forty p.m. New York time Saturday, the NFL official and the barrel-like little fullback sobbed together across a desk high up at Four-ten Park Avenue. Hake was a confused football player after the four-day ordeal, and Donnelly was an accomplished actor. At twelve-fifty, they ended it. Donnelly smiled, thanked Hake from the bottom of his heart for his cooperation under difficult circumstances, and handed the player a plane ticket to St. Louis.

They shook hands. As Hake turned to leave, Donnelly clicked on the big-screen TV. Ohio State at Penn State.

* * * * *

Hake sat in seat Three-B, first class. He felt self-conscious, in that he was wearing his old gray glen plaid suit. It was sour with sweat. He was the only passenger not in sports clothes.

"What would you like to drink, sir?" the flight attendant asked. "Our white wines are –"

"Nothing," Hake told her. "Nothing. Thanks."

"Nothing I can get you?"

"Well, yes, as a matter of fact. How 'bout a late score on the Ohio State-Penn State game."

* * * * *

"I haven't slept in four days," I groused, keeping up a front, seconds after he walked through the front door. "You'd better have lots to tell me."

But no gambling, please, Christ.

"I've gotta get out of these fucking clothes," he said, three steps up the staircase. "Give me a couple of minutes. I'll tell you all I can."

"Wanna beer?"

He nodded and continued up the staircase.

Not my betting, thank Christ! I fairly sprang to the kitchen for two Buds and had them on the breakfast table coasters by the time he came back down.

He had scrubbed his face and changed into a yellow Cobras running suit.

"You're not driving to Kansas City tonight, are you?"

"No. Tomorrow, probably," he said, rotating the beer can in his powerful hands. "I don't want to be a distraction on game day. I'm disqualified for this week. It's not like being suspended for fighting or for shoving a ref. This pisses me off, Paul. Until now, I'd never missed a practice – high school, college or pro. I was proud of that. And until this week, I never really knew what happened to my dad and my brother."

He looked up at me, eyes intense. The Bud can stilled in his grip.

I drank six, I believe, and Chesty downed twelve during his telling of his New York revelations. Mr. Irrelevant from years past became very relevant.

"You're the only person who's going to hear everything."

Neither of us was an actor; neither of us a Donnelly. We talked across the table till ten.

184

* * * * *

For all the hurt Hake had endured, he had learned so much. The wrapping paper came off all those boxes of tragedies, the ones kept in the emotional closet for years and years. Chesty learned in New York:

* The drug-dippy fat man believed to have ravaged Chesty's mother was anally raped and strangled less than two years later in the maximum-security penitentiary at Chester, Illinois, allowing St. Louis area police to close the case. The four-hundred-pound assailant, staying with relatives five blocks away on Mary Avenue in Brentwood, had learned Hake's mother's maiden name was Rockefeller, and he wanted to be remembered as having done something special to someone special. He bragged of this to guards and inmates. He kept bragging when he went before prison officials. His fate was, they said in Chester, not unexpected.

* C. J. Hake, probably five-foot-six, never loved his elder son, David, almost a foot taller by the athlete's freshman year at the University of Missouri. Only rarely did David have any contact with his father or even his mother after he left for college. C. J. went to David's Brentwood High games on Friday nights, but only to make certain he would be seen by Cadillac Mutual policyholders and prospects.

* David Hake never suspected his million-dollar-plus Cadillac Mutual life insurance policy, issued within four or five weeks after he had been the Chicago Bears' first-round draft choice, never had a change-of-beneficiary form submitted to the home office, thereby leaving C. J. Hake – who wrote the policy, of course, and received the commission – as the primary beneficiary and Chesty Hake as the first contingent beneficiary. Rory Rifkin, as companion and business partner, was to have been named primary beneficiary, with C. J. as first contingent beneficiary and Northern Illinoians Against AIDS as sec-

185

ond contingent beneficiary. Forget Chesty, of course.

* C. J.'s Cadillac Mutual production went from that of a consistent Million Dollar Round Table performer to that of a journeyman agent, and several policyholders in both Missouri and Oklahoma complained to the Cadillac Mutual home office that he failed to return phone calls or to take care of service requests.

* Cadillac Mutual's Vice President/Agencies, Denny Johns, summoned C. J. to the home office to review an alarming job performance and encountered a small man in the throes of depression. Johns ordered C. J. to get psychiatric help and told him a change of scene and routine would be beneficial as the new CMAL general agent in McAlester, Oklahoma. Johns quickly made it clear to C. J. his general agent's contract would be voided if he didn't comply.

        * If C. J. had lost his Cadillac Mutual contract, another agent would've been assigned as servicing agent for David's substantial policy. C. J.'s oversight – refusal to submit to the home office the signed change-of-beneficiary form – would've come to light quickly, and the senior Hake would've been vulnerable to a charge of insurance fraud. We're talking *felony* insurance fraud.

* Chesty never had shown a strong interest in a career in life insurance, and his father long had felt anxiety about Chesty's ability to succeed in the adult world; hence, he felt he needed a foolproof means of insuring – literally – Chesty's future.

* The selection of Hake by the Cobras as the Mr. Irrelevant in the NFL draft, coupled with his graduation from college a month later, provided C. J. with a reason to insist his two sons be "reunited," even if for only a weekend in late May in central Missouri.

* * * * *

Except for pee breaks, I sat for almost two hours and listened.

I have no idea how many times I shook my head. I just remember doing it. I was awed.

But he didn't mention gambling. And, dammit, he didn't say anything about the pistol.

"Now you know, Paulie," he finally said. "Now you've learned everything I learned in New York. And I don't know how to handle it. I don't know who would. I'm rich, I guess, with money I don't deserve. But I'm not a crook. I didn't know what my dad was going to do. The money's mine, the law says, but I don't deserve to have it.

"If I turn those death benefits back to Cadillac Mutual, somebody'll find out, and we'll have all kinds of stories about collusion, about my knowing Dad was going to do what he did – what the league tells me he did. We wouldn't have any privacy after that, you can bet.

"I just don't know how to deal with this," he went on, fatigue in his voice. "We've got our employee assistance program in Kansas City, so I guess I'd better ask the Cobras to get me some psychiatric help. I've been in therapy before, so it won't be all new to me. But I'm not gonna talk to anybody in the organization about this. They'll find out from New York what they need to know. People really don't need to know how my mom died, or my dad or my brother, either."

For just a moment, he looked privately amused.

"And no one 'cept the IRS needs to know I've got 'bout three, four million bucks," he said. "Tell ya this, Paulie: Not one fucking dollar is going to the Northern Illinoisans Against AIDS."

"Do you believe everything you were told in New York?"

"I guess I have to, even if I don't want to. They had things carefully documented – little things they couldn't have made up. When I went through Dad's files, I found correspondence between Dad and Denny Johns, his boss in the home office. I guess I was too naïve and too emotional at that time to know Dad was in some kind of trouble. So, yes, I think what the league told me is true. Somebody else knew

187

what was in those files. No doubt about it. But dammit, when I accepted those big death benefits, I didn't know what had happened. I was blind, I guess."

"Did your Donnelly guy believe what you told him?"

"I don't know. I told him everything I could, as honestly as I could. If I had lied, he would've caught me. I just wanted out of there. I couldn't make a phone call! Shit, I'm not accustomed to picking up the phone and getting short-circuited. The hotel operator was nice, but that's the way it was."

Hake crushed his beer can into a ball and went to the kitchen for two cold ones.

"One more thing, and then I'm going to bed," he said from the kitchen. He came back into the breakfast room and handed me my beer. That huge upper body leaned forward, and he put both elbows on the table. I really didn't know what to expect from him. One of those scary times.

"We've gotta talk about money," he said.

"While I was in New York, one of the league's lawyers told me I'm an idiot for not having a current will. So I'm not going back to Kansas City tomorrow. I'm going to have J. Billy Wingo do a will for me."

"Look, Chesty—"

"Now, here's what I'm going to do," Hake went on. "I'm going to will you my stamp collection."

"Aw, Jesus," I said. "I don't want your collection. Hell, I've got a nice collection of my own. Don't do it."

"Hey, jackoff, you may have to wait thirty, forty, fifty years. But I want you to have it. You'll appreciate it more than the Missouri Historical Society or some other museum will. Maybe you haven't looked around the house lately, but I don't have any kids. See what I mean?"

I tried to make light of it. After all, his collection was begun by his great-grandfather, a history professor at Amherst, I believe. A man who died decades before Chesty was born. Then the collection was added to by a late grandfather and his father. My collection was a source of pride, certainly. But even with Hake's stamp gifts at Christmas time, it was paltry by comparison.

"The collection will come out of my estate before any other property does," Chesty continued, and my mind struggled to catch up with what he was telling me. "I know it will. Then, after that, here's the way I'm going to work it.

"Forty percent of what's left goes to Blackwater College, because small colleges really have a tough time of it right now. Blackwater was pretty good to me. I was made to feel wanted and appreciated when other schools didn't want any part of me. Most schools wanted fast stallions, and my background chased away some of the big schools. That's all right."

Hake stopped talking too suddenly. He made a few jottings on a Cadillac Mutual Life note pad. He was tired, but he still had a lot to say.

I waited.

"Then another forty percent of my estate will go to Father Graham's Boys' Home down in Salem, Missouri."

"Father Graham's?" I asked, puzzled. "What's the connection?"

"Well, they made a good eighteen-year-old out of a bad, bad thirteen-year-old. My dad was an orphan, and he was in trouble all the time from the time he was seven or eight until Father Graham's took him. He told me about that when I was held back that second time in grade school. Dad said he'd never have gotten into college if it weren't for being forced to grow up at Father Graham's. I want forty percent to go there."

Chesty paused.

"Now, I know what you're thinking: I'm trying to build a monument to myself."

"I don't thing that you'd –"

"Anyway, I'm not. For Blackwater and Father Graham's both, it's going to be stipulated that nothing – no building, gym, scholarship fund or whatever – ever can have my name on it."

There was a scratch on the tabletop. Funny, I hadn't noticed it before. I looked for others.

"And the remaining twenty percent goes to Paul O. Tenkiller."

"Why? I don't *want* your money. I don't *need* your money. Living here, I have almost no bills. I make a decent living at the paper. My car's paid for. I don't pay any alimony. I'm okay, Ches. Really."

"Do it for me, not you."

He got up and walked with those powerful, choppy strides. Over his shoulder, he said: "Good night."

* * * * *

When I came down to breakfast, Hake was engrossed in the front section of the Sunday paper.

"Morning."

"Morning."

Brunch went okay. There was nothing wrong with Hake's appetite. New York hadn't affected that. I sliced and diced the makings for fruit bowls while Chesty handled eggs, Buerger's Famous thick-sliced bacon, and baked bagel halves with fresh-grated Parmesan.

We didn't reopen that sensitive subject that closed out the previous evening.

"When ya goin' back to K.C., Ches?"

"No rush. I'll stay and watch whatever games are on TV this afternoon, then see J. Billy Wingo about the will tomorrow morning, if possible. Lawyers tend to be busy on Monday mornings, but I'm not on a timetable. If I can get in to see him tomorrow, fine; otherwise, it'll keep. I'll just run and do some lifting."

* * * * *

The NFL, with no official media comment, reinstated Chester J. (Chesty) Hake Jr., fullback, the following Tuesday.

Thirty

That Sunday, Hake played what probably was the best overall game of his pro career. He had opening-day spring in his legs and renewed power in his upper body, while the Saints felt the tug, the drain of a long season and hundreds of hits that hadn't healed.

He controlled special teams play, recovering a fumble, making five tackles and being credited with three blocks that indirectly sprang Cobras kick-returners for two touchdowns. The forty-one-point victory come over the wire to my paper in seconds, but I didn't learn until the following morning – across the breakfast table – Chesty Hake had been awarded his first game ball as the team's most valuable player. Special teams coach Bob Wilmette glowed in the dressing room.

"Hake, we didn't know where you why you been in New York, but goddamn, we're glad you're back!" An inscription was on the ball by the time Wilmette tossed it to Hake.

Chesty remained on a crest as he left W. W. W. Weston Stadium through the throng at the high double doors. It was five-twenty-two. He clutched an overnight case in one hand and a football in the other as he walked to the all-alone Jaguar for his cross-state trek. The vast civilian parking lots were long since empty.

No one hailed him.

* * * * *

Hake was clear of the heavy traffic by the time he reached Concordia. He patted the football on the passenger seat as if were the thigh of a good-looking woman. He ejected the tape cassette from the console and inserted another. Gale Garnett again told him how long "We'll Sing In the Sunshine." He thought of Laurie Stanley, who, in all probability, wondered what she had done wrong.

It was rape and murder and a skinned dog, Laurie. No relationship can survive that. But you tried.

"I'll give you that, with your gorgeous fingers down my back," he said aloud at eighty miles an hour.

The Native American bodily remains container offered up a beer.

"And I'll be on my way," Hake reprised loudly, feeling at the same time good and bad about himself. Gale Garnett's six words trailed off, and he was glad. He had quiet highway time and wanted to ride in silence. The Bud grew warm in the console cup holder as he cleared Sweet Springs, the Marshall junction, the Blackwater turnoff, the Boonville exit, the Missouri River Bridge, all the Columbia exits. He blew past the U.S. 54 South exit at Kingdom City and drove on through the night. The cooler handed him one.

An hour from home, he thumbed in a Four Lads tape, then turned off to get gas at Grace & Ernie's Shell in Warrenton, as he did so often.

Once home, he was greeted only by the back stoop light, the light over the kitchen sink, and the upstairs hall chandelier. My room was dark. I wasn't there for his big moment. I bet he stood there, just cuddling the prized ball, then said: "To hell with it."

At breakfast the next morning, I wore my white Cobras jogging suit with the yellow and black trim. I thought I owed it to Hake.

Hake wore a yellow version, and he already was digesting the morning paper.

"Morning."

"Morning."

"How ya doin', Ches?"

"Never better."

"You're back!"

"You bet your ass I am," he said quietly.

"Hey, nice football!"

"I reached for his game ball, and that was a brief mistake.

"Don't touch it! Don't touch this thing!" Hake said as he scooped it up. "But I wanted you to see it. I earned it. Coach Wilmette was kissing himself: special teams MVP, Chesty Hake."

His smile was quite shy.

"Shit, I played well, Paulie."

"So let's go out and scuff this ball in the street."

"No!"

I had him, and he knew it.

"Well, shit, if you don't want to do that, we'll just sit here so I can read the paper. Congratulations, Ches."

"Thanks."

"Hey, how about New York?"

"You mean what I was told? I'm over that. I should've known it a long time ago."

"You're over it."

* * * * *

But his moods became erratic. No longer could I gauge him. He had some good games, after which he turned inward. Then he'd have a bad or so-so game, and he'd laugh and kid around. How to read that?

He'd laugh at a good joke but laugh uncontrollably at a stupid one. He'd race to the front porch when he heard the paper arrive, yet not move out of his chair when he heard the doorbell ring.

We were eating Chesty's *picadello*, a Mexican dip he makes for six people, and it takes a good hour to prepare because it contains something like twenty-seven ingredients – everything from chopped egg to white raisins. When two people instead of six tackle it, well, only two bags of flour tortillas are needed.

We neared the bottom of the big dip bowl.

"We need to discuss your will, " I said.

"No, we don't," he said sharply. "There's nothing to discuss. It's already drawn up."

"But I don't feel right," I snapped. "I'm a little embarrassed. I feel like a gigolo or something."

Hake scooped the last of the hash-style dip onto a tortilla chip, then held up his hand, traffic cop-style.

That was Hake's way of changing the subject.

"Ches, think about it," I pursued. "What – what if some asshole came over the center line and killed you? That will of yours would get held up in probate by somebody. A whole lot of investigators would come after me."

"You could handle it."

"I don't want to fucking handle it. Shit-can the will."

"No."

"The paper would do a story on us – *us*. That scares me. Give it all to Blackwater and the orphanage."

"You don't want to be rich? Buy a new car?"

"Not particularly."

"Own antiques like these? Own these? This house? They're also written into the will."

"Aw, shit! Chesty, what if you fall in love? What if you get married? What if – what if Sara somehow comes back into your life? That will of yours is gonna be as up-to-date as high-button shoes. Change it – for me. Let me get a good night's sleep, will ya?"

"Sara's not going to happen, Paulie, so I have no intention of ever getting married. I don't even date much. You know that. And it's always one-dimensional: Go to dinner or maybe a banquet, go back to her house and screw. As for Sara, she happened a long time ago and unhappened a long time ago, too. I suppose the biggest mistake I've made was idolizing her instead of loving her. There's a world of difference. I was in idolatry, not in love."

What do you say to that? I kept quiet.

"The biggest mistake I made was not breaking Hy Kassel's neck when he said I couldn't see Sara. But if I had put that jackoff out of his misery, we wouldn't be sitting here at the table playing Alphonse and Gaston. We wouldn't be haggling over my millions."

I squirmed, trying to dodge the issue.

"The will stands. If you don't accept what I'm providing out of friendship, then you don't get my stamp collection, either."

I gave in.

"Shit, Ches, eventually I'd love to have your stamp collection. But only if I outlive you. Okay, I'll accept the terms of your will, you sonofabitch."

He wore his wry little smile as he crushed his Bud can and went to the kitchen for fresh beers.

Thirty-One

"I can get him," the tall redhead said. "I know I can."

"Bedda, woman. You bedda. Else yo' regrit it."

"You don't scare me. You never have."

She hit the yellow throw rug just inside the kitchen doorway. It became a looped cotton sled as her fanny hit it. She slid into the doors of the cabinet under the sink, and then she hit her shoulders and head on the ersatz cherry wood. She glowered up at him.

"Bedda git 'im," the angular man repeated. He left her to pick herself up and find a mirror.

* * * * *

The St. Louis answering machine contained the usual messages and much more. But then, the season was just getting underway.

Hake listened to a kid who wanted to "stop by" and get a Cobras-Eagles program signed, a football trading card signed, and an *official*

197

NFL ball signed. And what is the address and what would be the best time to "stop by?" He had to chuckle at the kid's *chutzpa.*

That call was followed by one from a Mr. Townsend, a man without a first name, apparently. Three references were to "Mr. Townsend." Hake liked his pitch: "We need you to be our speaker next Tuesday or even the Tuesday after that." Mr. Townsend didn't seem to know Hake was in a team meeting Tuesday at eleven sharp and on the practice field by one. And he would be every Tuesday through December. Sorry.

Then came a call telling Hake the importance of and modest cost of his cancer insurance policy. He didn't bother to mention the Missouri attorney general was trying hard to get sales of such policies made illegal.

"Boiler room jackoff," Chesty muttered as he popped a beer. "Dad would shit if he could hear that sales pitch."

Then came a transparent call from John Fox Franklin, for Chesty the scourge of the playground at Mark Twain Elementary twenty-five years earlier. A bully from Chesty's first day of kindergarten, Franklin now wanted to renew a friendship that never had been anything warmer that a co-existence, even in high school. Hake recalled reading that the Franklin Furniture Showrooms in St. Louis and Kansas City had filed for Chapter Eleven a couple of years earlier.

"The world's full of jackoffs," Chesty informed the bedroom. "They're everywhere."

Then came the first of a series of calls, and the season – the season that was to be his last – was just one game old, just a few hours old. We began the slide down.

* * * * *

"Chesty, this is Sara."

He put down his beer can, slow motion, and didn't hear the message. He was numb. Before Hake could reach the replay, there came another message.

"This is Sara again, Chesty."

This time he listened intently. She spoke fast, and it was different from the Blackwater days. She implored him to return her call. He didn't know why she was in St. Louis, but the eight-six-three exchange told him the call had come from the University City or Olivette suburbs of St. Louis County – very close. What – what was she doing in St. Louis? Do I call her? That question skewered the pit of his stomach.

Hake went down to the refrigerator for another beer. His hand shook as he popped the top. He was perspiring. The skewers raked at his stomach, and he felt sick.

The lyrics of "We'll Sing In the Sunshine" popped into his mind for just a moment.

Am I going to call Sara and again risk being a madman, a zombie, the way I was as a rookie, using that mentality to make me one of the first successful Mr. Irrelevants? Am I going to call her?

Hake's procrastination cost him good hours of sleep that Sunday night. He had trouble concentrating on the paper at breakfast Monday. He took too many breaks from his videotape review, pacing, shoulders set for the hit that didn't come. No focus. He couldn't focus at all on Green Bay and the Bears on "Monday Night Football." The question remained: Am I going to call her?

At five-ten Tuesday, well before sunup, he showered without shaving. Before heading for the eleven o'clock team meeting, he checked his answering machine one more time. There was a message, the digital display said, but Hake hadn't heard the phone in the night. This time, the message was furtive.

"Chesty, *please* call!"

He vowed he would call her from the condo that evening. That would be safer.

He listened to the five-thirty news block on KMOX, then punched in a tape cassette. The first selection: "We'll Sing In the Sunshine." Unbelievable. He pushed the fast-forward.

A random thought drifted in, something from a saner world. He had left a bowl of his fine *jalopeño*-garlic spread uncovered in the refrigerator. Fuck it.

* * * * *

Hake arrived at his condo at five-twenty. He had a bad elbow scrape and a case of Budweiser. Instead of the bathroom pit stop, he ran upstairs to his desk to check his answering machine. It was there.

"You have to call me, Chesty," she said.

That gave him some kind of warped satisfaction – that he had immediately run up the stairs and been rewarded.

"I'm going to be in Kansas City on business Thursday and Friday, and I want so much to see you. We owe it to ourselves, Chesty, and Daddy won't stop us now. He won't hurt either of us, I promise. Please call tonight, or even early tomorrow morning. I get up early. Please?"

There were no more messages. Good thing. He wouldn't have been able to concentrate had there been more. Hake went fast down the staircase, popped a Bud from the fresh case, put on two pans of water to boil, inserted a video tape from Sunday's opening game into his VCR, and tried like hell to put Sara out of his mind.

His dinner probably smelled good, but he didn't notice. The stove timer alerted him to the tuna casserole and a dish of snap peas with cheddar. He left it half-eaten, no taste on his palate. Plenty of fragrance, though in his mind; she moved there, perfumed shoulders and green eyes.

He went back to Sunday's special-teams game tape on his VCR. He spent three hours running and rerunning it. He took notes, made many X's and O's on a yellow legal pad. He drank beer but worked nonstop. As long as he was working, he was able to keep her at bay.

When the kitchen clock read nine-fifty-five, he shut down the VCR to watch the local news. He didn't want to be seen or mentioned on TV during the Cobras report, and he never was. That Foamcore sign – the warning to reporters who might approach his locker —took care of that.

By the finish of the local news and the hype for the late-night talk shows, Hake was tired from pushing her away, holding her off. He was glad he had brought home a case, not a twelve-pack.

Thirty-Two

S mooth Watkins came into her bedroom. She doubted he had eavesdropped.

"When ya callin' again?"

"I just did."

"Ya gonna git 'im?"

"I got his answering machine in Kansas City."

"Keep tryin'. Ah need money – soon. You do, too. Lotsa money, ya hear?"

"I'm going to Kansas City Thursday and Friday."

"Git 'im."

* * * * *

Public relations firms are smart. They make use of all kinds of services to get the job done for their clients, including media monitoring. Sara Kassel worked for the St. Louis office of See Hear & Reed

Media Services.

She had tried repeatedly to get Chesty to return her call. Finally, she called the Cobras' switchboard.

"I'm sorry, Miss Kassel, but we have a strict policy that we cannot give out players' unlisted numbers," said Becky Shular, receptionist of all receptionists.

"Oh, *c'mon!* This has to do with media monitoring," Sara argued into the phone. "Give me that number!"

Shular paused a moment, bent on maintaining her composure. She checked her master phone list at the same time.

"Miss Kassel, I promise you I don't have an unlisted number for Chesty Hake. I have the published numbers for him in both Kansas City and St. Louis, but I imagine you – in media monitoring, of course – have both, don't you?"

"Yes, yes, I have. Well, thanks," Sara said, trying to sound defeated and reconciled to ending the conversation without having gotten Chesty's unlisted number. "Listen, miss, I'm sorry I raised my voice."

"That's all right, Miss Kassel," Sheller assured her. "I hear worse every day."

"Bye."

* * * * *

Sara vowed she would persevere. Chesty *would* call back, and she thought she had a way to make him do it.

* * * * *

Becky Sheller was the best receptionist the Cobras could hope to have. Tall, leggy, reasonably buxom, schooled in karate, wonderfully patient, discerning, stern. And nobody got by her desk to the dressing room complex without authorization. She was tough; therefore, well-respected at Weston Stadium.

Shular was the best, and Hake could vouch for the fact that she was discreet. But tough as she was, Shular wasn't prepared for the onslaught from Sara Kassel. Two inches taller, two inches wider, a few years older and maybe nastier.

"I'm Sara Kassel," the six-foot redhead began. "I'm here because I need to see Chesty Hake. No. No, I don't *need* to see him; I'm *going* to see him."

Becky Shular got up from her receptionist's chair, ready to rip her skirt up to the seams, just in case her karate training might be needed.

"Here's what you take down to the dressing room for Chesty. You tell him Sara has multiple sclerosis, and I don't need financial help, but – but he should call this number."

She handed Shular a dog-eared business card with a Lake Lotawana number and the eight-six-three St. Louis number written on it, both in copper ink. Shular looked at the numbers, then up at the tall redhead. The ink and the hair were a match. Shular said to herself: She's tough, but she's a showboat.

"I'll make certain he gets the card and the message. And I hope you feel okay."

Sara Kassel strode regally to the giant wooden doors.

Over her shoulder, Sara said: "Forget the multiple sclerosis. That was a lie."

* * * * *

"Chesty, a strange one for you here," said Shular, being front-desk professional. She looked at his wet-from-the-shower hair, then watched his face as he read the business card and the message. She knew not to try to embellish what she had written. He looked ready to smash his way through the high double doors.

"You can tell I've got yet another problem, can't you?"

"Chesty, I have to tell you, Your girlfriend's a – a bitch."

"Don't worry about it, Becky. This goes back a lot of years."

"I didn't want to pop her in the throat or anything."

That was Shular's way of conceding.

* * * * *

"You handled it just right, Shular. Nice job."

"I wasn't going to go to the throat of someone you love, Chesty," she said, then paused for a long moment. "Do you love her?"

"Women."

Shular lowered her voice and scanned the Cobras' lobby.

"I feel better about saying this now, Chesty. Would you think about – about maybe going out for a drink next week? Tuesday night, maybe?"

"Well, yeah," he said after a long pause. "But I don't want you in trouble with management. You know the rules."

"Don't worry about that."

"Okay, we'll go to Danny's on Nolan Road. That'll be safe."

Her touch on his arm was light.

* * * * *

Danny's was a quiet, classy spot, dark in the corners and most of the booths, frequented by the forty-and-over crowd of K.C.'s eastern suburbs.

"Shular – Becky – nobody's going to know about this, right?

I don't want you in trouble."

"No, Chesty, that's not going to happen," she said. "Yes, employees of the Cobras can get fired or at least disciplined for dating players. But that won't be a problem. My dad was big on trust. He was a K.C. cop for thirty-three years."

"This has to be very one-on-one, okay?"

"Okay. But one question: What do you want me to do when that big redhead shows up again?"

Becky saw in Hake's face the kind of pain he would've shown with a torn Achilles tendon. She slid around to his side of the booth.

"That came out the wrong way," she said, putting her arm around his shoulder. She was relieved to see his eyes clearing.

"Look, Chesty, why don't we just drink these, go home, and smile at each other in the lobby tomorrow?"

Chesty watched her. Nightclub lighting softened her profile. She was exquisitely feminine, no phone, and no note pad. Another time, maybe. When he had it together.

"I'm gonna be jealous now, every time some guy looks at you."

"You wanna talk about jealous?"

They walked across Danny's parking lot to their cars. Becky was going home to an empty bed, which she dreaded. Chesty was going home to an urgent message on his answering machine, which he dreaded.

* * * * *

"Where ya bin?" Smooth Watkins asked.

"Out of town. I told you I was going to Kansas City for a couple of days. I was covering for my boss."

"Ah'm yo' boss, bitch! Ya better grab 'im damn soon."

"Damn you, Smooth! I want him as much as you do, and you know it. I've been working very hard at it. I even tried to see him at the stadium while I was in Kansas City."

"Listen, woman, ya gotta wrap 'im up soon. Mah patience ain't a-gonna las' fo'ever, and bad shit happens when Ah run outta patience."

"I know, Smooth," she said, showing her own impatience.

Thirty-Three

B y the time I awoke, Chesty was working out in the basement. When he came up to the breakfast room, he was breathing hard. He sat and mopped sweat from his face and neck.

"Morning," he said.

"How you doin'?"

He got some milk in a large crystal tumbler sporting an etched Cobras helmet.

"I'm going to shave and shower," he said. Milk in hand, he started from the breakfast room. "Gotta lot to do today."

"No breakfast?"

"Not today," he called back.

I went to the pantry for some Cheerios or Rice Krispies. Those were my morning staples when Hake wasn't home to make eggs benedict, omelets, or what he called eggs kingsbury.

* * * * *

HUT-HUT, northbound on nearby Bemiston Avenue, made its stop at the intersection and then made a leisurely right turn onto Carondelet. A classified advertisement in the paper a week earlier had caught his attention, and he hoped he wasn't too late responding to it. The ad, under the FOR SALE – COLLECTIBLES heading, began:

KANSAS CITY CHIEFS MEMORABILIA

The agate lines told Hake the items were from nineteen-sixty, the first year for K.C.'s "other" franchise, then known as the Texans and based for three seasons in Dallas: a wallet, a silver money clip, ball-point pens, glassware, stemware, enamel and crystal ashtrays, a waste basket, letters, copies of player contracts, and an unopened box of Texans letterhead. Chesty thought at least some of these items would be interesting to have – despite their roots.

Every parking space in the seventy-seven-hundred block of Carondelet was occupied, as usual, so Hake planned to park in the Aragon Place building's garage. That would make toting purchases easier anyway, he figured. Then he asked himself: Did I get enough cash at the back? I have no idea what kind of prices are being asked, even if stuff's still available.

He was fortunate to be moving at no more than fourteen or fifteen miles an hour. An old white BMW suddenly darted from its space in front of the Clayton Radisson and narrowly missed getting tagged by HUT-HUT. The driver of the BMW had picked the wrong day.

* * * * *

We already were on the downward slide, of course. Kinda like that continental shelf on the coast, that gentle incline before the falloff into the depths. I hadn't wanted to face it, although the reporter in me tracked the changes, those dumb jokes and the too-loud laugh, the way he'd sit and ignore the doorbell, and the twitchy moods, especially the moods. Phone messages setting him off, brooding; that whole Four-ten Park Avenue thing, muckraking around his graduation, the deaths of his dad and brother. Those images of his mother tied over the dining table, the skinned dog.

All of it must have swirled inside him, along with the body hits in Cobras games. And always the rolling over in bed, the groans throughout the night. Not just body pounding, maybe. What about emotional pounding, traumatic pounding, of a kid who ate sandwiches in the john, who got shoved down because of his size, small, now smaller?

How had his mind worked on that will, giving money to the small college that gave him a chance that built him up? Body pulverized and twisting to ugly memories. It had to happen, of course.

That fucking pistol. Nobody could keep in what Chesty Hake was trying to keep in. In the end, it was easy for him: Shoot your way out …

* * * * *

Hake followed the small car to the Hanley Road intersection, missing the Aragon Place entrance. When the BMW stayed in the right-turn lane, Chesty chose the left-turn lane. He stopped the Jaguar with its front bumper even with the BMW's rear bumper. Then he reached into the cassette carrier on the passenger seat; the one marked FOLK MUSIC, and removed the silenced pistol. As the white car completed its right turn on red…

A little fellow named Joseph Tilley held desperately to the wheel, a tire gone, on heavily traveled Hanley. Horns began to honk. Hake made his left turn and returned the piston to FOLK MUSIC.

"Hope nobody I know gets caught in that shit," he said aloud, surveying his rear-view mirror.

210

He was two-for-two.

* * * * *

Chicago's weather and Hake's mood were a morning match.

A cloud-cluttered day confronted him when he awoke Sunday. His first thought was of the synthetic turf over at Soldier Field. If it rains or snows or sleets, the Bears would have an advantage.

Actually, Hake's low, wide stature would give him an advantage. Those tall, fleet, long-striders suffered on a slick or a muddy surface. Low-to-the-ground grunts like Chesty often did their best work.

Hake pulled himself out of bed determined all the parts that needed to move were moving, then slipped into shower shoes. He trundled into the bathroom.

"Hi, handsome."

He looked at his reflection in the bathroom mirror. Rain began to bang furiously on his ninth-story windows. He turned on the hot water in the sink and the shower.

The Cobras, eleven-point underdogs, upset the Bears, nine-three, in intermittent freezing rain. Exemplary special teams play by the Cobras was the difference. After K.C.'s field goals in the second quarter, the Bears fumbled the ensuing kickoff. The rookie lined up in the R-Four slot, just inside Chesty's spot, made the recovery. The Cobras also blocked a Chicago field goal attempt from a mere thirty-nine yards, and the Kansas City punt team never let the Bears start a possession from outside their thirty-five-yard line.

Curiously, Hake didn't spearhead the special teams on the Soldier Field turf. He had only one assisted tackle, and some of his blocks on the return team would be graded fair to poor by his coaching staff after review of the game tapes. Everybody has an off day. No cause for alarm.

* * * * *

I couldn't gauge Hake's moods. Sometimes, instead of drinking a couple beers and going to bed, Hake would stay up all night reading a mystery novel, then sleep for a couple of hours late Monday morning. Normally, that would have been time devoted to his stamp collection or at least jogging and stretching.

I got home a little after six that Sunday and skipped dinner. I drank a beer and fidgeted for four or five hours until Chesty returned from Chicago via Kansas City. I heard the Jaguar pull into the garage.

"Hey, Paulie, never better!" he called out, as if he hadn't seen me since a class reunion. "You're probably not hungry this late, but I am."

He held up six perfectly ripe avocados.

"These are going to be the guacamole of all guacamoles."

I smiled, but I was off balance. Fifteen minutes later, we dipped white corn chips into the serving bowl. God, the son of a bitch was good in the kitchen!

Hake explained it to me: Billy Petrocelli, a Blackwater College graduate who owned four Chicago area produce markets, had given him the avocados as he left Soldier Field to catch the first of the Cobras' two blue buses to O'Hare.

Down to the last chip. Billy would've been proud and happy. He hated the Bears, anyway, he'd told Chesty.

I asked my question.

"What are you doing about Sara?"

"Dinner tomorrow night."

He smiled, pleased he had tricked me, and proud he had conquered his own reticence.

Thirty-Four

S ara suggested he pick her up at about six-thirty. He arrived at six-twenty, which may have said something he didn't want to say. But she opened the door before he could ring the bell.

"Chesty, finally. It's been too long," she said. She grabbed both his hands with hers and bent slightly to kiss his cheek.

He smiled nervously.

"Come on in, and we'll both take a deep breath."

She obviously was more comfortable than he.

She went to the kitchen and turned on the light over the stove, then came back to the living room and turned on a table lamp. She switched on a radio, and he tracked her as if she would fumble and he would make the play of the day.

"I think I'm about ready," she said, picking up her purse. "But I need to say something."

"All right."

"Chesty, you've got a hard look about you. Did you always have that, and I didn't realize it? Or did I do that to you?"

In the kitchen, the refrigerator began to whir. He could hear it over the radio.

"I guess what I'm saying is: Is it my fault?"

"Don't take the blame, and don't let your father claim the credit. Let's just say I'm no longer twenty-three. I've taken a lot of hits on Sunday afternoons, in training camps, during practices. Not sleeping well does it, too. Not hard, Sara, just banged up. That's the hard look you see."

He gave her the litany: the knees, always throbbing, aching; elbows so scuffed they looked like shoe leather; the swelling left eyebrow; the partially torn biceps; the knuckle of the little finger, popping in and out of joint. The two a.m. shuffle to the medicine cabinet: Tylenol, bandages, and tape.

"It's not very glamorous, Sara. Pro football is brutal, and I wish I didn't love it. I've scared away some good women because of it. Maybe that's what you see."

He didn't add that she, too, had aged twenty years in seven. The wonderful, towering posture was gone, her weathervane breasts had been victimized by age, and the sheen had gone out of that wonderful red hair. Only the fragrance remained. What did she think, seeing herself in the mirror and spraying that wonderful scent?

The most pronounced change was in her shoulders. She saw a hardness in Chesty's face, but he saw shoulders that had been wide and square and strong, but now were tired. Defeated, maybe.

God, how I hate Hy Kassel! Chesty said to himself. What he's done to Sara. If we had been allowed... I could kill him, Hake thought, then wished he hadn't. Had he killed Hy Kassel, tonight couldn't be happening.

"Let's go to dinner, Jumpshot," he said.

Sara checked the dead-bolt lock of her front door as they left, then twice tugged on the outside knob after closing the door.

"Is this yours?" she asked as they reached the curb. "A Jaguar? No Cadillac?"

"A lot of things have changed."

"Since we were in love," Sara said, as she ducked her head and settled into the bucket seat. Hake walked around to the rear of the car and climbed behind the wheel. "I should add, Chesty: 'Since Daddy ruined my life.'"

"Is Chinese all right," he asked. They had gone a quiet couple of miles south on I-170.

"Still my favorite." She paused. "But you couldn't know that after more than seven years. Think back to school, Chesty. So many Chinese dishes popular now that we didn't even know about eight years ago. Even when I went back to Kansas City after I graduated, I don't thing I ever had Szechuan. Now, it's the hotter, the better."

They exited the Interstate and continued south another mile on Brentwood Boulevard. Szechuan. Seven years, defeated shoulders, and Szechuan.

"This is close to where you grew up, isn't it?" she observed as Hake wheeled the Jaguar into a parking slot at Hunan Wok. He was pleased she remembered.

"Yeah, six blocks from here. It's changed, but you remember."

They went in, and Hake signaled the young Chinese waiter after they were seated at a corner table.

"What would you like to drink?"

"A Chinese beer, of course. How 'bout you?"

Hake looked at the waiter.

"Two Tsingtao, please."

They talked, and Hake felt nervousness and anxiety drain from him. Comfort came, like oil on shattered nerve ends. He had fought this – all her calls – and now wished he hadn't.

And tonight his knees didn't hurt.

Things were good. Bowls and plates were cleared and dessert declined. They looked at each other in silence.

"One more beer?" Hake asked. "I'm going to."

"I'd better not. I don't drink very much, Chesty. Actually, I can't afford to drink very much."

They split his fourth Tsingtao. He knew what was coming, and he headed it off.

"Sara, don't go there. I got over my sorry and hatred both. I don't wanna hear about your father."

She talked anyway, because Chesty was lying. She explained that her father's best friend, legendary Kansas City attorney Melving Gross, had forced her to sign documents. She relinquished all claims to the estate of Hyman Aron Kassel if she should have any contact whatsoever with one Chester J. Hake Jr., a.k.a. Chesty Hake. In return for her signature, she was to be named assistant sales manager at Hy Kassel Motors after graduating from Blackwater College a year later.

Not put into writing by Gross were references to "parties" who would kill or cripple Hake if Sara didn't earn that assistant sales manager's job. And she couldn't sell Hake a car. That last was "Uncle Mel" at his most cunning. He enjoyed it, like a kid pulling wings off a fly.

Sara had had a total of six years of college: a washout year at Kansas and a mixed bag of courses at Blackwater. The hallmark path of a woman basketball player, she would tell Hake.

"At the dealership, I was a figurehead. Chesty, I didn't give a shit about the car business, but Daddy and his store paid me well. He also could keep track of me. He even helped me buy a little house at the lake," she said, sending Hake's thoughts back to those college weekends and summer weeks at Lake Lotawana, easily the happiest times of his life save for the occasional presence of her father. "That little house I bought strengthened his hold, of course. He loved to remind me I needed six years to get through school. And how often would he hint he could have you killed or crippled!"

Hake watched her reach for his beer glass.

"Finally, I'd had enough. I not only hated going to Daddy's store – dealership – every day; I was embarrassed the whole time I was there. Everybody, even the kid in the paint shop – the one with the wet, dreamy eyes – knew I wasn't on the payroll because I was good at approving trade-ins or telling people we'd throw in custom floor mats. Fact was, I didn't approve anything in five years, and didn't throw in a single floor mat. I just walked, sat, and smiled. This fig-urehead."

Another sip of beer from Hake's glass.

"Remember Phil Melman? You roomed with him your freshman year, my second year at Blackwater?"

"Sure. From Lee's Summit. You were classmates in high school. He always was calling you in the middle of the night for advice. He was scared to death of me, Sara."

"Phil's a member of Mom and Daddy's temple, and at some plan-ning committee meeting or whatever, he saw just what kind of bully Daddy is. Anyway, Phil manages the Kansas City office of See Hear & Reed, a company that provides media monitoring services for large and medium-sized firms.

"He called the store one day and said he knew of an opening in Reed's office here in St. Louis, and he thought it might be a good job for me. We had lunch. He showed me the way the company's Kansas City office did business. He also told his St. Louis counterpart, Ray O'Neill, I would be a good addition to his operation. I came over for my interview the following week and was packing a U-Haul a week later."

She paused. The beer glass was between them, some odd totem. "I don't make the money I did, but that's okay. And I'm not in prison anymore. How's this for irony: Phil Melman bought my Lake Lotawana house for about *a time and a half what I paid for it!* He likes Mom but really tries to ignore Daddy."

"What's media monitoring?"

"What? Oh. Basically, we fill in gaps in public relations. No company really has a P.R. staff big enough to keep track of what's being said in every major newspaper, news magazine, on every network, big television station or radio station.

"We can provide a client with video tape of any TV show on any station anywhere in the U.S. or Canada, or audio tape of just about any radio broadcast. Sometimes we work directly with corporate P.R. Other times, we deal with the firm's P.R. vendor. It's interesting, and it's a relatively new kind of service. I'm just glad I took several communications courses my last two years at Blackwater. And, of course, I worked really hard on the yearbook after you were gone."

"*The Blazer?* Really?"

"I was the sports editor, and no figurehead."

"We need more beer."

"Now it's your turn, Chesty."

Hake had questions still hanging inside him on hooks. Did you ever marry? Do you have kids? Did your mom ever talk about me? Did I mention I've missed you every day all these years?

"You were in Kansas City, so you knew I made the club the hard way: on special teams," he began. "Because I was the last draft choice, that year's Mr. Irrelevant, I knew I wouldn't get many opportunities to run the ball – even for the expansion team. Each day, I waited for the axe to fall. But I was a pretty damned good blocker, and I worked to refine that for the pro game. A fullback who can't block is on his way to a Sunday morning flag league.

"And then the special teams. I'd never been on a kick team or return team in high school or college, but the Cobras' coaching staff gave me a chance. I fell in love with special teams. I love knocking would-be tacklers on their *keisters*, and I love making an open-field tackle. I mean, I *love* it! And that love has kept me in the NFL for better than seven years, so I guess you'd call it an affair of long standing."

Sara looked hard into his eyes.

"I used to see your name in the paper every once in a while, before I came to St. Louis," she said. "Not often enough, of course. I always had to be careful to avoid conversations at Daddy's store when the subject came around to the Cobras. When the sports pages were out and the coffee was hot, I got out of there. I didn't need to complicate things. I remember one headline, early in your career, and I saw the replay of that TV interview with your magic word bleeped out.

"And the funny thing for me about it was that a lot of people I knew told me they wished somebody had done that earlier. You were very popular with the common man, you know – our mechanics, our sales people, our janitors."

"I shouldn't have sworn at him, Sara. I came off being as stupid as he was."

Hake went on to tell her of his first interview with Paul Tenkiller and how well they meshed. He explained that I, like Hake, had graduated from McAlester High and that our housemate relationship over more than six years had been nearly ideal. He said nice things about me, but he was honest about it: He paid the bills, and I was quite willing to accept that, to serve as house-sitter, errand-runner, grocery-shopper, appointment-maker, and, yes, interior decorator.

"Paul's got a fine sense of humor, likes his Budweiser, is more flexible that I am, knows a lot about antiques, decorating, stamp collecting – and can't cook worth a damn," Hake explained. "When I'm not home most of July through December, he must live on my leftovers – plus Big Macs, Domino's, and happy-hour chicken wings, when he gets out of work early enough."

She didn't laugh.

"He's Indian. Paul's half-Choctaw, which is why his family wound up in McAlester. The Trail of Tears thing. His great-great-grandfather – or maybe great-great-great-grandfather – took what probably was a Cherokee name. He went way north of the Choctaws."

"It has a certain romance to it," Sara said. "You call him Paulie?"

"Yeah. It just seems to fit. He's okay with it."

"Sounds like a nice guy."

Talk mellowed, softened around beer and quiet surroundings. That's when secrets are told, if the timing's right and the listener's right.

Chesty talked about the graduation-day deaths of his father, his brother and his brothers' business partner-lover, how they were a spectacular murder-suicide. He told her of his New York grilling.

"When I came back from NFL headquarters, I was a whipped puppy. I didn't give a damn about my brother, and I admit I was embarrassed and defensive when somebody talked about David being gay. But my dad – my *dad* – I always tried to be good to him. I didn't want to be in insurance, and to this day I don't want to be. But Dad wanted me to be. You knew him, Sara. He was a good guy. He died knowing I could live very, very well because of what he was doing.

"I have a lot of money, Sara, and it doesn't mean shit."

"You should've married, Chesty."

"No. No, I shouldn't have. If dating doesn't mean much, how the hell could I put everything into a marriage?"

"But you do date," Sara said, half-concluding and half-questioning.

"Oh, yeah. I dated a very nice woman for a while, an elementary school teacher, and she probably would've been good to me. Very down-to-earth, compassionate. But she wanted us to be in love. So it ended. She loves pro football but can't afford tickets. She gets two in the mail the Tuesday or Wednesday before each home game. I don't care if she takes a girlfriend, one of her students, or even a date."

"She's not going to forget you."

Hake drank his Tsingtao. He wanted to tell Sara how he nearly hurled his spent condom onto the roof of Hy Kassel Motors. And he avoided the nightmare, the unspeakable, which had been spoken to Laurie that night; while she went rigid and the soothing fingers on his spine stilled.

"Chesty, what are you going to do after football?"

"I should be thinking about that, I guess," he acknowledged. "Haven't, though. And I've already told Paulie this is my last season. I don't have anything more to prove except maybe that I can finish my career without having blown out a knee or snapped a tendon. Mr. Irrelevant has survived.

"So I don't know what I'm going to do after I quit. I could go into business for myself, I guess. I don't want to coach. Maybe I should concentrate on charity work. I know about a place called Father Graham's. Maybe that's my future. I've made a good, six-figure income playing ball as a non-star. And the proceeds from my brother's insurance policy and my dad's policies were considerable. My dad left some money, and my brother had the antique shop in his estate. That came to me, too."

"So you're comfortable."

"Oh, yeah."

"A million?"

"More."
"Much?"
"Much more."

* * * * *

Cruising north on Brentwood, Hake laid his hand over hers. She had been waiting for that.

"Are we going to your house?"
"No. Yours."
"Oh, let's go to yours," Sara said, her voice husky. "I'd love to see it: four bedrooms for two bachelors! And I don't steal silverware or towels."
"No," Hake said firmly. "Maybe Paul hasn't cleaned up his supper dishes. Maybe he's got company."
"C'mon, Chesty, why can't I see your house?"
"Nobody sees it, to be honest. Nobody. Paul and the meter readers are the only people who've been in it since I bought it six, seven years ago."
"Why, for heaven's sake?" She watched him concentrate on traffic. "I've never heard of anything like that. You've never even had friends over?"
"Nope. Paul hasn't, either. When he came to live with me, that was the only condition I had: no rent, no visitors."
Sara considered that.
"What would you do if the woman next door knocked on your front door and asked to borrow a cup of sugar – turn her away?"
"No, I'd tell her to wait there on the front porch, and I'd go to the kitchen and get the sugar. Or, if Paulie were home, I'd ask him to get the woman a cup of sugar while I chatted with her on the porch."

222

Sara pulled her hand away.

"Look, you have to understand, Sara. I don't need buddies. I don't need a date on a regular basis. And Paulie can afford a motel room or the gas back to his date's apartment. Somebody's invited into my house, and my unlisted phone number is compromised. I don't need jock-sniffers in my life, and I sure don't need gamblers.

"I could get set up. I have some very, very delicate antiques that had been in my mother's family for a century of two. A small copper box reading on the bottom 'Jacob Lynn, Boston, Mass Colony' and dated seventeen-seventy-five could be in somebody's pocket or purse before I could get back to the living room with beer. I own three Lock Cortlands, Sara – three originals Paulie says probably are unknown in the damned art world. And both Paulie and I have nice stamp collections – *very* nice collections. Those are *our* collections, and we don't want them to become someone else's."

"Okay, Chesty. So my father screwed up our lives, and now you're a recluse. I see it. After my father, you wouldn't be trusting. Protect your stuff – things you care about, the way you cared about me. Protect your unlisted number. You've probably got one in Lee's Summit, too. Just don't slide. Just don't spiral down."

"I won't spiral down. You're back."

She put her hand over his.

"My apartment."

* * * * *

Chesty Hake had known quite a few women, come to think of it. Even as he hid himself away in his home with his beer and his furniture and his stamps, women threw themselves at him in public. They came in all shapes and sizes, and he took them in varied and some-times-exotic places, like airplane lavatories and a couple of Kansas

City's beautiful fountains. And there always were the hotel rooms, the anonymous couplings crowned with a mint on the pillow. Many women, probably, but he didn't know them. He kept them at arm's reach even as he held them close in his arms. He took: gave, too, maybe. But these women never touched him. He kept his worlds separate, his heart private.

So being with Sara Aron Kassel at last was not easy. He wanted her; he needed her desperately. But as she lay under him, this athlete, now tired of body and beaten in spirit, locked up.

They lay quietly in the dark.

"What is it?" she murmured, fingers caressing.

But that only reminded him of the schoolteacher's fingers down his spine and his ultimate disclosure about his mother. That had cost them both.

"Chesty?"

"Give me a minute."

"It's all right."

"Just give me a minute."

A car's headlights strobed the curtain, intruding. Then it was gone.

He made love to her then, but they both knew that part of him was locked away, unreachable. Part of her, too, probably.

Each of them fell asleep knowing the damage Hy Kassel had done.

* * * * *

"Uhhh!" came from Hake's throat as he turned painfully onto his left side.

The red digits on Sara's bedside clock read four-fifteen. After dressing, washing the sleep out of his eyes, and tapping some Binaca onto his tongue, he went and stood on Sara's side of the bed.

"Have to go," he said, loud enough to bring her half-awake.

Sheets moved. Tousled faded copper.

"We've got a team meeting at eleven and practice at one," he explained. "They'll wonder about the slacks and blazer at the meeting, of course, but it'll be worth the abuse."

"Will you call me tonight?"

"Only if you think I still love you and respect you this morning."

"Kiss me."

* * * * *

"I've got him. You can stop worrying," she said and slammed down the phone.

Thirty-Five

Hey, gas company! Yeah, you! Welcome to the nineteen-fifties! When Harriet Nelson and Donna Reed sported pearls and wore nylons to vacuum while they wondered when that smiling meter reader might knock on the aluminum storm door. Any time would be fine.

St. Louis, like every community, has a two-income, maybe-I'll-get-home-for-supper environment a half-century removed from Ozzie and Harriet. The Gas Company telling customers they must have their meters read "weekdays between eight a.m. and four p.m." is – is bullshit.

Over dinner one Monday night, I told Hake of my indignation. The anger still was in my voice.

"Appliance and furniture deliveries are handled on the same basis," Chesty observed.

"True, but the difference is that we can buy a Kenmore stove from any number of Sears stores. We can get our washer-dryer combination from the dealer who's closest or has the best delivery reputation.

We have leverage on delivery time. Hell, nobody's so important that he or she can't set aside a half-hour or an hour sometime. But the utilities? Hell, no! They want you to block out a morning, an afternoon, or a whole day! That's the mentality of a monopoly, not a public service."

I got that small smile of his.

"I'm glad you take this sort of thing seriously, Paulie. You're a good housemate."

* * * * *

Call it Fate, a first encroachment into our lives where our table talk merged with that real world beyond our Nobody Allowed house. Fate would hit later with an unimaginable violence, but for now that Bitch Goddess settled for a gold-and-blue gas company pickup. It ran the left-turn signal from eastbound Litzsinger Road onto northbound Brentwood Boulevard.

Chesty rested the pistol's silencer at the front of the right-side window frame. He waited for the service truck's right front tire to come into his sights. A silenced pistol trades velocity for suppressed noise, which for Chesty was a fair swap. The round went into the front tire. The truck sagged to a stop. It stopped in the outside lane of Brentwood Boulevard, directly in front of the Brentwood Fire Department's driveway. The bullet passed behind the Roll of Honor commemorating Brentwood's war dead and become a subject of interest for the nearby police department.

He drove away, replacing the pistol in FOLK MUSIC, and waited for the exhilaration to hit him. It dissipated for a precious moment all thought of dead mothers and dead dogs, of dead fathers and dead brothers, and lifting body pain from deep in his bones. He was not disappointed.

227

"Ches! Ches! Look at this! My wish has been granted!"

"You mean that Choteau Gas truck leaning badly to starboard? Yeah, I thought you'd like that," he said, recalling the picture in the front section. "The story's on Three-B."

Choteau Gas Truck Ambushed

The blown tire on a Choteau Company truck that snarled lunch-hour traffic at a busy Brentwood intersection Monday resulted from a gunshot, Brentwood Police said.

The service vehicle was completing a left turn from Litzsinger Road onto Brentwood Boulevard when the right front tire went flat, the driver, Richie L. Persley, twenty-three, of High Ridge, told Brentwood authorities.

"The nature of the holes throug outer walls and the tread of the tire indicate they were made by a bullet from a small- or medium-caliber weapon," said police Lt. Ronald Kurre. "And we needed to push the vehicle onto the shoulder quickly because it not only was impeding traffic, but it was blocking the driveway of our fire department. If fire vehicles had been called out immediately, we would have had quite a problem."

The story continued, pointing out that Brentwood, a quiet, middle-class suburb of eighty-two-hundred, had not had a police report of a gun-related incident in almost four years. Kurre said he saw no motive for the shooting.

"What timing," I mused. "Now, if this guy would shoot the tires out of about ten more Choteau Gas trucks, maybe they'd come to realize I don't appreciate their high-and-mighty ways. Maybe – maybe somebody would call the switchboard and say: "The meter reader's here at eight-forty Thursday morning or another truck gets it. And no coppers, or it's curtains."

Hake smiled. It had been easy, and he'd pleased someone.

* * * * *

EDITOR'S NOTE: The way Chesty walked always bothered me. Even when he was seventeen years old, he told me, his calf muscles and Achilles tendons were that tight. He wanted to be a tall man and couldn't be. When I watched him walk, I knew: one, that he wanted to be tall, rangy; and two, that his legs always hurt. Sensing his pain was what bothered me most, I guess. But he never wanted to discuss it. And he refused to project what would be the condition of those knees twenty, thirty, forty years down the read, when, as my mom would've said, "He'll be visited by ol' Arthur It is every day."

The day we read of the Chateau Gas truck, Chesty seemed to bounce on his toes a little more when he walked. It was noticeable.

Thirty-Six

In the May before Chesty's next-to-last season, he scared me.

"My great fear is I'll have to go someplace else, play for some other team," Hake said, surprising me at the breakfast table.

"What brought this on?"

"I'm going into my seventh year. That's what brought this on. And I'm hearing trade rumors in Kansas City all of a sudden. I've heard it at the deli counter when they didn't know who I was. I've heard it at Danny's, and yes, I've even heard it in the dressing room the other day during mini-camp. I don't want to play anywhere else. If I'm nothing else, I'm loyal. I belong with the Cobras. I'm one of the originals on the team. Management knows that. They know what happened to my family, and they know my money situation, obviously. I've never had an agent, and I've never bitched about the terms of my contract."

"Don't get soap boxey, Ches."

"If we had a little more loyalty and a little less bitching about salary and signing bonus and that bullshit, we'd have a good team by now. But loyalty doesn't mean jack shit any more, and money means everything."

"Money doesn't mean anything to you," I noted. "But loyalty doesn't mean anything to other people. That's the way the game is now in all major pro sports."

"I'm getting out after one more year," he said. "I don't need to be remembered as somebody who played ten, twelve, fifteen seasons. I'd rather be remembered as a marginal guy who did a decent, conscientious job and then got the hell out. I don't want to go out as a cripple, and we both know that's gonna happen if I keep coming back year after year."

Hake paused.

"One more year. But only for Kansas City – only for the Cobras. And then that's it. Hey, I guess you won't be with me after that."

I let that alone.

"And I don't want some broad to be my wife just to rub my knees when they hurt in the night."

"Sure."

One more solid news story I couldn't write.

* * * * *

It was serendipity. For those years Hake and I were housemates, as I say, we complemented each other. He knew nothing about color and structure despite having all those antiques, and I couldn't whip up anything that would appeal to a troop of hungry Boy Scouts. But it worked.

Think about it: On his mother's side, he came from a heritage of billionaires. On my father's side was a heritage of people who had to work and work to make their foodstuffs stretch to the next *tenk* house.

The roles should have been reversed. I should've had a middle-class father who married a socialite, and that would've allowed me to study the fine things people had in their fine homes and their hermetically controlled storage lockers. Chesty could've been a Choctaw – Chesty the Choctaw – who constantly got lectures from ugly Uncle Horace and equally ugly Aunt Coley, whose great-grandfather was Coleman Cole, the chief of the eighteen-seventies who opposed the Choctaws' coal-mining operation around McAlester. Oh, Choctaw Chesty would've loved hearing those lectures. Survival on the Trail of Tears.

Could you've handled it, Chesty? For Hake's sake, could you've handled it?

* * * * *

"I bought us a blanket chest today," I said when I returned from an antique show. "You'll like it, I think."

"Why do I – we – need a blanket chest?" he asked as he took off his yellow and white windbreaker and hung it on the hall coat rack. "Where the hell are we gonna put a blanket chest? I mean-"

"Hey, at the top of the stairs, adjacent to the deacon's bench, of course," I said, pissed. "We've got a lot of nice things still in the basement and in the storage locker, but nothing's quite right up there. We need something significant right at the top of the staircase."

The blanket chest, probably crafted between eighteen-forty and eighteen-forty-five, sponge-painted a red-orange and in terrific condition, cost me – cost Chesty – a little more than eighteen-hundred. He could afford it. I didn't bother to explain to him the primitive, eight-foot deacon's bench, circa seventeen-sixty and in quite fine condition, would be worth at auction considerably more than most people earn in a year.

Hake started up the tall staircase.

"I had to struggle to get the damned thing up the stairs," I told him.

"Yeah, yeah."

"Check it. Give it your approval, then tell me what we're going to do about dinner."

"You want me to tell you I like it?" he called down. "Okay, I like it."

Serendipity. I, and the blanket chest, created a pleasing decorative arrangement. Ready for the world to come tumbling down.

"Now, what do you want for dinner?"

"Veal something," I said. "I bought some today on my way back from the York Woods Antique Show. You would've enjoyed it, Ches."

"I'll enjoy the veal. I wouldn't have enjoyed your antique show."

Thirty-Seven

O ur nineteen-forty house had thick walls, but I always felt the difference from late winter to spring, to summer, to early fall, to deep fall and early winter.

Seldom did Chesty moan in the night from late January through June. Seldom did his knees, ankles, ribs, or shoulders really pain him then, despite the running and the weightlifting. If he moaned and twisted, it was those other demons. From mid-July to the end of August each year, because of training camp, I seldom saw him. But on Monday nights from early September into January, I prayed I would sleep through the night and not hear the groaning. I always heard it.

Once, when I asked him about it, his response was: "Groaning? Naw. Probably just beer farts. I don't snore or groan. My legs feel better this season."

All I could do was look across the breakfast table at him and not argue with his lie. Those were *his* knees, *his* ankles, *and his* shoulders. That was *his* pain.

My greatest pain was in using "further" when I should've used "farther" and catching my error at six-fifteen the next morning – along with a great many readers. It was different from rolling over onto knee joints that scraped cartilage, sending pain up your spine and into your brain. I didn't groan in the night.

* * * * *

Hake had worked awfully hard in this training camp, his eighth, because he had determined it would be his last. But there were some things he didn't do as well as he had a couple of seasons earlier. Even W. W. W. Weston, the team owner, spotted it. Coach Turk Madigan's decision to keep Hake was overturned by the general manager and the assistant G.M., at the owner's behest.

The three of them sat at one end of a conference table while Madigan's nine assistants sat down both sides. It was not a round-table discussion by any means. Rather, it was the afternoon devoted to chewing up the lives of five football players – five pretty good football players.

It was the first Sunday of September, the final Sunday before the start of the regular season. In the NFL, each team had to be down to forty-six active players the Monday before the season. The Cobras had had fifty for the fourth and final exhibition game two nights earlier in Cleveland.

Four players. Four names. Four talented athletes. Except to the fan who reads the paper diligently, listens to radio call-in shows or debates at Janie's Fun-Time Lounge. For him, those four names won't have great significance. Then those were the four players, their psyches and their families, if they had families. For them, the impact of being waived is like a seven-point-two earthquake.

The head coach, the G.M., and the assistant G.M. did almost all the talking at this Sunday session. Assistant coaches, some around the table and others roaming the large room, are to speak only when spoken to.

"The owner wants to get Hake out of here once and for all," said General Manager Shel Bergman, himself a lame duck. "He's pretty well worn out his welcome here, we feel. He's still pretty efficient and pretty smart on special teams, but he can't run the ball. He didn't average two-point-five yards a carry when he got to play last year, and what he did against the Browns the other night shouldn't be done by a damned rookie. Seven years in the league and he fumbles twice against those pussies! Twice! If he had any speed at all, I'd fight to keep him. But–"

"But he's the one I want to keep," said Coach Turk Madigan. "He's still got smarts and guts – and class. And I can't say that about a whole lot of these turkeys."

Pudge Muskopf, the assistant general manager, spoke last.

"Fuck the owner," he growled. "Keep Hake. I know he's gonna make too much money this year for what we're gonna get out of him, except on special teams occasionally, but I remember when Chesty and I went out on the town in San Diego one night and –"

"Awright! Awright!" snapped Bergman. "We keep him. But not because you and Hake got laid in the swimming pool at the Hotel del Coronado back when you were a washed-up wide receiver and he was a mediocre running back who liked to get laid in interesting places."

"I'll be able to smooth it over with the owner, I suppose," Bergman added, toning things down.

"Good," Madigan said. "That's one out of the way. Now, what are we going to do about Champ Dillon?"

The conference room exploded with voices, each determined to be heard.

"Hey! Hey! Hey!" the general manager shouted. "We'll never get out of here tonight if you guys keep this up. C'mon, I wanna get home and–"

"Where?" one of the assistant coaches asked.

"Awright, so I may take the long way home, but–"

Laughter this time. Everyone in the Cobras' organization knew of Bergman's indiscretions. For an overweight fifty-five-years-old with cancer in remission, a heart condition and an assortment of chins, the G.M. did awfully well with nurses, librarians, teachers, cocktail waitresses, even clergywomen and telemarketers.

Madigan came to the G.M.'s rescue.

"So what about Dillon?" He looked down to the other end of the long table. "Davey?"

The linebackers coach leaned back in his chair and stared at the lighting panels in the ceiling. He wanted his words to be fair and have a convincing strength.

"Champ was one of the better 'backers in the NFL just a couple of years ago," the assistant said slowly. "Then something happened. Now even some of the younger players refer to him as 'Chump.' His reactions are slower. His best hits lack something. Everybody in the league knew we were lying when we put in the media guide he runs the forty in four-eight, so we can't even think about trading him. And Shel, I'm sure he's doing drugs – and maybe selling."

"Try that again, Davey," Turk Medigan said quietly.

"I said something I didn't want to say, Turk. But my verdict? Dump him before he does some serious harm to the young players around him. Maybe he already has. I don't know. Training camp and pre-season don't tell us as much as we need to know."

"Coach?" Bergman asked, turning to Madigan.

"Yeah."

"What?"

"Yeah. I mean, yeah, get 'im outta here. Now, who's next for the Turk. And I don't mean *me*."

The Turk, on the Cobras as on many NFL teams, is the assistant general manager or an assistant coach. In the Cobras' case, Pudge Muskopf had the thankless task of notifying a waived player he's to see the head coach, turn in his playbook, and pick up an airline ticket or gas money on his way out the door.

"Diarrhea is more fun," Pudge Muskopf once was quoted as saying. "At least you eventually get *that* out of your system."

It wasn't until early evening that Pudge went from the conference room to the men's room and then to his office. He activated the FAX machine. His message to league headquarters read:

KANSAS CITY COBRAS REPORTING 9/3
PLACED ON INJURED RESERVE 9/3: DONOHUE, THOMAS P., QUARTERBACK.
CLAIMED ON WAIVERS: NONE.
PLACED ON IRREVOCABLE WAIVERS 9/3: DILLON, DON-NELL
D. (CHAMP), LINEBACKER; NAULLS, WILLIE D., JR.,
WIDE RECEIVER: KLINK, TODD L., TIGHT END/FULLBACK.
FOLO UP COMING WHEN ALL NOTIFIED.
END KANSAS CITY COBRAS REPORT 9/3.
GOOD NIGHT, NEW YORK.

* * * * *

The mid-evening call to the Donohue kid didn't cause any undue pain for the assistant G.M. The youngster was a rough, raw, roughish free agent with a strong arm and a willingness to learn. Those traits enabled him to stay around training camp and the four-game exhibition season.

And hell, going on injured reserve isn't like being cut, Pudge ratio-nalized. The kid knew the elbow of his throwing arm had been hyperextended in the last exhibition game in Cleveland. He also knew he was going to get a nice paycheck every Monday he was on I.R.

Klink and Junior Naulls were easy to locate that Sunday night because each was staying with a veteran or a relative while waiting to learn whether or not he had made the club. Klink and Naulls handled the news philosophically. Klink would go back to Bloomington, Indiana, to be groomed to take over his family's three motels, to be active in the IU alumni organization. Naulls also understood, but he told Pudge he dreaded facing his father after falling a little short.

Champ Dillon? There was no telling where the Champ might be by mid-evening on a Sunday. Pudge Muskopf dialed his number – and hit "redial" at least a half dozen times. Each time, he had to lis-ten to Dillon's singsong voice on a recorded message:

"This is the Champ, and I ain't in – obviously. You jus' leave yo' name, number and any ol' thought ya got f'me. If the Champ thinks yo' worth talkin' to, he'll call ya. Sure. Now, baby, you talk at the Champ when ya heah mah hmmmmmm-m-m sound. Ya'll ready? Heah comes. HMMMMM."

He dialed another number. The answering machine in Lee's Summit began its message, but Muskopf was certain the phone was being monitored. He identified himself.

"Oh, no, Pudge," Hake said, coming on the line.

"Chesty? Wait! Wait! I'm not playing the Turk with you."

"Then what is it?" he asked, relieved he had not worn Cobras jer-sey No. Thirty-three for the last time. He had trouble concentrating on what Pudge had to say.

"I need to find Champ. Know where he might be?"

"No, not really. I – I know he's not at his apartment very much these days, but I really haven't run with him since training camp started."

"Well, I know he still thinks of you as his friend, and I've gotta find him tonight," the assistant G.M. confided. "You can figure it out."

"I can figure it out."

"The league can't release it to the news services, the papers or radio and TV until I tell him. That's the way the commissioner has to have it. He says it's like the media giving out the name of a murder victim or a traffic accident fatality before the police let his family know he's dead. That's why I have to tell him."

"I'll find him. Pudge. At least I'll give it a try. You in your office?"

"Naw, I'm heading home. I've had a bellyful for one day, believe me. Listen, if you find him, have him call me at home. I'll be there in about forty, forty-five minutes."

"Right."

"You have my number?"

"Pudge, you know damned well I have your number," Hake said.

"Chesty?"

"Yeah."

"Thanks. I appreciate this. But don't tell him what it's about. That's my job."

"And a shitty job it is, too. How could anybody be willing to be the Turk?"

"Walk in my shoes, why doncha? Have him call."

The phone went dead.

Hake changed to blue slacks and a yellow golf shirt. No Cobras logo. He hustled down to his car in the underground garage.

By the time the Jag moved to the street, Hake knew where he probably would find the Champ, a.k.a. Donnell D. Dillon. He wouldn't be at Janie's Fun-Time Lounge, not with coaches likely to be there. Hake headed for a singles bar frequented by young ballplayers who liked to finish up an evening with a free beer and a free lay. The place was listed in the phone directory as The Three-Dollar Opera, but every regular referred to it as Inflation. Champ would be there.

* * * * *

"I ain't gittin' married 'gin, mind ya," Champ said as he tried to make his eyes focus on the young white women. "But if'n I happen to, this man – this man name of Chester J. Hake Jr. here – he gonna be my bes' man. 'Cause he is the bes' man."

One woman smiled at Chesty. He didn't smile back. He wasn't in a bimbo kind of mood.

Champ introduced Hake and the women – by first names, slurred – then raised a meaty arm. Hake pulled down the arm and looked into Champ's eyes.

"Champ, I've gotta talk to you. It's a helluva lot more important than a good time tonight."

The young woman whose eyes had been at least sympathetic now was hurt, and those eyes showed it.

"C'mon, Ches."

"No, Champ, I mean it. We have to talk."

Hake turned to the expressive young woman, rather plain and with brown hair. "How many beers has he had."

"Two or three, I guess, He came in right after my friend and I did. He plopped right down, and she wanted to leave. I don't know what he had before he got here."

She looked uneasy, as though her answer might not suit the sandy-blond man with the strange face and the huge arms and shoulders. The dark woman left the table abruptly and headed for the bar.

"Has he said anything about drugs?"

"Well, he said he knew where–"

Hake quickly turned back to Champ. He took in the sagging shoulders, the empty eyes. He wanted Champ out of The Three-Dollar Opera, and he wanted him out of there immediately. Chesty drew a fifty-dollar bill from his right-front pocket, put it on the table, and gave the order: "Champ come with me."

She watched as Hake all but carried Champ out the back door. They slowly stumbled to Chesty's car, and he dumped Champ into the bucket seat. Champ was limp and compliant, muttering something.

As Hake turned to go around to the driver's side, there stood the brown-haired woman.

"Drugs?"

"That would be my guess."

"I'm a nurse. Alice Camp," she said strongly. "Let me check him. Just to make sure he's okay."

"Sure. I suppose that's the smart thing to do."

Alice knew what to do. She checked Champ's forehead and pulse. Then, by the car's courtesy lights, she looked at the insides of both elbows for needle marks. She also pried open his mouth for a long sniff. From her bulky purse she took a pencil flashlight and looked into those vapid black eyes. Then she turned to Hake, who was bent over her shoulder.

"Beer and cocaine: a bad mix," she pronounced. "Will you take him home?"

"Not to his; mine. And if you'd follow me in the Champ's car, I'd really appreciate it. It's a condo on a private drive. I'll take it easy so I don't lose you, Alice. It's Alice, isn't it?"

Hake tugged a key case from Champ's jeans. Champ grinned, slack-jawed, at nothing.

"He's the white Lincoln over there."

* * * * *

Hake awoke at five, as always, and realized Alice, R.N., had been the first woman to share his Lee's Summit bed. When he came back from the master bath to put on a jogging suit, a bedside lamp was on. Alice was wide-awake and staring at his stocky, strangely muscled body.

"Good morning," he said, too brightly.

She continued to stare.

"We need to check on Champ."

* * * * *

They'd gotten Champ settled down in the guest bedroom and forced two Tylenol down his throat. That was at eleven-thirty. It was midnight before Hake called long-suffering Pudge Muskopf and told him of the situation.

"Look, I'll have him at Weston Stadium before eight in the morning – before nine, New York time. I told you, didn't I? Well, I will. Then you can thank me."

Hake cradled the phone. He walked to where Alice stood guard, nude.

* * * * *

They were a misbegotten threesome around the breakfast table: Chesty, Alice, and Champ. Chesty wore leather sandals. His guests were buck-naked.

* * * * *

"These clothes: Wore 'em yistiday," Champ observed as the Jaguar wheeled into the players' lot at W. W. W. Weston Stadium. It was seven-thirty-nine a.m. "An' wha' 'bout ma car, Ches?"

"It's in front of my condo, and your key case is behind the left visor. I'm sure Pudge will get a cab to take you to it."

Thirty-Eight

Hake took a break from his game tape review and called Sara at mid-evening Tuesday. They talked for only five or six minutes and he was ready to end the conversation. She sensed it.

"You still don't like the phone, do you? You used to call at school, and, after a couple of minutes, you'd say, 'Honey, your dorm's only thirty seconds away. I'll be there in twenty.'"

He said he's call again before Saturday's flight to Minneapolis-St. Paul. And he did: Wednesday night, Thursday during dinner, Friday night before calling me, and then late Saturday morning before driving to K.C. International.

When Hake called me after talking with Sara Wednesday, he didn't hide his emotions, didn't downplay the fact his life was running in reverse, to put it into football parlance.

"Something tells me you'd better be thinking about changing that will of yours," I told him. "And don't ask me to be in your wedding. I'm not going to rent a tux for you or anybody else."

"It's not going to be like that," Chesty protested. "It's just something that seems to be happening. It could be over in a flash, believe me."

"You'll be late Sunday night. It'll keep till breakfast Monday. Oh, and you'll call me Friday night, right?" I half-asked, not telling him. As usual on Fridays, I was going to probe ever so gently for inside information concerning the Cobras' health, attitude, and game plan for Sunday. Those sixty-four-dollar paydays from office pools no longer were attractive to me. But I never, never could let Chesty know that.

Besides, the Friday night call always gave him a chance to tell me what to put on my grocery list for Saturday.

* * * * *

EDITOR'S NOTE: I was up fifty-five-hundred dollars for the Cobras' first six games. If I – if Chesty – had known more about the Bengals going into the fourth week of the season, I probably would have put down my usual thou on that game. But five hundred dollars buys me about eight thousand miles worth of gas, the way I figure it.

* * * * *

It was a nice double room on the tenth floor of he Radisson in Bloomington, Minnesota, a hotel that had an eight-foot-wide fireplace in the lobby and accommodated teams of three-foot-wide football players. The Cobras and the Radisson were one of those comfortable marriages the NFL teams try hard to arrange. There were oversized beds and no-call rooms and a nice bar where a veteran player, age thirty-two, could go and order a beer in a booth and not have to worry.

He sat in a back booth with his beer. He bothered nobody, offended nobody. Eleven o'clock bed check was a second pilsner away. He never minded sitting alone.

No barflies seemed attracted to him, and that was good. He could sit and think of Sara, knowing how she would enjoy that big fireplace out in the lobby. And he could weigh his options.

He downed the beer.

Earlier, his mind had been grooved on a review of the Vikings tapes he and his teammates had watched for a couple of hours, right through prime-time Saturday night TV. Hake knew what he would have to do at twelve-oh-three the next afternoon in the Hubert H. Humphery Dome: Lock out the fan noise and keep track of Burl Vaughn, the fastest kick returner in the NFL. That's all.

The difference between a stout thirty-two-year-old who could run forty yards in five-point-one-eight seconds and a human gazelle who could cover that same distance in four-point-two-seven seconds. Doesn't sound like much. But the difference in eighty-eight hundreds of a second is remarkable. He also had told me Friday night on the phone all he did Sunday was his best. A bad sign.

Amazing, what happened. The Vikings had figured, on the opening kickoff, should it come to Vaughn, he'd run it to his left, toward K.C.'s R-Five guy, the one closest to the sideline over there: Chesty Hake.

* * * * *

Hake told me at breakfast Monday only a couple of the Cobras' front guys had not been intimidated by Burl Vaughn, and Chesty had no great faith in last-hope tacklers.

He had paid the bar waitress for the two drafts and two more. He went to his tenth-floor room to review his special-teams notes one more time – with a friend, a twenty-ounce go-cup.

* * * * *

Vaughn took the kickoff at the goal line and made his cut to the outside at the ten-yard line, heading for the Cobras' R-Five guy as expected. The furious collision was at the nineteen.

"Damn!" Cobras coach Turk Madigan and Minnesota coach Buddy Battles said simultaneously from their respective sidelines. Turk was concerned Hake wouldn't get up. Battles was saying: "How bad? How bad?"

Hake's reputation for being a cunning, vicious special-teams madman was extended into his eighth and final season. Hey, he was my housemate. For the time being, at least.

Hake got up. Vaughn got a gurney ride through the stadium tunnel to the Vikings' dressing room.

Thirty-Nine

For once, I beat Chesty down to Monday breakfast. But then, I didn't get my body smashed up Sunday afternoon, didn't fly from the Twin Cities to K.C. International and didn't drive home two-hundred-forty-five miles through the night. When Hake arrived at the breakfast table, he announced he'd rather make eggs benedict than discuss events of the past week.

We talked at length, but I could see a change in him. He used words like "appreciate," "comfortable," "confused," and "happy."

But he stayed in character: private, given to understatement. I didn't bother to ask how Sara looked, had she changed much in eight years, did they make love. Some questions, however, my newspaper mentality forced me to throw at him.

"Has she married, Ches?"

"I don't know," he said, preparing what he called his hurry-up hollandaise sauce. "I didn't ask."

"How 'bout kids?"

"Didn't come up. And I didn't see kids or photos at her apartment."
"Going to see her tonight?"
"Yes, definitely!" he said with uncharacteristic enthusiasm, coming
loud out of the kitchen. "I'm taking dinner, in fact."
"Aha! What is m'lord going to prepare for Lady Kassel's
approval, if I may ask?"
"What do you think of this: my beef *bourguignone* over some nice,
wide egg noodles with a marinated salad of fresh asparagus, toma
to slices, chopped egg and diced scallions?"
Before I could respond, he added: "And I'll get that wonderful
lemon cheesecake with the red raspberry syrup swirling through it."
"And you're telling me you don't know whether or not you want
to rekindle this thing?"
"I've gotta get busy," he told me. "If I get to Schnucks by ten, I
can have my grocery shopping done by ten-thirty or so and get out
to Ray Briere's shop by eleven. He'll shit when I tell him I want
a coupla bottles of that forty-four-dollar burgundy for cooking."
I could see the tattooed little Frenchman yelping in pain.
"I'm due at Sara's at five-thirty, and the *bourguingnonne* needs
three hours if I do it at five-hundred degrees. I'll still have plenty
of time to run a little, shave, shower, and take a nice, long
Jacuzzi."
"I imagine the 'Cooz will feel good after that hit on Vaughn yesterday."
"Yeah, but even more than the 'Cooz, I need to stretch and run. I
really am stiff this morning."
"And tonight?"
"You're still a jackoff," he replied.
"I think you're going to need your buddy Wingo to rewrite that
will of yours," I added while the opportunity was there.
"As I said, you're a jackoff."
"Oh, by the way, I'm due at the paper before eleven o'clock, so I

probably won't see you before you get back from your shopping. Just remember to leave me your list of what needs to be done and bought this week."

"I will."

He cracked six eggs into ramekins. Six eggs: six unbroken yolks. He began to pour them carefully into the boiling vinegar water.

"Look, I hope dinner goes well tonight."

"Thanks, Paulie."

We were reflective as we ate eggs benedict.

* * * * *

Dinner didn't go well. In fact, dinner didn't go at all.

Hake arrived at eighty-seven-seventy-seven Brookshire, less than a mile from his home, at five-forty-six. He noted the time as he went to his trunk to get the oversized picnic basket, and he hoped Sara would rave about the *bourguignonne*, with its wonderful sauce containing bits of orange peel and bacon. There was extra marinade for the salads; plenty of noodles from Palozola's little shop, and then the cheesecake. Oh, and two bottles of wine from Briere's, slightly cooled.

Sara was holding the door for him by the time he reached the stoop. She extended her arms, and he hugged her as best he could. Don't drop anything, jackoff. She kissed him hard.

"This had better be the finest baloney available," she told him, a lovely sparkle in her eyes. "Your roommate just called me from his paper to warn me. He said baloney sandwiches with American slices, Dijon mustard and sweet relish are your specialty when you make dinner for a woman. I told him you were out front, and the basket looked awfully big for baloney sandwiches."

"That dirty son of a bitch," Hake said in mock-anger, then imme-

251

diately wished he hadn't. From the back of he apartment came running a gangly, mocha-skinned boy of four or five, his hair tight and orange. The Hidden Agenda. The Surprise Package. The Dreaded Answer. The Relationship Change.

"Chesty, this is Kisho," Sara said, singsong. "My little boy."

"I didn't–"

"Of course you didn't."

She tried to gauge the questions he would ask.

"Don't be alarmed, Chesty. As they say, it happens."

Sara looked at the big basket and the canvas tote bag containing the two bottles of wine. "Let's take all this to the kitchen."

The child fled back down the hallway.

"Are you ready for a beer, Chesty?" Sara asked. When he didn't answer, she asked again.

"Uh, no. No, Sara, I brought some wine," he said, still struggling. "The burgundy is good, the same I used in the *bourguignonne*. And there's a nice merlot."

Sara poured merlot for each of them, and they went to the living room sofa. She knew she needed to do something – and quickly.

"Don't be upset, Chesty. Please don't be," she said, gathering his hand in both of hers. He stared down at her hands and remembered marveling, a dozen years earlier, at how large they were. "Kisho is something that just happened. It was in Kansas City, and it was a long time ago, love. I'm a different woman now. I don't hate everyone around me the way I did six years ago, after you – you were gone from my life and I was helpless to do anything about it. It's different now, believe me."

He sipped his merlot.

"Were you married? I need to know."

"No, no. Oh, no. If you think my father hates *goyim*, just imagine how he feels about *schvartzes*. No, Daddy knew I had a biracial baby. How could he not know I was going to have a baby, seeing my belly every day at the dealership? But he never has seen Kisho. And he never knew who Kisho's father was."

Hake stared at the carpet. As Sara raised her glass to her lips, her hand shook slightly. He noticed.

"We can handle this, Chesty. Let's not damage this wonderful thing we've got started. That would be unfair to both of us, I think."

Kisho romped back into the living room. He stopped in front of Hake and stared at him with curious eyes, as if he never had seen a white man.

"Kisho, why don't you sit down and talk with us," Sara suggested. "Tell us what you did at school today."

The orange-haired boy continued to stare, but he moved slightly to Hake's side, as if seeking a three-quarter view or a profile.

"He'll talk at the dinner table, I'm sure. He always does."

"Kisho, I'm Chesty. You wanna shake hands?" Hake asked, offering his hand.

No words, but the boy took a step toward him. Instead of shaking hands, Kisho stomped on Hake's shoe.

"Goddammit!" Hake bellowed, shocked. "Why the hell'd you do that?"

Hake grabbed the child by his upper arms.

"Why'd you do that?" he yelled into the boy's face. "I haven't done anything to you, have I?"

Kisho wrenched free and ran to safety at the back of the apartment.

"Oh, Chesty, I'm so sorry! I have no idea why he did that. He's always so well- behaved."

"I'll buy him a goddamned shoeshine kit for Christmas," Hake said, checking the scrape on his highly polished shoe. Then he realized the inadvertent racist nature of his remark. "That came out wrong."

"I know."

Hake and Sara turned as the front door opened. In came a thin black man, and they rose to confront him. Confrontation occurs in many and varied ways, as Hake quickly would learn.

"Smooth, what are you doing here?" Sara asked indignantly.

"Ey, Ah jis' thought Ah heerd some trouble goin' on in heah," Smooth answered. "Thought Ah'd bedda check an' see."

Hake waited, catching the burst of adrenaline in Sara. Fear was what it was.

"Chesty, this is Smooth Watkins, a – a friend of mine. Smooth, this is Chesty Hake, also a friend."

"Hello, Smooth," Hake said, extending his hand. The wiry black man ignored it.

"Woman, we gonna talk," Smooth said, gesturing toward the hall way. *Now.*"

"Hey, sport, what the hell do you think you're doing?"

Hake took a step forward.

"Chesty, sit and drink your wine," Sara said with a calmness that surprised him. "Please. I'll be right back."

Hake watched Smooth hurry Sara out of the living room. He could hear their voices down the hallway, loud and animated and emphatic, but he couldn't make out what was being said. After a minute or two – or an hour or two, in Hake's mind clock – he decided to check on Sara. She came back into the living room, this time shaking and perspiring as well.

"Chesty, this is awful, but you're going to have to go," Sara said, rushing her words, silently pleading as she looked into his eyes. "I'm sorry – sorry about this. I really am. But you have to go. I mean it. I'll be fine. I wish I could explain this to you, but I can't, not right now. Just bear with me and – and go, if you love me. I'll call you if you won't call me. But please, *please* do this for me."

Hake was frozen. He allowed her to push him toward the door. Then the door closed quietly behind him.

Numb, he drove home. What power does that black son of a bitch have over her? He asked himself that question three or four times and came up with no answer. How does he just stroll on in? Does he own her? Is he her drug source? Is he the father of that bastard kid? Is he her pimp? Jesus Christ!

He had acceded to Sara's wishes. He surrendered. And he surrendered Sara a second time in eight years, and he felt the same rage he had felt eight years earlier.

Back then, he was twenty-four and a rookie-to-be, not thirty-two and a retiree-to-be. Back then, his anger, hurt and indignation were converted into resolve, resourcefulness and determination: ingredients that allowed him to become the rare Mr. Irrelevant to make an NFL roster. This time, he was grappling, off balance.

* * * * *

"What the hell?" I exclaimed when I drove into the garage and saw Hake's car there.

I listened closely when I opened the kitchen door. I could hear nothing, so I took two cans of Bud from the refrigerator and started up the staircase. I padded up the ginger-colored carpeting and got almost to my door when I heard Chesty weeping.

Back in my room, I put down the beers and sat on the edge of my bed. I stared at the terra cotta paint on the wall across from me. What went wrong? I kept asking myself that question.

* * * * *

Hake was due for a team meeting that Tuesday morning. I

knocked on his door.

"What? Yes?"

"Chesty, it's six o'clock. You need to be on the road."

I knew he would catch the alarm in my voice.

"I'm not going back today, Paul."

"You're not?"

"Come on in."

Hake looked like hammered shit. He held up a hand.

"Don't ask. I'm not gonna explain it to you right now. Just under
stand that, right now, I'm not fit to play professional football. I'm
gonna sleep an hour or two, then I'm gonna call Kansas City."

"Okay."

There was nothing else to say.

* * * * *

I had "early slot" at the paper that morning, so I was gone by
the time Hake arose at nine. He squirted some saline solution into his
eyes, didn't bother to gargle, put on a running suit, and went down to
get some milk. Because the Cobras would be playing the Raiders on
grass, not artificial turf, Hake pulled from the hall closet an old pair
of yellow football shoes with what the players call "grass cleats."
The cleats are slightly longer than the ones most players prefer for
playing on synthetic turf, Hake once explained to me.

* * * * *

EDITOR'S NOTE: I had the same intense interest in
cleat lengths I had in the excretory systems of the
Borg fly and the Atrebates moth.

* * * * *

Hake returned from his run and to his milk. The wall clock said nine-ten. He turned on the TV and flipped to CNN Headline News. Then he dialed Turk Madigan's direct line at Weston. He didn't feel up to talking with Becky Shular, so he told the coach's secretary he had a serious personal matter to attend to. He would get back to Kansas City when he could.

Hake hadn't eaten in some twenty-six hours. After breakfast Monday, he was too busy shopping and then cooking and then working out to bother with lunch, and then there was the dinner that wasn't. Twenty-six hours.

What was missing, though, was the Vikings tape or a Raiders-Patriots tape. No rewind. No fast-forward. No concentration.

Forty

Hake was more than one hundred feet from the Maryland Avenue intersection when the green went to amber, eight feet when the amber went to red. He eased to a stop but realized he was in the right-turn lane, not the through lane. In hundreds – maybe thousands of trips so close to home – he never had made that error. Fate, the Bitch Goddess, doing her thing.

He looked left, then right before starting his automatic right on red. From his right, westbound, came a car gaining speed despite facing an amber light gone to red.

Hake scarcely realized how quickly he had yanked the seven-point-six-five-millimeter from the FOLK MUSIC tape case. He really didn't know he had rested the silencer on the leather cushion of the door.

Evelyn Koster, sixty-eight, retired accountant, conservative Jew, had no idea why the left-rear tire of her silver Buick Skylark blew out. After all, she had run that traffic signal on Maryland at about noon virtually every Monday since she had retired from the office supplies shop, since she had gone to work part-time at her son's drapery shop out in Ladue.

Evelyn was embarrassed to see her hubcap continuing ahead of her car, rolling through the Brentwood Boulevard intersection, up a curb and onto a grassy strip just short of a shopping center parking lot.

Hake finished his right turn and looped around to Kingsbury Boulevard, four blocks north.

At mid-afternoon, bored by the *de ja vu* of CNN Headline News and his stamp collection, Hake remembered he was about out of Lavoris. Why then? Why Lavoris? But instead of driving a half-mile or so to his new Schnucks store, he chose to drive to an older, smaller Schnucks almost two miles away.

By the time Hake returned to the Maryland-Brentwood intersection, Mrs. Koster's tire problem from midday was nothing more than a notation in the "Calls" log at the Clayton Police Station on South Central. This time, he was in the proper lane to get him the few blocks home.

Northbound drivers could see the lights for westbound traffic change from green to amber, and then they could say "a thousand one," "a thousand two." It was a game. But Hake was having none of it.

Judge Herb Kornblet, Eighth Circuit, age sixty-three, goosed the Seville. Stopping for that light at Maryland and Brentwood meant another eighty-five or ninety seconds before he could get to his six-bedroom home in Ladue or to Busch's Grove for happy hour with his judicial peers. The hell with that!

He had no idea why his left-rear tire blew.

Hake drove on, past the brick entryway with a brass plaque reading:
CLAYTON GARDENS
NO THROUGH TRAFFIC

And in the ensuing forty-eight hours:

Roy R. Sibby, twenty-seven, with known Ku Klux Klan ties, fire-wood cutter and salesman from southeastern Missouri, en route to visit ex-girlfriend in St. Louis County jail on drug charges, ran a red light at the intersection of Forsyth and Meramec, Clayton, and spun out.

Tory Lynn Taylor, sixteen, lukewarm Roman Catholic, Ladue High School junior, leaving Lord & Taylor department store and Galleria Mall in white BMW 325i convertible, fishtailed to a stop and caused braking by traffic in three lanes on Brentwood.

Richard R. Rabin, forty-one, reformed Jew, Ph.D., faculty member in Washington University School of Architecture, forced his way from outside lane to inside lane, forced another car into near-accident with oncoming traffic at seventy-two-hundred block of Forsyth, University City. Then he crabbed to a stop on rubber ribbons.

Bertram B. (Bert) Conley, thirty-three, non-practicing Lutheran, blocked one-lane alley and underground garage exit with his Alderson Foods Inc. delivery truck, then left vehicle to make delivery; between Carondelet Avenue and Bonhomme Avenue, Clayton; ticketed by Clayton Police.

Hell of a day, Chesty said to himself, hell of a day. The Lavoris was on the seat beside him.

Forty-One

Hake didn't get much sympathy form Turk Madigan when they met in the coach's office at a little after nine Thursday morning, but he wasn't fined. Madigan, who'd had his own troubles with wives and assorted women and teenaged girls over four decades, told Hake his punishment for missing two practices and two meetings would be reduced playing time against the Raiders on national TV.

" 'Monday Night Football,' " the venerable coach said. "Stings more, don't it? You'll be in for the openin' kickoff, kick or receive, but don't expect to play a whole helluva lot after that."

"That about it, Turk?"

"Yeah, that's about it." After a pause, Madigan said: "No. Coupla more things, Hake. One, make sure you get those ankles taped good and tight this morning', 'cause you're gonna work real hard in practice. And two, why doncha just find yourself a nice lady here in Kansas City, maybe over in Lenexa or down in Lake Lotawana or wherever, some little lady who'll treat ya right and wancha to bang her a coupla times a week? Why doncha?"

"Unfortunately for me, I think I have."

"Whatcha mean by that?"

"See ya at meeting time, Turk. I'll make sure my ankles are real tight."

* * * * *

Eleven hours later, Turk Madigan sat at the bar at Danny's, happily downing fan-bought Chivas Regal and laughing heartily. He regaled his audience with NFL war stories. Twenty-three feet away, in a darkened booth on the periphery, a couple sat with their backs to the bar and drank a pitcher of Bud. In contrast to Turk, they talked seriously.

"Any idea at all what her relationship is with this Smooth guy?" Becky Sular asked, staccato-tapping the back of his hand with her index finger.

"I wish I did, Becky, but I don't," Hake said. "A strange situation – a little frightening."

"Frightening? For you?"

"Oh, I wasn't afraid of him. No, that's not it. But the situation. I was playing out of my league, Becky."

"Chesty, from what you're telling me, I'm glad you're above that shit."

Her fingernail, tired of staccato tapping, now ran soft circles on the back of Chesty's hand. He looked from her eyes down to her busy fingernail and wanted so much to add something like: I wish I could love you instead, Becky. Turk would approve.

But he didn't love her.

And he wanted to brag to her about his marksmanship, too, but couldn't. He was happy being with Becky, even if it was against club rules. Happy with Becky? Yes. Satisfied? If it weren't for Sara…

*****

"Why do they call me Turk?" the coach asked rhetorically, getting louder by the sip. "Cause when I was an assistant coach, I kep' missin' lunch when I hadda go tell guys they'd been cut. Hey, that's why. Mad'gan's not a Turkish name, y'know."

Becky looked at the animated head coach at the bar, then back to Hake.

"Noisy, huh?"

"That he is."

"And it all comes down to the Turk."

"What the hell are you saying?" he asked.

"The Turks. First, eight years ago, you made the team and avoided the Turk. But not until that turkey who would've been your father-in-law had cut you. Now you've been cut by another kind of Turk, this one named Smooth. And still, for eight years, you've risked being cut by that Turk over there," Becky concluded, pointing to the bar.

The woman bartender, pretending to be paying attention to Madigan, peered over his shoulder in time to see Becky's gesture. She came over with another pitcher of Bud.

*****

Pete Parent's Pistols was, if nothing else, convenient. Next door, there in the unincorporated blue-collar section outside the K.C. suburb of Raytown, was Parental Custody.

Parental Custody was a saloon with an oft-ripped Naugahyde bar, now more silver than black, with all those duct tape repairs. Pete would sell a fella a pistol and then a six-pack if the customer were in the mood to go home and argue with his old lady. Oh, don't worry about the waiting period or the license to carry; catch up with that when you can, podner. Or Pete would sell you a quart of hundred-proof and a buck-sixty plastic flask, then take you next door to sell you enough twelve-gauge shells to blow apart most of the Canada geese in Nodaway County. But at least that bourbon would keep you from catching cold, right?

Pete Parent, on cozy terms with every cop who might happen into his premises, also sold boxes of seven-point-six-five-millimeter. Chesty bought three boxes, the paper work would keep. He put them in HUT-HUT, then went next door and had three beers before starting back to his condo.

* * * * *

For more that two decades, "Monday Night Football" had been a bonanza for TV and the NFL, the bane of coaches and players and other personnel.

"It just slices up our week to where we cain't git nothin' done the following week," Turk Madigan once lamented. "Even if you win on a Monday night, you don't have no momentum goin' for you the fol-lowin' Sunday."

Hake and many Cobras understood. But the NFL schedule-maker had seen fit to pit the Cobras against the archrival Raiders on the West Coast Monday night. Kansas City's "other team" – not the Chiefs – hadn't had a Monday night game in two years, and the Raiders had-n't had one in three, as the network boomed in its promos.

Sunday, Hake drove north on State Highway 291 out of Liberty on his way to I-435 and K.C. International. His watch read nine-fifty-five, and he was in good time for the eleven o'clock charter to the Coast. Turk wanted to be at the hotel in time to see the second half of the Jets-Dolphins game.

On a deserted two-lane stretch of Route 291, Hake spotted an old Dodge pickup backing out of a dusty farm lane. Then, too quickly, it was about to back into the northbound lane, just ahead of HUT-HUT.

* * * * *

Hake put away the pistol and watched in his rearview mirror as the truck collapsed on a tire. Would the Clay County Sheriff's Department compare notes with its St. Louis County counterpart? Hake doubted it. Then he realized, on the back end of his thoughts about Sara, the exhilaration was fading, no longer belonging. He wasn't up there, free of his mother's corpse and dead dogs and other festering things.

He knew a profound sadness.

* * * * *

In the back of the plane, Hake drank his two beers, the young receiver's two, the young punter's two. Two were gone before the plane left the gate, and the other four were down by the time the Seven-Twenty-Seven reached cruising altitude. Hake slept until the flight was into its descent over KCI at four-thirty a.m., but he awakened quickly. There were miles to travel and things to be done.

He reached the far suburbs of St. Louis as rush-hour traffic was winding down, and he drove toward Sara's apartment instead of heading home. He would have gotten to Eighty-seven-seventy-seven Brookshire several seconds earlier if it hadn't been for what an Olivette Police Department spokesman later termed an "accident" in the ninety-nine-hundred block of Olive Boulevard. Lorenzo Wheat, fifteen, no professed religion, dark blue Lincoln Town Car, no driver's license, claimed no one to post bond when charged. There was no registration, no insurance liability card, no knowledge of vehicle's owner. After cutting close to Hake, he rocked into an Amoco station with flashing red-and-blue lights behind him. The flattened tire saved him from continuing headlong into a fuel pump.

The City of Olivette pretty much grabbed him by the scruff of the neck.

Forty-Two

**Gambling Figure Charged
In Chesty Hake Shooting**

Tyrone W. (Smooth) Watkins, a prominent figure in organized gambling in North St. Louis, was arrested Tuesday and charged with armed criminal action, carrying a concealed weapon and parole violation in the shooting of professional football player Chester J. (Chesty) Hake Jr.

Watkins, thirty-six, of the sixty-one-hundred block of Vernon Avenue, University City, was being held under police guard Tuesday night at an undisclosed area hospital. Bond was set at one-hundred-thousand dollars by Circuit Judge William X. McPeak.

Hake, thirty-two, a running back for the Kansas City Cobras and a resident of Clayton, was shot in the left shoulder Tuesday morning at the doorstep of an apartment in the eighty-seven-hun-

---

dred block of Brookshire Lane, Olivette.

A spokesman for the Olivette Police Department said the apartment recently had been emptied of furniture, clothing, and all other belongings. The occupant was not present at the time of the shooting, said spokesman Sgt. Scott Brendel.

* * * * *

The story went on to say police sources indicated Hake had no known gambling connections. Hake, after being wounded, smashed Watkins' jaw and three ribs and pounded his alleged assailant's right eyeball virtually out of its socket. The story failed to say Hake broke a bone in his left hand doing it.

"Aw, sweet Jesus, Chesty! You're a mess!" I exclaimed as I went through the kitchen door and took a first look at him. He was standing at the stove, stirring something with a wooden spoon. "What's with the hand?"

"I broke it on Smooth's head. He shot me twice, Paulie. I had to go for his face. That was the only way I could keep him from shooting me again. But it's just one of the small bones down here." He pointed to the back of his hand, which was under an inch-thick wrapping of Ace bandage over gauze and tape. "The doctor at Jewish said the club's medical people probably will clear me to play week after next at Miami. It'll need a light cast, though."

Hake continued to stir at the stove.

"At least I'm alive. And I'm probably lucky I broke my hand, Paulie. Otherwise, I would've killed Smooth. I know I would've."

"So who the fuck is Smooth?"

"Oh, right."

Hake took a minute or two to fill me in concerning the picnic bas-ket debacle. How could I explain I had known Smooth – explained my gambling? I listened, two-faced, and I didn't like myself.

Then Hake explained, all too graphically for my taste, what he had done to the rat-like little bookie with three punches: the jaw, the ribs, and the eyeball. When he finished, I wasn't hungry. I looked past the man to see what he was stirring.

"How's your shoulder?"

Hake pulled back his running suit to display a four-by-four gauze bandage attached with lots of adhesive tape.

"It's not much more than a graze, but it sure a hell burned," he told me.

"And all that crap on your ear?" I said, taking a sip of beer and looking at the glob of gauze.

"They gave me a tetanus shot and some prescription Tylenol and told me to stay away from the beer. But that was quite a few hours ago. Ply me with one, will you? I'll keep sweating over this chick-en-lemon-wild rice soup. And if you'll dice, slice, and chop a few ingredients for me, I'm going to try a new salad. What do you think: tomato chunks, roasted red, green, and yellow bell pepper slices, red onion, black beans, corn, and a little bit of garlic, tossed in Italian dressing."

I was supposed to visualize the taste possibilities, but all I could think about was my gambling and Chesty's rib-breaking fists.

"I had it at a little place in Lenexa, Kansas, a couple of years ago. Well, anyway, you'll like it."

Becky Shular would appreciate this salad, Hake thought, if they made it together in her kitchen at Two-twenty-nine Kinsman Circle, Lenexa, Kansas, ZIP Code Six-six-two-one-five.

I popped Hake's beer and handed it to him.

"You never stop, do you?" I said. "Why the hell couldn't we just order a couple of pizzas? You're hurt, and Sara's on your mind, and-"

Chesty belched, his thick, bandaged hand around the spoon, stirring. "Y'know, with the broken hand, I didn't have to sign a single auto graph at the hospital. I told them I'm left-handed."

"What about Sara's apartment?"

"Empty. Cleaned out. Even the nails for hanging pictures and whatever had been yanked. And then to suddenly face that jack off and his gun on the front porch..."

"Did neighbors or anybody see her leave?"

"Not that I know of. When I went back to get HUT-HUT, I stopped at the apartment office a couple of blocks east on Brookshire. The two women there said the first they knew of the apartment being empty was when they came to see what the ambulance was about."

Hake called the phone company to determine whether or not Sara had a new number. The number hadn't been disconnected.

"I went over to the Olivette Police Department, and they treated me well," he told me. "They were surprised I was out of the hospital, but they couldn't give me much help."

They couldn't let Hake file a missing person report for two reasons: One, Sara hadn't been missing for twenty-four hours; and two, he wasn't a relative, guardian, step-relative or key business associate. Suspicion of kidnapping? No, because kidnappers don't remove picture hangers from walls.

"But she's my ex-fiancée, and she doesn't have any relatives in the St. Louis area," Chesty explained to a sergeant who seemed interested. Over the sergeant's shoulder, he could see two uniformed officers edging closer to the doorway for better hearing.

"Could she have taken off because you broke up?" the sergeant asked. His question seemed natural.

"Nah, we broke up seven years ago. We were just getting back together, believe it or not. That's why I've got to find her, Sergeant. She's pretty damned important to me."

"Okay, Chesty. Gimme your phone number, and I'll personally get back to you if anything turns up. Best I can do for ya."

Hake wrote his listed number, Sara's license plate number, and a description of her Nissan on a scratch pad.

"Thanks, Sergeant." Hake started to leave. "About Smooth Watkins: What's his background?"

"Smooth's nasty and always has been. I first arrested him twenty, maybe twenty-one years ago, when I was with the University City department. Since then, he's done a couple of stints at Jeff City for bookmaking and at least a couple shorties at Gumbo for carrying a concealed weapon. Those are just the ones I know of. He's an opportunist and a slug. We know he's part of a good-seized bookmaking operation on the North Side."

Hake was mute.

"And he's gotta taste for white girls. I figure some white guy's gonna kill ol' Smooth someday."

"I tried this morning, I guess," said Hake, holding up his bandaged left fist. "But his skull was tougher than my third metacarpal."

* * * * *

"What else can you do?" I asked.

"I don't know." He slowly shook his head. "Wait till Smooth gets out of the hospital."

We stared at each other.

"But then again, this could be Sara's doing," Hake said. "She may not want to be found."

His belch resonated.

"I did some checking," I told him. "Smooth's out of ophthalmological surgery. They've got a guard on his room. He's listed in serious but stable condition at St. Louis University Hospital."

I didn't like Chesty's look.
"I won't ask how you know that."
"Hey, I'm a newspaperman."
My belch matched his.
"Help me with the salad, will you?"
And that was it – for the time being.

* * * * *

Only Chesty heard the gun.

Joey Cerutti, thirty-nine, Roman Catholic, roared eastward on Maryland Avenue at Brentwood Boulevard, through the red light in his haste to get to his appointment at nine with the assistant vice president-purchasing at Barnes-Jewish Hospital. Cerutti was certain he wouldn't be on time after parking at the huge medical complex. He was right. The air leaving the left-rear tire of his dark red Lexus pretty well proved that. Hake steered HUT-HUT around it.

Who arrived at the hospital first? Hake, of course. He went in to have his dressings changed and his hand x-rayed and re-bandaged.

Traffic out of the hospital garage and onto busy Kings highway was difficult northbound, virtually impossible southbound. And Hake hurt.

HUT-HUT sat to the right of a black Porsche in the left-turn lane. When the Porsche's driver saw an opening, he pulled in front of Hake, who had been waiting patiently in the left-turn lane. Hake went two feet before braking. He didn't bother to honk.

There's no Rx for a flattened tire.

Christopher Crowell, M.D., fifty, a deacon at Emmanuel Episcopal Church in Webster Groves, took his first Demerol at eight- fifteen and his third just before heading out to give a speech to directors at the Yeatman Health Clinic on poverty-plagued North Grand Boulevard.

When Crowell didn't arrive, there was considerable agitation: "White doctors don't care. See, I told you! Dude didn't even show!"

Meanwhile, another busy street became congested.

Carol Braxton, twenty-four, no known religion, never thought backing onto busy, narrow-laned Lindell Boulevard should be a problem. After all, her husband just about *owned* this town, didn't he? He was the most influential radio personality since Jack who ever he was, who just happened to have lived in the Victorian house a few doors down when he died. Jack had had a circular drive. Carol Braxton was ticketed for obstructing traffic, and, when she called her husband on the air to tell him of her flattened right-rear tire, she erased her anger with a news-block of epithets that got Bobby Braxton a letter of reprimand from his station and another from the Federal Communications Commission.

One lane per vehicle, Hake said to himself. He waited for the emotional kick that would free him. It didn't come.

Mary Luke Lansing, Society of the Obsessed Sisters (S.O.S.) or something, sixty-nine, never had been issued a Missouri driver's license or any insurance coverage but had been the beneficiary of a rusted-out green Chevrolet station wagon. It now straddled the centerline of two westbound lanes on Forest Park Boulevard. With Tylenol not handling his pain, Hake honked repeatedly. He put her right-rear out of its misery.

Hake should've gone home and taken more Tylenol. Instead, he scrambled past the wagon and, two miles later, exited at Olive Boulevard and went to lunch at Ken's – close to Sara's apartment.

He sat on a stool at the L-shaped bar and called to the legally blind bartender: "Only eleven o'clock, Nikki?"

" 'Fraid so."

"Oh, well, it's noon in New York. A long-neck Bud."

Now, if Hake ever were questioned as to his whereabouts that

Wednesday morning, he was at Ken's having a beer by eleven sharp. Nikki also would say that. Chesty had a corned beef on rye, a bowl of Ken's fine turtle soup with some sherry splashed into it, then two more long-necks. He ate quickly and drank the second and third beers faster than he normally would, then was ready to head home by eleven-fifty-three.

"Told ya I'd be out of here by eleven-thirty, Nikki," he said, putting two extra singles into her hand before climbing off his barstool.

Hake walked to his car and wished he had provided himself with time crutches for the previous tire shootings. By the time he closed the garage door with the remote control in the kitchen, he felt the fear of detection closing in for the first time. Angry as he was, he knew, he couldn't continue to blast away at tires. Cops look for patterns.

But...

But another athlete couldn't be spared. Chad Thomas, twenty-seven, Cincinnati Reds pitcher, Lutheran and active in the Fellowship of Christian Athletes, evidently hadn't been reading much other that the Sports Section and hadn't learned running a just-turned-red at Maryland and Brentwood Boulevard was a dangerous undertaking. His black Ferrari didn't clear the intersection after a seven-point-six-five-millimeter slug chewed into the right-front Pirrelli. Hake had to negotiate carefully to get around the sports car to make his right turn onto westbound Maryland.

Clayton police still were on the scene at the intersection when Hake returned from the nearby Schnucks market fifteen minutes later with a case of beer and a four-pack of nicely cut pork loin chops. He navigated the maze of residential streets: Topton Way over to North Forsyth. Then, on the off chance HUT-HUT's presence had been noted, he went quickly north to Kingsbury. He had seen enough. And, as the Clayton police chief would've attested as they worked on a horrific traffic problem, he had done quite enough, too.

The *Region/Local* section the next morning would contain an item pointing out that pitcher Chad Thomas had been arrested for D.W.I., having a blood-alcohol level of zero-point-one-eight, almost double the legal limit in Missouri, and assaulting a police officer investigating a traffic accident. Oh, and Chad also had been driving with an invalid Missouri license.

All this by early afternoon.

FCA do-gooder or not, the son of a bitch was a real menace, Hake mused, turning to the obituaries and the funeral notices.

Forty-Three

I looked up from the paper as Hake came down the stairs. "How you feeling?"

"Tylenol helps."

We read in silence for a minute or two. He glanced over page One-A and turned to Two-A.

"These tire shootings are strange," I said as he checked out the celebrity comings and goings on Two-A. "There's a story here we haven't heard. Whoever's doing it is smart and shrewd. Must have something to prove, I guess."

"I guess," Hake said absently, picking up the *Region/Local* section. "I dunno. Do they think there's any connection? The location? The time? The make of car, maybe?"

"The cops are getting pissed off. The County Police Chief was in the executive offices at the paper the other day. Obviously, he wants a strong campaign for the editorial page—an extension of the 'neighborhood watch' program."

"Then they don't know who's doing it," Hake said, his face in the *Region/Local* section. "Surprising."

"Whoever it is stays cool. No cowboy chases. No attention drawn to himself. No, this tire guy is bright and patient, I'd say. It'd be fun to sit here at this table and drink beer with him some night. Find out what goes through his mind. Doncha think?"

I waited.

Hake turned to the Op-Ed pages and looked for familiar names among the *Letters to the Editor* contributors. He found none, so he flipped back to the funeral notices and the obits. No familiar names there, either.

* * * * *

The departments of several suburbs and the St. Louis County Police Department determined they would pool their resources and theories. All they knew was somebody out there, somebody pretty accurate with a seven-point-six-five-millimeter handgun, had been playing hob with tires in St. Louis County, primarily the Clayton area, and therefore playing hob with traffic on some major arteries.

His continued success had the cops pissed off.

One high-ranking police official speculated on TV the Tire Killer was a would-be kidnapper or extortionist who, eventually, would try to extract money or something else of value to end the shootings. That official's brother, the police chief of their North County suburb, suggested publicly there must be a deficient gene in their family.

Another officer of significant standing suggested the Tire Killer must be a trained marksman and, therefore, the National Rifle Association and local gun clubs should be asked to assist by screening recent competition winners. And the Air Force should be asked to investigate expert/sharpshooter qualifiers from Scott Air Force Base, just across the Mississippi River from St. Louis.

"That's bullshit!" reasoned Clayton Police Chief Royal Parsons. "It would be a rare NRA member who drove around brandishing a weapon that fires seven-point-six-fives. And the military doesn't even mess with seven-point-six-fives. Let's cut the bullshit. Let's not even waste time or resources trying to find some staff sergeant or a card-carrying member of the NRA. It's somebody else, somebody very different."

With that no-live-mikes pronouncement to the media, Parsons went in to face the Clayton Board of Aldermen. He knew his words were going to be wasted.

"Traffic's down at the Maryland-Brentwood intersection, and fewer people are going through on red nowadays. We haven't worked a multiple-vehicle accident there in weeks. But, yes, because of the Tire Killer, we've devoted too much time to that intersection."

The Chief looked at Mayor Spiegel and the board members. The faces were somber or stony or sour.

"We'll get him," Parsons vowed. "That's all I can tell you, all I can promise you. I've had a unit—a unit there—a car—virtually every minute during daylight hours-"

"Chief Parsons!" snapped alderwoman Cynthia Bemiston Todd, a personification of old Clayton money. "Just catch this criminal."

* * * * *

EDITOR'S NOTE: I had beaten the spread on six of Kansas City's—the Cobras, that is—first seven games, but the early line on the Cobras-Seattle game in the eighth week was going to be a toughie: the Seahawks by five. With that spread, I had no strong feeling either way.

Just then, I got a call from Chesty at Barnes-Jewish Hospital. He told me he had been shot, was okay, and was going to take a taxi from the hospital to Sara's apartment to get his car. He would see me at suppertime. That became a three-thousand-dollar phone call, as it turned out.

I immediately called a "friend" of mine, made certain the spread hadn't changed from five points, then put down the biggest bet of my life, taking the Seahawks and giving the Cobras those five points. I estimated it would be eight by kickoff Sunday. It was nine.

Chesty's loss was a half-point, perhaps. The remainder was the gossip around the dressing room, in the weight room, on the trainers' taping tables and rubdown tables, across players' dinner tables, on their pillows with their wives or girlfriends asking tough questions.

The Cobras wouldn't go into the game as they should've. I didn't bother to watch even two minutes' worth on the Sports Department's TV that Sunday afternoon, so confident was I that I made a savvy wager. Seattle won, sixteen-ten, beating my spread by a point but not the closing spread of nine.

Perhaps Hake's absence and the short week and the speculation didn't increase that spread by four points. Who knows? But I'll be sure to dwell on those theories as I count my thirty hundred-dollar bills.

Forty-Four

The political big guns of Clayton and St. Louis County grew impatient. The mayor of Clayton, the county executive, Clayton's police chief, chiefs of other area suburbs, and the chief of the St. Louis County Police Department realized they had to do something— and quickly. The natives were getting restless about having someone variously tabbed by the media as the Tire Killer, the Tire Man, the Marksman of Maryland Avenue, the Tire Changer, and some other names.

Saul Spiegel, Mayor of Clayton, called a former college friend, Dr. Ted Fischer, to see what could be done. Dr. Fischer, from Wisconsin A&M University at White Falls, was internationally known as an expert on vigilantism. His expertise had helped authorities with that awful situation in Omaha a couple of years earlier, and before that, he had shown police in Biloxi how to find the guy who killed those eleven prostitutes, making a fine living off servicemen at Mississippi's Keesler Air Force Base and the Navy Seabee Base in

Gulfport.

"Ted, we've got a strange situation down here," said Spiegel. "I'd say we've got a killer who doesn't kill anybody."

The mayor went on to explain the Tire Killer was shooting regularly, a small-caliber gun was used each time, each of the victimized motorists probably had violated one or more traffic laws. They talked for another ten minutes.

"Saul, I can't get there until the weekend," said the psychologist from his office in White Falls. "But I'll be there Saturday. I prom ise. It sounds interesting."

"That's wonderful, Ted. A lot of people are frightened—and embarrassed—and a lot of cops are pissed. We'd all appreciate your help."

"Okay. Plan on working Saturday afternoon and Sunday. Call a press conference for Monday afternoon early. That way, we make the drive-time news on radio and the dinner-time news on TV."

"Why do we need that?" Spiegel asked. "What'll that accomplish? I was thinking-"

"Just have your people call the TV, radio, and newspaper types," Fischer said. "I know what I am doing. Support me on this, Saul."

* * * * *

I called Hake from the office, something I seldom did. I knew he was home and could monitor his answering machine.

"Ches, watch television at five o'clock," I told him. "They're going to have a press conference about the tire shooter. This may mean they've caught him. Should be interesting."

Hake thanked me and hung up.

* * * * *

The news conference was a disaster. Every politician on hand thought so. None of them was allowed to posture, to make any statement whatsoever. Dr. Ted Fischer was a twenty-four-carat camerahound with a stack of crudely done, eighteen-by-twenty-four Foamcore graphics. The forty-minute session was his. Not the mayor's, not the county executive's. It didn't belong to any of the half-dozen law enforcement officials. Fischer was large, loud, gruff, and imposing, and everyone seemed willing to back down from him.

Public relations people scrambled to make the shooting incidents themselves paramount, while Fischer used his expertise to ensure the spotlight—and the cameras—remained on him. Mayor Spiegel's long-endured diverticulitis acted up. He wished he never had dialed Fischer's number in White Falls. County Executive Brian McGee glowered at Spiegel and anyone else who happened to be within ten feet of Fischer's podium. McGee was not accustomed to hearing: "Shut up!" At least not from anyone but his very wealthy wife, or perhaps the governor on occasion.

"Then could this be the doing of a jealous person, Dr. Fischer?" the woman from the ABC affiliate asked.

"A good question, but the answer is 'no.' If it were jealousy, our gunner would have killed somebody by now. Our friend is a vigilante. Our friend doesn't want to hurt anybody. He just wants to see justice done once in a while. So he shoots out tires."

"Doctor, what's he like? We want to see a profile," said a reporter from the Fox Network affiliate.

"All right. If he's a male, he's probably a very small man, an irrelevant man. Over thirty, but a guy who has tried long and hard for attention. He's a person who first shoots a squirrel in his back yard with a BB gun, then knocks the poop out of a parking meter when it won't accept his dime, then gives the finger to a guy in a pick-up truck when he gets cut off at an intersection.

"But this fellow focuses," Fischer said. "He no longer gives the finger. He shoots out a tire."

Two dozen media people and perhaps a dozen technicians kept their eyes on this academic type. It was a news conference with no movement, no animation.

"Dr. Fischer, you've said that the Tire Killer is small. Other than that, what can you tell us?"

"That's tough. Let me go at this slowly, please," he said. "Awright, we've got a thin man, no more than five-three or five-four, a guy who's had several jobs, a guy who did well early in college and then had problems of some sort, a guy who is heterosexual but has some sort of problem achieving heterosexual orgasm, a guy who lives alone and doesn't let others into his private life, a guy who wants everything to be precise."

"Does he want to be caught?"

"No," said the psychologist. "If he did, he wouldn't be using a silencer. He'd want a big bang, so to speak. A forty-five or a three-fifty-seven magnum."

"How can people protect themselves from this person?" asked a television type, a thin black man with an extra-large head of dyed-black hair.

"Well, what I am going to say is going to sound like I'm caving into your vigilante, but I'll make the recommendation anyhow: Don't run stoplights. St. Louis is known nationwide for its 'St. Louis stops,' those rolling stops. This doesn't seem to bother your shooter. Rather it seems to be mostly affluent people who feel the amber light gone to red doesn't apply to them.

"He probably had an accident with somebody above him, financially and status-wise." Fischer went on. "I've been given a list of vehicles that had their tires shot out, and they tend to be cars driven by affluent people: two BMW's, a couple of Cadillacs, a Lincoln

Town Car, a Porsche, a Ferrari. On the other hand, there was a big delivery van, a panel truck, a black minister's clinker, and a nun's station wagon.

"The perpetrator probably is a small person. The perpetrator probably has been wronged in the city of Clayton or perhaps by someone who lives in Clayton. The perpetrator doesn't live in Clayton because he's obviously too intelligent to poop in his own back yard."

* * * * *

I called Chesty again.

"Channel Four at six, Ches," I said hurriedly. "Tape it for me, will ya?"

"Sure."

* * * * *

We sent two City Side reporters to cover Fischer's press conference. Our urban affairs columnist and a photographer went along, too. They all came back to the paper shaking their heads.

"Un-fucking-believable," Tim Rich responded when I asked him in the men's room how the news conference went. "Twice he told the county executive to shut up. That was the highlight. Too bad I can't lead with that. The mayor of Clayton is gonna wish he'd never heard of this guy. Un-fucking-believable."

"Spiegel," I said blandly. "Mayor Spiegel."

"Yeah. Well, excuse me, Paul. I've gotta go write. Thing is, no matter how I work my story, those people out there reading the paper tomorrow morning aren't gonna believe what this zany fucker said."

"Quote him accurately." I said. "Your only defense."

* * * * *

Watching two minutes of the ten o'clock news, I realized what Tim Rich was saying in the men's room. Fischer was willing to adjust his thinking, his logic, his instincts to suit the most recent question. For instance:

"How do we know the perpetrator is a man? Perhaps it's not. Women can be just as accurate with a gun as men. Here in St. Louis, you have a significant number of women taking marksmanship courses because of your high violent-crime rate. As for the Tire Killer, you might just have a woman."

Which way next? Fischer paused and looked around, either to check the camera angles or to find someone with another question into which he could introduce some new, quirky, titillating element.

Clayton patrolwoman Sharon Klippel entered the conference room and crossed to Chief Royal Parsons' chair behind Fischer. She handed the chief a note and left. A detective quietly followed her.

"What was that all about, Sharon?" he asked when he caught up.

"The chief wanted to be kept up to date. The Tire Killer has struck again. Four times this afternoon."

"Oh, shit!" Dave Loomis muttered.

"That's exactly what the chief said."

They reached the sidewalk as media people began to exit.

Forty-Five

Hake was filling his tank at the Warrenton exit Shell station when he witnessed a pre-dawn event. The black Jag, without the right-of-way, cut off a pickup truck on its way into the pump area. The truck was forced to bang into one of the protective concrete bumpers. A teenage girl driving the pickup was shaken, Hake could see. He paid for his gas, went to his car, and made a U-turn around the island of pumps. When he reached darkness, he pulled HUT-HUT to the meeting of cement and grass on the exit tarmac, perhaps seventy-five feet from the lighted pay window.

As Hake might have predicted, the black Jaguar Sovereign was traveling at least thirty when it passed him.

His aim, as usual, was true.

The sedan continued no more than twenty or twenty-five feet into darkness before coming to a stop. It listed at the aft starboard.

Hake waited for the portly driver and his companion to go back to the lighted pay window. The pickup truck, in leaving, narrowly

missed them and sent them scrambling. Hake was proud of the girl.
Then, with his lights still off, he shoved the floor lever into "drive"
and smartly maneuvered around the stricken vehicle.

The conversation at the window was going to be colorful, Hake
knew. Jag driver versus Ernie's sister. Could Ernie's heavyset sister
sing "We'll Sing in the Sunshine"? Hake wondered that as the gun
went back into the tape case.

He flicked on his headlights as he crossed the south outer road and
started onto the overpass leading to I-70 westbound.

* * * * *

"Come in," Chief Royal Parsons called out.

Sergeant Nelson Marler from the communications room came in
and handed his boss a message.

"Looks like the Tire Killer has broadened his target area, Chief,"
Marler said, holding in his smile.

Parsons read the message from the Warrenton Police Department:
A motorist's right-rear tire was shot out at zero-five-fifty-eight hours
this date as he left Grace & Ernie's Shell on the south service road off
I-70.

"How many does that make now, Chief?"

"Hell, I don't even know anymore, Nellie. I can't keep up with the
ones we've had here in Clayton, much less other suburbs. And now
Warrenton." Parsons chewed at his lip. "We've got to get him soon."

"Could this have been a copycat, Chief?" Marler offered.
"Warrenton doesn't say what size slug. And besides, this guy never
seems to venture more than a couple of miles. Look at your map
there. He's hit Olivette, Ladue, Town and Country, Richmond
Heights, U. City, and Brentwood. Not many people would spend their
days in Ladue or Clayton and their nights in Warrenton."

"A copycat? Shit, who knows? Other than Mayor Spiegel, I mean. He's got all the goddamned answers."

* * * * *

In Kansas City, the only man Hake felt close to was the Cobras' longtime trainer, Obie O'Brien. Obie was in his late fifties when Hake met him, and he explained that his own father, like Hake's, had been the victim of a fatal accident on that high-speed stretch of I-70 between Columbia and Kansas City, back when it was old U.S. 40.

"Changed your life, didn't it?" Obie asked, not waiting for an answer. "I know it changed mine. I thought I was gonna be rich. My dad had a pharmacy in Sedalia. He built it, and I was going to take it over when I got out of the College of Pharmacy in St. Louis. I had some good marketing ideas, and I was gonna make it grow. Then Pop got killed, and I wound up not being able to pay my way through my last year of pharmacy school. We had to sell the store.

"I never thought I'd have the balls to ask the Chiefs for a job, much less the Cobras, but this has worked out real well." O'Brien wrapped Hake's right ankle. "I did my penance, though, before I became head trainer. Wanna guess how many ankles I've wrapped?"

Obie yanked harder on the two-inch athletic tape and drew the surgical shears from his hip pocket.

"But you know," O'Brien went on, "there are days I get so frustrated I think I could shoot somebody."

* * * * *

**VIGILANTE EXPERT SAYS: TIRE KILLER
IS TINY, BUT MY APPETITE SURE ISN'T**
Psychologist Theodore T. Fischer burned a

few calories during a news conference in Clayton Monday, then ordered a room-service dinner that cost the Clayton Police Department twelve-hundred-fifty-four dollars, a Clayton spokeswoman said Tuesday.

Fischer, known as an expert on vigilante crime, is from Wisconsin A & M University at White Falls. He was here to work on the perplexing case involving more than a dozen incidents in which drivers in Clayton and nearby suburbs have had tires shot out by an unidentified marksman. But neither the City of Clayton nor the Ritz-Carlton knew Fischer had an appetite for fine food and drink to match his appetite for crime cases.

Fischer's room-service bill at the Ritz for one dinner—one very long dinner—was twelve-hundred-fifty-four bucks, including tip. And he dined alone, said the waiter who took care of the big eater in Suite Eight-Eleven.

The twenty-six-year-old waiter asked not to be identified.

"That sumbuck could eat," said the waiter. "He started with champagne and caviar and then went on and on. I made four trips up to his suite. Each time, he wanted more champagne. I thought he must've had some other people in there, he was eating and drinking so much. But he didn't."

Subsequent paragraphs mentioned his two entrees were Peking duck and roast pheasant, and the waiter was quoted as saying Fischer had left a bite or two of one of his two desserts: chocolate cheesecake topped with shaved chocolate. Oh, and maybe a little of the *calamari*, one of his three appetizers.

* * * * *

"The son of a bitch does a forty-minute news conference, confuses everybody, makes a lot of political enemies for the mayor and me, tells us almost nothing we didn't already know, and then he stiffs us for almost four thousand bucks for his suite and his limousine and his fucking food." Chief Royal Parsons was cold with rage. A vein pulsed in his neck. "Well, we know when we've been screwed, don't we? Four thousand bucks!"

Mary, the chief's secretary, straightened her yellow pad.

"Call Mayor Spiegel and tell him how damned dumb his Fischer idea was."

"I can't do that, Chief Parsons," Mary protested.

"No, you're right. I'll call him. In fact, you'd better get outta here."

She left the chief's plaque-walled office when the yelling into the phone went from one exclamation point to two.

Forty-Six

In an opposing-opinion story of almost fifty paragraphs, the paper quoted a local psychiatrist from the faculty of Woods-Avery University who disputed much of Fischer's on-again-off-again vigilante theory. The story was done as a reaction to a television news piece two nights earlier featuring the psychiatrist.

"No, our vigilante really isn't a vigilante," we quoted Dr. Simon Jaffe. "I've told the authorities that. Yes, we're dealing with a little person, a little, insignificant person. We're dealing with a male— probably a short, effeminate man. He's a person who desperately needs to accomplish something in his life but never has. But he's doing this for himself, not for any cause. So he's no vigilante."

Jaffe also noted: "I don't think the Tire Killer is military or ex-military, but perhaps he's been involved in law enforcement somehow. He may be an ex-cop despite being effeminate, perhaps somebody who has had his badge lifted, and now he wants to show that bagging him was a mistake."

And the guy was a good shot. At least there had been no reports to the Clayton Police, St. Louis County Police or other suburbs' authorities of any shots that hadn't found a Michelin or a Goodyear or a Pirrelli.

* * * * *

Snow-blowing the driveways of their adjacent, posh Alexander Drive homes, two Clayton physicians who normally didn't talk "over the back fence" found themselves in conversation that Monday morning.

"Nothing's growing with this damned snow."

"Simon, nice piece on TV the other night about the Tire Killer," said Dr. Bernard Greenman. Then, quickly: "You *schmuck*! You love TV, don't you?"

"No. The police *need* to go after a little person, a male, a person who has been sexually rebuffed more than a few times, a person who got off to a bad start in life and never felt fulfilled," said Dr. Simon Jaffe, like Greenspan a psychiatrist.

Jaffe paused for effect.

"Probably a virgin."

Greenman chuckled lightly.

"I'm almost embarrassed."

"Don't be. I'll get your Tire Killer for you."

"Simon, that doesn't become you. In my practice, I don't need lies or exaggeration."

"No, believe me. I'm sure I know who's been shooting out the tires," said Jaffe. "I'll let you know a week from now. Not by name, of course, but whether he's my patient."

Damn, I wish I'd been driving past Alexander Drive off Wydown Boulevard the morning those two *schlumps* had their conversation!

* * * * *

"No, goddammit!" Clayton's chief of police, Royal Parsons, roared into the phone. "We can't do that!"

"Just why not?" Mayor Saul Spiegel asked. "Just why not, Chief?"

"Because no murder has been committed, you dumb sumbitch!" the cop exploded out of exasperation. "You can request the Greater St. Louis Metropolitan Major Case Squad be brought in only in the event of a murder that's going to be difficult to solve, or maybe some high official's wife gets iced. And that's only a maybe. You cannot – I repeat, *cannot* – ask for the Major Case Squad just because somebody shoots out tires. We're just gonna have to deal with this ourselves, Mr. Mayor."

"Well, get it done, Chief Parsons. This has happened how many times now? Twelve? Fifteen? This is an embarrassment to me, Chief."

"And my department's four-thousand-dollar tab for your friend Fischer is an embarrassment to me."

The mayor went on as if he hadn't heard.

"Our traffic problems here in Clayton are – are difficult. I don't need to remind you this is a fine community of some thirteen-thousand, but up to two-hundred-thousand people may come into our city each day to work, shop, eat or conduct business. Now, we can't have these people staying away simply because they risk having a tire shot out from under them.

"Why, when I played golf at Algonquin not long ago, one of the boys in my foursome said he was to have had an appointment with his attorney over on North Meramec this week but told his lawyer to come out to his office park in Kirkwood if they were going to do business.

"We can't have that kind of scenario," the mayor went on. "It'll mean the death of Clayton. Or what if some company from New

York of Dallas or wherever hears about our tire shootings and changes its mind about moving its world headquarters to Clayton? This all gets very dicey, Chief."

Parsons took a break and guessed the mayor was doing the same. Each needed one.

Forty-Seven

Coaches and officials of the Cobras deliberated as to how they would deal with the tough game scheduling: at Seattle for the late Sunday game in the twelfth week. Fly back after the game and figure on getting to K.C. International at or about twelve-thirty a.m. Central Time? Or stay over at a hotel near Sea-Tac International, early wake-up, and in the air by seven a.m. Coast Time? Either way, the players would need Monday and most of Tuesday off before resuming practice.

And either way, a short week of preparation, everyone knew.

"Let's just get the hell out of here," Coach Turk Madigan grumbled, smarting from the loss to the Seahawks. "I've seen enough of the goddamned Space Needle. Let's go home."

Upon boarding the plane, Chesty picked up his customary plastic bag containing two cans of beer in ice and started down the aisle to the seat occupied by Kansas City's punter, Rex Polymus.

"Oh, Rex," Chesty cooed.

The rookie automatically handed Hake, bandaged and gauzed, his two iced cans of Olympia. Polymus happily paid protection to keep helmeted prowlers off him.

Hake, second in seniority among the current Cobras, was given the seat of his choice. Ol' Muldrow, an offensive tackle who had been around the NFL much longer, always took an aisle seat halfway back in the cabin, where he always could find a gin rummy game. So Hake had the aisle seat/back row/left awaiting him and his overnight bag and his six cans of Olympia that night.

The first was gone by the time all the overhead compartments were secured and the veteran flight attendant began her spiel.

Skipper Scales, a young receiver, handed his beer over his seat back to Hake.

"Thanks, Skip."

He slept soundly on six beers until the bounce of landing awakened him.

"The local time is twelve-eighteen. We'll see you guys Saturday afternoon for our flight to Boston."

Boston. Well, he'd eat well at Legal Seafood Saturday night. You know you've been around a lot of seasons when you rate the restaurants on the road instead of rating your opponents or the stadium facilities.

* * * * *

Shortly after flowing from I-435 southbound into I-70, Hake rolled past Weston Stadium, past Arrowhead and the Royals' adjacent ballpark. He was just minutes from an all-night convenience store. With six beers buried in his CONTENTS: HUMAN REMAINS cooler, he was ready for his trek through the night. Surprisingly, five cans remained unopened when he pulled onto Kingsbury Boulevard a minute before five.

* * * * *

The answering machine spun out its tape.

"Mr. Hake, this is Earlene Watkins. Smooth's sister? I work with Sara at See, Hear and Read. She wouldn't want me to be telling you this, but she's been shot. I'm sure that brother of mine did it, and I guess that's why I'm calling you now. She told me she really cares about you, Mr. Hake. Our office opens at nine. Call me if you want."

Hake set his alarm for eight-fifty-five. He could get almost four hours sleep. Then he fell back on the bed, still clothed. He hadn't done that since the day the football season ended his sophomore year at Blackwater.

* * * * *

Earlene Watkins was understanding, comforting, apologetic. She said she wasn't certain what kind of relationship Sara and Smooth had, but she knew he somehow had persuaded or forced Sara to regain Hake's affection.

Smooth's objective: to obtain, from Hake through Sara, confidential information concerning the Cobras. He wanted information like bonafide injury status, players' moods, the types and lengths of practices, new players, subtle changes in defensive alignments, the likelihood any starters or key substitutes could be distracted by legal or police situations, wives' pregnancy problems, or a grandfather's hospitalization back in Elizabeth City, New Jersey.

Factors of that sort can have a heavy bearing on the outcome of a pro football game. Every bookie and every serious gambler knows this.

297

"Tyrone's been into gambling since we were kids, I'm ashamed to say," Earlene admitted. "Nobody can stop him. He always thought gambling was easier than honest work. He even found ways to get into gambling when he was in jail."

Earlene went on to tell Hake that Sara was in Barnes-Jewish Hospital, room six-sixteen. Two bullets had all but torn apart her pancreas, and it had been removed several days earlier.

"I talked to her yesterday 'bout this time, and she sounded pretty good, I guess. But she told me she doesn't want any visitors for at least a couple more days. So I'm just warning you, Mr. Hake."

He rushed his words to thank her and said goodbye.

Forty-five seconds later, with the dashboard clock showing nine-oh-six, the Jaguar was emerging up from the garage.

* * * * *

"Chesty."

He loved hearing her exclamation the moment he walked through the extra-wide, blond wood hospital door. That, in a flash, proved to him he did love her. The door locked back on the hinge.

"How – how did you find me?"

"I just had to find you, Sara. It's been weeks. What happened? Why did he shoot you?"

She shook her head.

"You look awful, Chesty."

"I hurt a little from Seattle," he told her, his fingertips going from his swollen jaw, then to a bad, knotty bruise.

"No, I mean you look awful."

Hake looked down at his mussed clothes, then turned to look into the mirror over the hospital-style dresser.

"I see what you mean," he said, smoothing his hair. "I put on these clothes yesterday morning. Then I flew back from Seattle in them and drove home from KCI in them. Oh, and then I slept in them."

He turned back toward her.

"Sorry."

"Keep your breath out of range," she told him.

"I'll do better next time. Promise. When do you get out of here?"

"I don't know. They haven't told me. Daddy said he and Mom are going to try to speed up the procedure as much as they can so they can take me back to Lake Lotawana for a while. Daddy can't be away form his precious cars for very long, of course."

"Has that son of a bitch ever taken a vacation? I mean –"

"What do you care?" Hy Kassel boomed as he moved into the room. Hake could hear Sara suck breath.

"What do you care, you *goy* bastard? And what're you doing here, anyway? Here you have no business! No business whatsoever! I want you out! Out! Out!"

His face was red and sweaty. He reached for Hake, as if he would forcibly remove him from the room. Hake swatted him away.

"Still the heartless bastard you were twelve years ago, Kassel. I'm here to see Sara, and you're not gonna do a damned thing about it."

Foolishly, Hy Kassel went at Hake again. Chesty used a football technique some coaches still call the "forearm shiver." The heels of Hake's hands came upward and into the indentations below Kassel's shoulder bones. The force sent him reeling into the stainless steel table containing Kleenex, Q-Tips, cotton balls, tongue depressors, a flashlight, a rubber knee-knocker, and a glass vial containing a ther- mometer. The table rolled away from his weight, and Kassel tumbled onto his wide ass. A seam ripped.

"No, Chesty!" Sara cried. And then: "Don't! Daddy, quit it!"

Into room six-sixteen marched a still-attractive Lotzey Kassel, followed by a female nurse, a male nurse and a Polynesian-looking security guard.

"Sara, are you – oh, hello, Chesty. I – I didn't realize you would be here."

"He won't be in another minute!" Hy Kassel said loudly, puffing to get to his feet. To the security guard he said: "I want this *nudnik* outta here immediately! Do you hear me? This is my daughter's room, and we want him out!"

Through the sudden silence came a resigned voice.

"Go, Chesty. It's for the best. I want you to go – again."

Sara's eyes were closed. Hake could see her hands clenched, shaking. She shook the same way she had that horrible evening, the evening that should've been the most wonderful little dinner party he'd ever catered. It scared him.

Hake knew both nurses and the guard were eyeing him. Lotzey stood wide-eyed, obviously wondering what her role should be. Her disheveled husband watched Hake. Sara's eyes remained closed. The tremor in her fists didn't subside.

The Polynesian-looking security guard gave Hake ample berth to stride silently from the room.

* * * * *

"Good afternoon. Kansas City Cobras," said Becky Shular.

"Becky, this is Chesty. Everything okay?"

"Things are going as well as can be expected, I guess, considering we're four-and-eight and counting. You in St. Louis?"

"Yeah, and I think I may be here for some time, Becky. My soap opera gets stranger and stranger. A lot has gone on, believe me. Or maybe I should say a lot has gone wrong. I'll tell you about it when I get there. Maybe Tuesday night at Danny's?"

No response.

300

"Well, for now, will you connect me with Turk? I need to tell him I'm going to miss tomorrow's practice."

"Chesty, I'll connect you, but you don't need to tell him. Don't you remember? He cancelled Wednesday's practice. On the charter back from Seattle. You're due Thursday at eleven. Didn't you hear the announcement on the plane?"

"I slept. I'll call you tomorrow if I'm not going to get back Thursday morning."

* * * * *

Hake was angry and confused. He had planned to explain to Turk Madigan, as best he could, he wouldn't be worth a shit at practice Wednesday, and he knew Turk would understand. Turk had had a few problems dealing with women, Hake knew. The week was screwed up anyway, from a coach's standpoint, so Madigan thought it better to give his players extra time before going to play the Patriots.

And Hake was doubly fortunate to have Wednesday off.

* * * * *

The doorbell rang at nine-thirty that morning. Rarely did the door-bell ring. He tensed.

"Chester J. Hake, Jr.?" the mustachioed woman on the other side of the double-screened outside door asked.

"Yes. Why?"

"I'm here from the St. Louis County Sheriff's Department, Mr. Hake. I'm here to serve you with this," she said as she opened the outer door and handed him a white envelope bearing his name and address.

Hake was ripping open the envelope by the time both doors were closed.

* * * * *

"Mornin,' Chesty. What's up?"

"J. Billy, I've got a lawsuit on my hands," Hake said into the phone. "I need to see you."

A civil suit had been filed by Sara Aron Kassel on behalf of her minor son Kisho n/m/n Kassel, claiming violent shaking of the child by the defendant on or about Monday, October sixteenth, which caused brain damage and resulted in extensive medical bills, loss of some of plaintiff's income because of work missed, and immeasurable suffering by both plaintiff and her minor child.

The suit sought damages of two-hundred-fifty-thousand dollars, plus treble punitive. Total, one million.

* * * * *

J. Billy Wingo slammed the pages of the suit onto his desk.

"Smells a whole lot like bullshit, Chesty."

Hake nodded.

"And you don't think this is her doing?"

"It's not her style, J. Billy. Besides, she was sitting right there on the couch with me when I grabbed the kid's arms—when I *held* the kid by his arms, I should say. Sara knows I didn't hurt him. This is her father's doing, and Smooth may be in for it."

"Smooth?"

"Tyrone Watkins: slime lizard."

J. Billy Wingo wrinkled his jowly face.

"Awright, Chesty boy, tell ya what. I'm gonna be over at the County Government Center this afternoon, and I'll look into this dang thing. But for now, you tell me everything you can 'bout your relationship with this woman, 'cause I need to determine if *mebbe* this attack isn't *her* motive.

"Okay, let's start with her full name, her address, her employer's name, and both home and business phone numbers. Oh, and the nature of her job."

"Don't have it all, J. Billy," Hake said. "Her full name is Sara Aron Kassel, Sara with no 'H' and Kassel K-A-S-S-E-L. She's thirty-one years—no, make that thirty-two years old. As far as I know, she's still with a company called See, Hear & Reed—the name of the guy in Dallas who formed the company. The St. Louis office is over on East Lockwood in Webster Groves."

Hake gave Sara's business number, then added: "But I can't give you her home address or phone number. When I went to her apartment the week after this—this shaking supposed to have happened, it had been cleaned out. Her co-workers told me they didn't know where she was. Believe me, I've been trying to find her since the middle of October. Then I got a call."

Hake detailed for Wingo the answering machine call from Earlene Watkins, the difficult scene in Sara's hospital room, and the violent second meeting with Smooth Watkins.

J. Billy rotated a pencil in his pudgy fingers.

"Now, you'll be goin' back to Kan' City tomorra?"

"Yeah. I need to be at practice, J. Billy. I haven't done shit this week. No running or weight work at all. The Seattle game seems so long ago, and we need to play well at New England Sunday. So I'll go back tomorrow morning and just hope for the best at practice."

"You' some stud, Ches," Wingo said, getting to his feet. "Bona fide stud. I'll let you know what happens here. But git your mind back on football. This thing'll be weeks and months, not hours or days. Just gotta learn to carry on, work around it."

"A million-dollar lawsuit hits hard. I'll check with you when I get home next Monday. Oh, and right now, I'll make certain your secretary has my Lee's Sumit number. Don't hesitate to call. I'll pick up your call off my answering machine and get right back to you."

Forty-Eight

When Chesty called Friday night, I didn't quite know how to direct our conversation. He had left me a photocopy of the lawsuit when he headed back to K.C. before dawn Thursday. I was thankful to have been in Cape Girardeau Wednesday and Thursday to do a good-sized piece and a sidebar on a seven-foot-one basketball player at Southeast Missouri State University. Talking by phone Friday evening was going to be taxing enough.

Chesty told me both days of practice had been spirited, and I made a note of that. He said the workouts had been therapeutic for him, had allowed him to put Sara and the suit out of his mind for at least a couple of hours each day. I took note.

"I've told myself I'm just going to have to have a strong finish to this lackluster career," he said. "I've got only four more Sundays, Paulie, and I'm going to discipline myself as if I were a damned rookie fighting for a spot on the roster. I mean, it hurt last Sunday when I wasn't on the field for the opening kickoff. I hadn't been benched like that since my second year, and I'm sure I deserved it. It'll be different at New England. I'm back on all the special teams."

"Great," I replied, writing. "That's great."

I could hear him swallow. I guessed some Bud was going down.

I thought it might be wise to change the pace of our conversation somewhat.

"It's the first of the month," I pointed out. "Did you remember to send your check to Blackwater?"

"I wrote the check Wednesday and mailed it yesterday. But I appreciate your reminder."

"Did having the extra day off help you and the older guys?"

"Oh, definitely. 'Ol' Muldrow's ankle has responded to treatment just fine, but they're still listing him as 'questionable'. You don't want to give away any secrets, y'know. He was kept out of contact work yesterday and today, but he's going to start Sunday," Hake noted, and so did I after changing to the next page of my scratch pad.

"And Skip Scales, the young wide receiver out of Ole Miss? He's going to get his first start. We didn't announce that, for one obvious reason: The Patriots' cornerbacks play so far off the receivers that Scales—a good, solid, possession-type receiver—should do very well with crossing patterns, 'outs,' and underneath-type stuff."

I quickly translated that data into a half-dozen words.

Finally, we got around to Sara.

"I didn't hurt the kid, regardless of what the suit says. The last thing I'm going to do is alienate Sara by hurting her kid. If I have to lose her again, I want it to be my doing, not the kid's and not Smooth's and not her goddamned father's."

"You're handling it right. But listen, Ches, I'm going to cut this conversation short," I added, hoping I sounded genuine. "Yes, I actually have a Friday night date. Amazing, huh?"

"Good for you, Paulie. Who is it?"

"Oh, it's Sandi again. That's S-A-N-D-I, which probably is one more reason we shouldn't be dating. I have no idea where we're going. That little club was fun last time, and so was the Sheraton Westport. Maybe we'll—"

"Never mind, never mind," Hake interrupted. I could tell he wanted me to hang up.

Within a matter of seconds, I called a "friend." And it wasn't Sandi, spelled S-A-N-D-I. Just maybe, if I'd called Sandi, things would have been different. But I didn't and the slide continued.

* * * * *

EDITOR'S NOTE: After striking out on the Cobras three times in four weeks, I was doubly delighted Hake was back in uniform for the New England game and dedicated as well.

I took Kansas City with seven points and watched as other people and their "friends" obtained some late information and brought the spread back to five-and-a-half points at kickoff.

No matter. Those underdogs from K.C. played their best overall game of the season and won by nineteen points. The Patriots' only touchdown came on a special teams breakdown, a missed open-field tackle on a punt return, but Hake's people blocked a punt and a field goal and recovered two fumbles.

My "friend" suggested to me, as I pocketed his ten hundreds, I might like to find another "friend." Oh, how I like to make "friends."

* * * * *

For the next couple of weeks, Chesty's moods were dice-rolls. He admitted to his erratic ways, at least. Situation Sara and Farewell

Football had him wishboned. He came from a thirteen-ten victory over Dallas in a strange, ebullient mood. I felt off-balance, almost distrustful. There was much more than the how-ya-doin'/never better greeting.

I had had the warm Sunday off, a kink in the Sports Department scheduling for November. Sandi and I had picnicked and swigged the afternoon away at Bee Tree County Park, at the southern tip of St. Louis County, on a bluff providing a terrific panorama of the Mississippi. We drank my beer. However, most of the food was from the freezer, leftovers of dishes prepared by Chesty during off-days of weeks past. Sandi loved it. She also loved making love, so I was in a touchdown kind of mood myself by the time he arrived home.

"We were up by three with forty-one seconds to play when I recovered the fumble," Chesty said. "It was—it was almost unfair. It was as if the ball just sat there on the turf for me. Ah, why can't every moment be that enjoyable?"

"We'd get bored real quick," I replied, meaning it.

Into his eighth beer and an egg salad sandwich, he mentioned he had not tried to contact Sara since the hospital debacle. He said he was afraid he might kill Hy Kassel if they collided again. The mere mention of the car dealer's name turned Hake's emotional switch to "hate". I headed off to bed.

* * * * *

EDITOR'S NOTE: To my way of thinking, Chesty Hake never made a bigger play in his eighth NFL seasons than he did with that recovery to end the Cowboys' final possession.

See, I called an auxiliary "friend" early in the week. I had deduced K.C.'s special teams were back in synch, what with the return of a full-speed Hake. The Cowboys were getting two points at that time and four by Sunday morning. The margin of victory: three.

Thank you, Chesty Hake!

And "friends," just wait till this week!

Forty-Nine

As befits the weeks leading up to the final home game for every NFL team, the media do features, bytes, and retrospectives. In Kansas City, there were subjective pieces about both franchises. Would the Chiefs go for some All-Pro talent? The Cobras had likely free-agent movement and the imminent, long-since-announced retirement of Ol' Muldrow and a couple of others.

Another popular topic: Will Cobras General Manager Shel Bergman's cancer, if in check, allow him to be back for another season?

But nobody seemed to consider—even for a paragraph—Hake would be calling it a career. That's exactly the way he wanted it. He went about his work with diligence and a rookie's enthusiasm as he prepared for his Weston Stadium farewell. Running the periphery an extra time after practice a couple of days, doing more lifts than were comfortable. By late Friday, Hake was "jacked," as players describe a motivated comrade or opponent.

* * * * *

On his oft-made trip down I-470, he took his oft-made detour along Rellerson Road, west off the Interstate, to Relly's Lee's Summit Emporium.

"How many points, Chesty?" Relly Rellerson asked before "hello" even occurred to him.

"That's your worry, Rel," Hake answered. "My big worry is making certain the Steelers don't get to my punter."

The liquor storeowner laughed at that.

Hake cradled two cases of Budweiser cans in his left arm, then went into the adjoining video department and returned with a black-and-white John Wayne classic.

"Good combination," said Relly, surveying the spoils. "Anything else, big guy?"

"Yeah, a pack of AA batteries."

Relly reached to the battery rack behind him. He tossed the AA's on the counter.

"Need those AAs," Hake said a he pulled a hundred-dollar bill from his right-front pocket. "I want to be able to hear 'God Bless America' or 'From the Halls of Montezuma' loud and clear on my Walkman at about eleven-fifty-nine Sunday. That's important to me. Or the Mormon Tabernacle Choir doing 'This Is My Country.' You know how hard I can hit somebody after listening to that?"

"Pretty hard, I bet."

"How much?"

"That's thirty-one-eighty, with your volume discount. And keep the John Wayne as long as you want, big guy."

"You going to the game, Relly?"

"Naw, I'll see it on TV. It was a sellout 'fore noon yisday, so they hafta lift that TV blackout."

Hake put the beer on the counter with the batteries and the video. He went to his wallet, and out came four tickets.

"Your granddaughters are painters and sculptors, both, right?"

"Gonna be. Both gotta lotta promise, people tell me."

"Do me a favor, Relly. Take them and your wife to the game Sunday."

Hake laid the four section two-sixty-eight tickets atop the cash register. "Have a good time. And please cheer. Oh, and by the way, you'll be sitting with a very nice woman named Laurie Stanley. Go ahead and introduce yourself. Tell her you're a good friend of mine. And tell her I said she's too good to be a friend of mine. She'll understand."

Rellerson carefully picked up the four tickets from atop the register. He studied them. Then he watched Hake load two cases of Budweiser into the trunk of HUT-HUT. He was sure the gold Jaguar was the only twelve-cylinder car ever to pull onto his lot.

* * * * *

"This is my county-y-y," came through the earphones.

Hake's shoulders might as well have been pistons, so powerfully and rhythmically did they pump while he listened to the Mormon Tabernacle Choir. Then he ripped off the headset and handed the whole Walkman to trainer Obie O'Brien. Hake was "jacked."

And then, from the second deck, came a giant white banner with black lettering. The bearers played to the TV cameras like Miss America contestants. Almost sixty-eight-thousand onlookers and a TV audience wondered at the significance of the words.

The banner read:

Chesty Hake
SEE YOU IN SEPTEMBER

The Tempos, 1959
The Happenings, 1966
PLEASE SAY YES!

Hake's hit on the kickoff return man was inspirational. The ball squirted free, did a cowhide pirouette, then landed in Hake's taped-up grasp.

The NFL's oldest special-teams captain, a fact that a network announcer pointed out after Hake's fumble recovery, waited less than a half before recovering another fumble. Three in less than a game and a half! No wonder the media hadn't bother to consider Hake as a retirement candidate.

And then, with the Cobras commanding a seventeen-zero lead midway through the third quarter, ol' Fate whispered into Hake's ear again. The four-foot-high snap from center was at nine feet when it sailed out of the Pittsburgh punter's reach. Hake tore past the "up" man and the punter and cradled the ball on the artificial turf for his third fumble recovery of the day.

In the pressbox, the onus was on Robbie Browning, the NFL observer/ombudsman assigned to Weston Stadium this week.

"Is that a record or isn't it?" many media minds asked anxiously.

"I'll have to call New York and let you know," the redheaded Browning answered. "We'll know in a few minutes."

Chesty Hake, Kansas City Cobras, the man who never scored a touchdown and never had a player agent to negotiate his contract, did in fact tie an NFL record by recovering three opponent fumbles in one game. That's page one-eighteen of the *"NFL Record & Fact Book,"* for future reference, if you need it.

Sandy/Sandi, a much better football fan than I, called me about the "See You In September" banner. That call, plus Hake's three recoveries, made my Sunday. Even the second snowfall of the season didn't faze me.

313

There was a new warmth between us. I could feel it. She didn't need to call me to tell me about the banner, but she knew I'd appreciate it. She may even have wanted to ask me whether or not I was responsible for it. No matter. Just the call mattered. Obviously, she knew I still loved her, and I think at least some love for me had come back into her heart.

Which way our relationship was going to lead I could not even speculate.

* * * * *

EDITOR'S NOTE: With a "friend" I knew to be a compatriot of Smooth Watkins, I placed the biggest bet of my life: five thousand dollars, taking the Cobras and two-and-a-half points. K.C. went into the game with a six-and-eight record, while the Steelers were eight-five-and-one, riding a four-game winning streak and angling for a wild-card spot in the American Conference playoffs.

I might've done better – three-and-a-half points, maybe even four or four-and-a-half – if I had waited until closer to game day, but I felt cocky. Despite the bad stretch while Chesty was sub-par, I went into the fifteenth week up by ninety-five-hundred dollars for less than four months' "work."

The same day I put the five thousand with Smooth's partner in crime, I FedExed a package to two of my former co-workers/beer buddies on the *Kansas City Register's* sports desk. They were going to be in the pressbox before going down to the dressing room sidebars, slugged *Dress* for the Cobras' quote story, *Steelers* for the visitors.

They promised me they'd make certain some responsible, second-deck, front-row, family-type spectators would unfurl
SEE YOU IN SEPTEMBER
Just before kickoff.

* * * * *

I knew at twelve-oh-five or twelve-oh-six I'd done a seventeen-none job. Easy job.

Fifty

St. Louis came apart one day. The oft-overlooked, oft-behind-the-times Gateway to the West changed overnight, as though it had been a pubescent prom-queen-to-be. It was a different town the day the top headline read:

Councilman's Wife, Chesty Hake Gunned Down

No story – not a presidential campaign, not a United Nations Security Council emergency meeting – could've supplanted that banner and the sub-heads and stories that came down from it that day. Somewhat drunk, the paper's copy chief admitted at a Press Club luncheon the next day: "Shit, I'd have played that head seventy-two-point instead of sixty, but we hadda get 'Councilman' and 'Chesty' in there. Why couldn't their identities have been 'Twat' and whatever?"

But the laughter evoked by this one-upsmanship was tempered. Every newsman at the big round table knew stories of that importance meant many hours of hard work. That was the thrill, the satisfaction of the news business. That also was why these ten men were sloshing liberally at the Press Club at lunchtime.

In the City Room, a thirty-year veteran became curious. He pulled up on his computer a story from twenty-one years earlier.

Mother of Bears' Hake Murdered

> Virginia Rockefeller Hake, mother of the Chicago Bears' David Hake and believed to be a member of one of America's most prominent families, was found murdered in her St. Louis Conty home Tuesday.

Brentwood and St. Louis County Police said she had been strangled and sodomized.

The St. Louis Major Case Squad was called in immediately.

The body of Mrs. Hake, forty-seven, was discovered by a son, Chet, eleven, at approximately eleven-forty Tuesday when he arrived home from Mark Twain Elementary School for lunch. Also dead was the family dog, which had been stabbed and skinned.

> The story went on to say survivors included her husband, C.J. Hake Sr., two sons, David Rockefeller Hake of Chicago and Chester J. Hake Jr.; a sister, Gwen Rockefeller Belva of Dover, Delaware; and a brother, Brock J. Rockfeller of Hot Springs Village, Arkansas.

* * * * *

Not long after that, C.H. Hake became obsessively worried about his younger son. It was guilt, obviously. David had been so big and so strong, while Chet had been...

* * * * *

"You don't need to worry about your son, Mr. Hake. He's doing fine now."

"How's he *really* doing?" C.J. Hake asked, leaning across the table toward the counselor and letting his tone show an edge. He really didn't want to be at Brentwood Middle School's parents' night.

"Well, he's doing – doing fine. Academically, he's probably seventh or eighth out of his class of one-hundred-ten. That's fine, isn't it? I mean, considering what he's been through?"

"Yes, Mr. Van Hecht, but how's he doing with the other kids, with his classmates? How's he doing with his teachers? The high academic rate doesn't tell me that. Other than football, he isn't in any extra-curricular activities, and that kinda bothers me. He doesn't bring kids home with him after school, and he doesn't go to other kids' homes. That bothers me."

"Well –"

"Listen, dammit, he's all I've got. He's fragile, physically and emotionally, and I know that better than anyone. But I've got a business to run, and I can't be here at school to monitor his progress. That's what you're getting paid for. I want to know when you see things that aren't right, dammit."

Van Hecht, who usually dealt with mothers, wasn't ready for this.

"Mr. Hake. Mr. Hake, I think Chet is going to be—going to be just fine," Van Hecht said. "His social skills really are improving, and his performance on the football field seems to be having quite a salutary effect. He's very goal-oriented. Coach Avena says that Chet enjoys practices as much as he does games, and that's a rare athlete. At least that's what Coach Avena says."

Van Hecht needed a way out of this difficult interview and saw one.

"You might want to stop by and visit Coach Avena before you leave. Coach really does seem very pleased with the progress your son has made on the field. I think he'll have some good news for you. From my standpoint, all I can tell you is: Make certain your son continues to work at achieving. In this day and age—and considering what he's been through—that's what's going to be required, Mr. Hake."

"Thank you," C.J. said softly. "Thanks very much. Sorry I yelled at you."

"I understand. You're a good father."

* * * * *

When C.J. Hake got to his car at the curb, he looked skyward and whispered: "I really needed you tonight, Ginny."

* * * * *

The transformation was remarkable. Chet Hake went from being a tiny, frail, withdrawn eighth-grader to being a developing freshman, to being a muscular sophomore, with a new first name to being a brute of a junior, a genuine high school hero.

Girls watched him intently. Coaches, in their purple and gold t-shirts with the EAGLES logo, drooled.

Fifty-One

Hake didn't really want to be caught, as most perpetrators do. I knew he had the gun somewhere, and the gun had a silencer. It also bothered me, when I last saw that gun, it was stuffed with a full clip, and there was another in that oversized console.

I hoped the pistol was in his trunk, or maybe on the top shelf of his bedroom closet. Either of those alternatives would be bad enough, but I didn't want it to be in his console—accessible. Bad enough he had that goddamned beer cooler that disparaged my people.

Think about it: Previously, I never suspected Chesty because he tempted me with hypothetical questions across the breakfast table, and he asked whether or not the Tire Killer had been apprehended. He would ask what they were saying at the Cop Shop, our office at St. Louis County Police Department headquarters. He never acted like someone who had done something wrong.

I thought I was a pretty good judge of human nature. Obviously, not.

No, for the longest time, I didn't suspect. Hake didn't want me to know; I'm certain of that. Otherwise, I...

Otherwise, shit! I don't know what I would've done. I believe in personal pride, family respect, shame, guilt, and all that stuff when required. So I'm not certain what I would've done had Chesty come out and said: "Paulie, I get pissed off and shoot the tires of drivers I don't like."

But he never said a thing. It wasn't until a long time later I realized what was happening—and that, indirectly, I was a part of it. That's what a slide does, when Fate, that Bitch Goddess, sends you down, and there's nothing you can do to stop it.

Then I asked myself: Am I guilty, in that I didn't know until very late? Am I the fool? Everybody knows but me?

No.

Before I absolve myself of guilt, I need to consider something: Smooth Watkins had handled several of my bets on the Cobras over the years. For Chesty to learn that would've hurt him—hurt him in two ways. He didn't need to know how much of his mess was a result of Smooth wanting to have the information I had before kickoff each weekend. And Smooth knew Sara could provide it if she took mental notes while her head was on a pillow next to Hake's. So I carried some guilt. I just didn't know how bad it was going to get, and where it was all going.

* * * * *

Hake received a million-dollar Christmas gift two days early. Sara's lawsuit against him, which had been Hy Kassel's idea and had Smooth Watkins' emphatic stamp of approval, suddenly was dropped late Friday, just before the courts closed for Christmas break.

Through my bookie network, I learned Sara had arched her back.

She threatened to blow the whistle to the St. Louis County Police, her friends in Kansas City, and, most threatening of all, to St. Louis and Kansas City media. She certainly could do that through See, Hear & Reed. She had credibility.

Hy Kassel backed down. Smooth caved in.

Hake hadn't injured the child. The kid had no brain, neck or spinal injuries. His only problem, as Sara threatened to tell anyone who'd listen, was he had a slight learning impairment.

* * * *

"We just got this from our people at County Courts, and I thought you'd be interested," said Mike Mabee, an assistant city editor, tucking his extra-wide derriere between the computers in the Sports Department. "The suit against Chesty had been dropped."

I thanked Mike and quickly dialed Hake's unlisted number in Lee's Summit. He had said he would be at the condo Friday evening. He picked up.

"I've got some—"

"What is it, Paulie?" he asked.

I realized I hadn't even bothered to say "hello."

"Anything wrong?"

"No. Sara dropped her suit against you."

"What?"

"That's right. We just got it from our County Courts people. Dropped without explanation."

"Whatever that means," Hake said. He thought for a moment. "Well, that's one hurdle cleared. Some day, I hope I understand all this shit. Now, what do I do to talk to Sara? I guess that's the next step. The hospital told me she'd been released, so I imagine she came back here to Lake Lotawana with her mother and the jackoff. I need some answers."

"Use good judgment, Chesty. Just 'cause you've been screwed over more than you deserve, don't screw up the rest of your life by doing something irrational."

"I know what you're saying."

* * * * *

"She'll be here a few more days. Please call again."

Lotzey Kassel obviously couldn't talk with Hake, he realized, after she hung up abruptly. Hy Kassel had to be nearby.

"Damn!" he said to no one as he hefted his flight bag and his CONTENTS: HUMAN REMAINS cooler and started down to HUT-HUT in the garage. The San Diego Chargers: his last trip as a pro, his last NFL foe.

* * * * *

The Cobras played dreadful football in Southern California. The Chargers played almost as poorly but won, twenty-fourteen. The thinking on both sidelines was: What do you expect on Christmas Eve?

Rex and Skip dutifully handed their beer bags to Hake as they took their seats on the charter for the trip back to K.C. Hake settled in with his six-pack at the rear of the plane. As he popped the first can of Busch, he stood in the aisle and held up his blue can, as if he were going to propose a toast.

"Hey! Hey up there!" he yelled and watched heads turn as far up as the eleventh row. When he had the attention of a few dozen players, coaches, staff people, and flight attendants, he bellowed: "Merry goddamned Christmas, everyone!"

With that, Hake plopped into his next-to-the-lavatory seat, enjoyed the reaction from up front and pulled on his can of Busch. The senior flight attendant began her recitation. Skip Scales was young, but he had memorized how the oxygen mask would come down and the seat cushion could be used as a flotation device.

Skip whirled around.

"Chesty, you gonna retire?" he asked impulsively in his Oxford, Mississippi, drawl. He was kneeling over the back of the seat and facing Hake, perhaps eighteen inches away.

"Why?"

"Well, ever'body wondered 'bout that sign at the stadium last week. Thet mean you're retirin'?"

"I've got some good news for you, Skip. Next year, you're taking over as special teams captain."

"But I don't – then ya *are* retirin'!" the young wide receiver exclaimed, his volume mostly wiped out by the whine of jet engines.

"Yes, Skip, at this point, I'm a retiree – a thirty-two-year-old retiree. But that's gotta remain our secret for a few weeks. I've got things that have to be done before it can be made public. In fact, you're the only guy on this airplane who really knows I'm finished. If it gets out, I'll know it was Skipper Scales, and I definitely will tell Turk you want to be considered for captain of the special teams."

"Not a word, " said the younger player, waving his hand in protest. "Not a word, I promise. Not a word. Jesus, Ah hate special teams!"

Hake chuckled. And I, the lesser player, have made what most people would consider a very good living playing on kicking teams these eight seasons, Hake mused.

"Skip, you're one of only a handful of guys on this team I even talk to," Hake said quietly as Scales continued to peer over the back of his seat. "All I have to say to you is: Keep that good attitude, and keep your good work habits. Work habits! I watch you on the field and say to myself: 'He'll never be an All-Pro, because he's not a flashy receiver, but he definitely can become a star.' That, Skip, comes from an eight-year special-teams grunt with damned good work habits."

"Thanks, Chesty."

Skip quickly turned around in his seat and buckled his seat belt. He heard Hake's second can of Busch being opened.

Chesty didn't get home until about six Christmas morning. If anybody had a good shot at spotting Santa Claus, it was he.

Very little goes on at a daily newspaper Christmas night, so it's traditional that most of an editorial staff stampedes towards the doors at about mid-afternoon. Our sports people departed even earlier, usually for the Missouri Grill.

When I arrived home, Hake was up and around, clad in a bright yellow running suit with a little black trim. What the hell, we didn't have Christmas decorations, outdoor lights, even a Christmas tree. The only indication it was Christmas was somebody on tape singing "I'll Be Home For Christmas."

"I just thawed some *jalapeño*-garlic spread for lunch," Chesty said. "Very Christmasy. You want some?"

"In a few minutes. And if it's all right with you, we're having a little different kind of Christmas dinner. I got a half dozen Cornish game hens and a load of wild rice."

"Yeah, that sounds fine," he said, sounding upbeat despite Sunday's loss at San Diego. See? I never knew what to expect from Hake.

"You know what goes well with wild rice? Budweiser," I told him. "You want one?"

"Uh-huh, and it goes well with *jalapeño*-garlic spread on crackers, too. At Turk's Christmas party for the whole team and all the employees, it'll be kegs of no-name beer and seven-foot deli sandwiches. Turk knew I wouldn't be at his party."

Chesty belched.

"And at Turk's Christmas party, too, I imagine."

I was happy, secure sitting at our big circular table and chatting with Hake. His spirits seemed good, and he seemed to have things he really wanted to say. I tried to be cautious.

"I haven't picked out your Christmas present yet," he told me, not really apologetically.

"Don't worry about it. Yours is ready, but I haven't picked it up. At least I know what I'm giving you."

Hake's mood went sour. The misshappen jaws tightened, and the slanted eyebrow took on more of a slant. The bullet-bitten ear looked like a chewed dog toy.

I knew Hake wanted to get serious, and I know the subject was going to be Sara. I probably wasn't a very good sounding board, but Hake didn't know that.

"I called Lake Lotawana and got her mom," Hake said, moving right in, "but she was very abrupt, I guess, as if the fat fart was lurking right there. She told me to call back, though, and she said Sara would be there a few more days. That was Saturday morning. I think I'll wait till I get back to K.C. to call. That way, I can drive by the dealership and make sure the jackoff's car is there. Doesn't that make sense?"

"Yeah," I had to agree. "But what if she's back here by then? How're you gonna find her?"

"I don't know, Paulie. I guess I'd try Earlene Watkins, Smooth's sister, at See, Hear & Reed. If she didn't know, I might call Dr. Whatshername, the very nice Emergency Room trooper at Barnes-Jewish Hospital who fixed me up after my one-rounder with Smooth. The pretty doctor would check the records for me, I know.

"Besides, Sara knows my number," Hake added. "She called

enough."

He got up to replenish our beers.

I couldn't help but look at his ear, and notice the flesh filling in. He was going to be all right, but he was off the list for *Gentlemen's Quarterly.*

"Dinner's going to take a while, so I think I'll get started," he said. "How 'bout I do some broccoli and cheese sauce?"

"Fine, fine."

"By the way," Chesty said as he went back to the kitchen, "this is my last big meal. As a retiree, I'm not going to need three or four Cornish game hens. I should eat one – *one* – and guys like me who retire and keep eating as if they're still playing wind up regretting it. I can name many, many guys who look great five or ten years after they retired because they retired, eat less, and weigh less than they did when they played. But for each of those guys, I can show you ten who didn't get the message and turned into fat old men. Heart attacks a-plenty.

"What we don't eat of those six hens I'll freeze. You can add it to a salad or something while I'm gone at the end of the week."

* * * * *

The day after Christmas: This Tuesday was the second nastiest driving day all year in St. Louis County, right behind the Friday after Thanksgiving.

Everybody with a cc of shopper blood in his or her veins was certain to be out and about. Between Christmas gift returns and day-after-Christmas sales, the pavement and the parking lots simply weren't safe.

Especially if one or more of those zealots happened to cross a notoriously bad shopper not yet known as the Tire Killer. Especially when the Tire Killer was feeling disillusionment, maybe post-career letdown.

* * * * *

Hake located the strip shopping center on Gravois in South St. Louis and waited for oncoming traffic to clear before venturing across the lanes and into the parking lot. He began the ritualistic hunt for a parking space, just in time to be met by a bright blue Miata coming the wrong way down the traffic aisle. Just a few feet in front of HUT-HUT, the little Miata abruptly wheeled left, into a spot clearly designated HANDICAPPED PARKING. Hake watched two teen-aged girls hopping from the car and jaunting into a clothing shop.

He knew he shouldn't do it.

The pistol's work was lost in the sound of carols and Salvation Army bells.

He found a spot within fifteen seconds and went into a shop specializing in football memorabilia. He bought a leather helmet – with questionable authentication – that Red Grange wore at the University of Illinois, then took with him to the Chicago Bears in their early days.

This is getting even with Paulie for the goddamned deacon's bench and the goddamned blanket chest and all that other shit he dragged out of the basement and the storage locker, Hake said to himself as he climbed into his Jaguar.

The blue Miata sat on a tilt as Hake headed back onto Gravois.

His only other stop was at Chaim Salinsky's stamp shop on Delmar Boulevard. He was late in purchasing the traditional Christmas gift for me: a rare, very expensive stamp.

The lot adjacent to Salinsky's, always cramped and never with more than a dozen spaces, had reduced capacity this noon hour. An old white Cadillac Fleetwood with vanity plates was parked across three slots, facing the wrong direction so the driver could exit a shop and step immediately into the car.

At the curb in front of Salinsky's stamp shop.

There was no expression on Chesty's face.

Bitch! That's the same bitch who runs the same stoplight at Maryland Boulevard all the time, too! Paulie would have to wait for his Christmas present. Dammit, I come here to spend a coupla thousand dollars, and some bitch keeps me from doing it! Damn!

He stopped in front of the Fleetwood and reached into the FOLK MUSIC case. As he pulled the piston from the plastic padded case, the owner of the Cadillac came out of the stamp shop. Hake froze. She was blond, dazzling, overly made up, nicely fitted into her fine wool suit with fur collar. She properly reflected her station: wife of a high-priced, *wunderkind* attorney now serving on the St. Louis County Council as well.

The pistol went back into its case.

* * * * *

That blonde in the white Caddy worked on him, sent him muttering to himself.

"That scofflaw bitch!" Hake said as he broke a sardine with a salad fork and put half on a saltine. He realized he had no audience and wondered if, perhaps, that weren't better.

She knows she can get away with just about anything. Any problem, she puts all that beauty to work, the wool suit, the fur collar, maybe. Then, if that doesn't work, she reminds the cop or any other antagonist just who her husband is.

Bitch!

Between sardine halves, Hake sipped from his can of Bud and

obsessed about the scofflaw ways of Mrs. Dexter Dillon III, a.k.a. Sandy, a.k.a. Sandi.

If nothing else, the blonde in the white Fleetwood had taken Hake's mind off the strange developments surrounding his relationship – his non-relationship – with Sara. He went to the kitchen for a second beer, a second tin of sardines, and a second waxed paper sleeve of saltines.

He spent the next two hours trying to develop a three-part strategy that would: allow him to locate Sara as quickly as possible; get him honest answers about her relationship with Smooth and whether or not that hold on her could be broken; and, finally, make his relationship with Sara what it should've been eight years earlier.

First things first. He called See, Hear & Reed in Webster Groves.

"May I speak with Earlene Watkins, Please?"

"Mr. Hake?"

"Yeah, I'm trying to –"

"Mr. Hake, I can't talk to you. I can't. I just can't. That's all. Sara's still with her mama. That's all I can say."

The phone went dead.

"Smooth. Smooth's doing."

Hake carefully balled up the saltine wrapper. His face held no expression.

He would make a drive-by of Hy Kassel Motors in K.C. Friday. With luck, Kassel's car would be there, and Hake could drive to the condo and call Sara. He would be no more than three miles from her.

He pushed that to the back of his mind. He had three days to refine that part of the plan. For now, though, Blond Fleetwood Bitch roiled in his brain.

And I had a problem of my own. I planned to stop at Schillar's Photo in Brentwood on my way home to pick up Chesty's Christmas present. But then I was told I would have to stick around the office for a while in case two minor college bowl games ran long and the AP was late. I called Hake.

"Chesty, this is–"

"I'm with you, Paulie. Everything okay?"

"I suppose. But will you do me a favor?"

"Sure. What?"

"I need to have a package picked up at Schiller's over on Manchester in Brentwood before six tonight. I promised them I'd be there by then, and now I may be stuck here. Would you go get it for me?"

"Sure. Of course. But I'd better tell you: Every jackoff and jack-ette in St. Louis County is out on the road today. And inconsiderate? I tried to get your gift, but I couldn't. Honest, Paulie. A bitch in a white Caddy Fleetwood took up all three parking spaces – *all three* available parking spaces at – ah, forget it. But I could've shot-"

"What?"

"Never mind. What should I tell them at Schiller's?"

I couldn't respond for a couple of seconds.

"Paulie?"

"Yeah, just tell them you're picking up a package for me. It's all paid for, so there won't be any problem. If there is, just give me a call here at the paper."

"Fine. Oh, and Paulie?"

"Yeah?"

"We're having small portions of chicken *a la orange* for dinner tonight.

I didn't need his new piety, his discipline. Not right now. I may weight more than I should, but I've grown accustomed to eating nice Monday night spreads and some pretty damned good Tuesday to Sunday leftovers.

"Okay. See you tonight."

For two reasons, I knew I wouldn't have an appetite: one, the bitch in the white Fleetwood; and two, Hake's "I could've shot..."

See, I learned quite a bit by accident. The tape cassette case didn't contain any tapes. And with Hake's temperament, I didn't dare remove that gun or tell him I knew about it.

Until the day after Christmas, that is.

* * * * *

Hake didn't know he was to be his own Christmas gift. The Cobras were wonderful about providing me with copies of videotapes showing almost eight seasons of the best and worst of Chesty Hake on special teams. And Schiller's was wonderful about making a composite tape. I had gotten the Cobras' property sent back to Kansas City ZIP Code six-four-one-two-nine within forty-eight hours, and the whole process had been completed within seventy-two hours. Through all of this, my only fear was Hake would save his greatest special-teams play of all for his final game. He didn't.

* * * * *

Chesty's watch read four-fifty-two.

Returning northbound from Schiller's, he missed the light on Brentwood Boulevard at Maryland. Surprise! He made the light at Forsyth, so it was inevitable he would see amber go to red when he still was one-hundred-fifty feet short of Maryland. That's a given.

Hake wondered if he would – no, *hoped* he would – see that nasty but gorgeous blond bitch go gliding through the intersection. It's about that time of day, he said to himself. He lowered the windows despite the cold and reached for the pistol. Almost on cue, here came the white Fleetwood, westbound, picking up sped as the light changed.

* * * * *

A mental alarm went off for me. He had said, "bitch in a white Caddy." That had to be Sandi. He was going to shoot out her tire if he got the chance at Maryland and Brentwood, I was sure.

I was able to leave the paper earlier than expected, so I drove pell-mell west to Schiller's in Brentwood, then north much faster than I should've as I tried to intercept Chesty. God, I had to find him first, head him off.

After I passed from Brentwood into Richmond Heights and then into Clayton, I knew I had to make the light at Forsyth to avoid a ninety-second delay. I did. And there was Chesty, sitting northbound at Maryland.

I saw him lean out the right-side window of his Jaguar, pistol bare-ly showing. Almost on cue, here came Sandi's white Fleetwood, picking up speed as the light changed.

* * * * *

Our light changed from red to green. All I could think of to do was ram the Jaguar.

The silenced shot was like nothing else Hake had done.

According to the County Police crime scene people, it's seventy-two feet, two inches from the east crosswalk to the west crosswalk on Maryland at Brentwood. If the Cadillac had been going twenty-five down the gentle grade, then forty-five as the driver accelerated upon seeing the signal go from amber to red when she was well short of the east crosswalk, then the big car probably was traveling at about fifty-two when it reached the other side of the intersection – when it plunged through a lot of glass and brick and into the Prentiss Gallery.

I leapt from my car and raced diagonally across the intersection. Maybe I got halfway before the explosion. The heat of it overwhelmed me. The force of it sent me backward, smashing me into the pavement. I lay there, watching the flames, trying to get my brain working again, trying to get back into focus. But I was consumed by loss, and this massive, violent ache overpowered me.

I cried out. When you scream out a name in anguish – be it a real Sandy or a contrived Sandi – it doesn't matter how it's spelled. She was gone, and with her went the best part of me. That's when the primal anger kicked in, when my brain got to working, dragging me to my feet. How long it took me to get to my car I'll never know.

Sirens wailed against flickering flames and the first nudging crowds. My car engine was running – which was good – because, with my hands shaking, I probably couldn't have gotten it started. One glance in the rearview mirror: hair and eyebrows singed, the stink of fire on me. But no pain. The rage numbed all that. Everything now was about finding Chesty Hake. Right now, the Jag was gone. Chesty was gone.

I took a guess he'd made a right turn toward Meramec, so I did the same. I then went north to Pershing, away from the growing congestion, made a left and then a quick right back onto Brentwood Boulevard up to Kingsbury.

HUT-HUT was in the driveway instead of the garage, and that was all wrong. Was Chesty so shaky, after having killed someone, he couldn't get down the narrow drive back to the garage?

I parked at the curb. I would be leaving soon. As I got out of my car, the sirens four blocks south were singing something sinister.

I was more frightened than I ever had been, but rage had the edge. As I walked past his gold car, I glanced in and saw the FOLK MUSIC case on the right front seat. I opened the driver-side door, leaned in, and took the pistol. I tucked it into the pocket of my trench coat. Then I closed the door, very quietly, and walked to our front door. How many times have I asked myself why I didn't know the gun was where fine music like "We'll Sing In The Sunshine" should've been.

* * * * *

"Chesty!" I yelled up the staircase. My voice was different. I barely recognized it.

Hake appeared at the top of the stairs, holding a brown-wrapped parcel, which I assumed, was what he had picked up at Schiller's: his NFL history. Yes, he held what a pro football fan would consider a treasure, a true collectible, wrapped in brown paper and carefully taped.

He stood up there, five-foot-eight, but he towered there, staring down at me, wearing dark green slacks and a bulky white turtleneck. My fright, along with my rage, banged at me.

"Paul, I just killed someone."

New sirens joined the fray.

"She may have been a bitch, an inconsiderate bitch, but I shouldn't have killed her. I shouldn't have."

"Hake, you killed my *wife*!"

"Bullshit! Wife! Ex-wife! Whatever! That couldn't have been your ex-wife!"

"Yes, it was!"

I was sobbing.

"But you didn't do it alone, Hake. I helped. I was the one who banged your car – intentionally."

"You?"

The deep tuba-like honk of a fire engine's horn down at our corner told us a University City unit had been called out to help.

"Hake, my wife was two different people. She was a political climber and the wife of a big-time lawyer and a St. Louis County Councilman. But we were working through it, you jackoff. We were getting back together, whether she wanted to be Sandy or Sandi."

Hake just stood there, holding the small package: the best and worst of him. He held his life with both hands.

I could hear one ambulance, then a second, four blocks south. I could imagine what rush-hour traffic was like. The grandfather's clock in our dining room five-bonged the hour for us.

"Paul, I saw her car over at Salinsky's stamp shop this afternoon, and that's what set me off. How long have you known?"

"Ten minutes," I said. "Or the rest of my life. Take your pick."

"She was taking three parking spaces, and I-"

"Shit!"

"She was!"

"She was at Salinsy's to buy me a Christmas gift," I said, staring up at him and wondering whether or not I hated him. "She told me she was going to give me something no other woman would give me."

"Why the hell did she have to take three parking spaces?" Hake asked, words unreasonable, logic gone.

"Shut up!"

I never had yelled at Hake before.

"My wife's dead, Chesty," I said, looking up at him towering at the top of the staircase. I pulled out the pistol. "And I guess both of us have to admit our careers are over."

The pistol's next-to-last shot.

It pounded into all that muscle in the left pectoral area, making a red blood-dot on his sweater and not moving him much.

"Aw, Paulie," he said, his left hand out, a plea for forgiveness maybe.

The pistol's final mark.

The last shot picked Hake's nose. The slug, only about three-tenths of an inch in diameter, rose into and through his brain and exited the skull where Hake showed something of a bald spot. It bounced to a stop atop that beautifully sponge-painted blanket chest I had so proudly bought. I didn't know until much later that's where it landed, of course, but at least the cops didn't have to dig and poke into the walls of our beautiful home.

And here came Hake.

THUMP-THA-THUMP-THA-THUMP-THUMP-THA-THUMP!

He rumbled and tumbled and tumbled some more, almost with a rhythm as he came down the stairs. Strong as he had been, his neck was broken at some THA-THUMP down those fifteen stairs. When he reached the Oriental rug in the foyer, his shoulder blades and fanny pointed upwards, and so did his blank-eyed face. That huge neck had been yanked around a full one-hundred-eighty degrees. There was not so much as a twitch.

"What about our stamp collections, Chesty?" I said into the silence. "What about all those fucking stamps?"

I didn't freeze. But then, I didn't want to call the paper or the cops right then, either. And I didn't want to call the Kansas City Cobras. That would've opened up all kinds of story ideas and column ideas for the likes of Hank Mather. And I wasn't ready to call nine-one-one.

I felt relieved he was dead. Never to get up, never to come at me, those big shoulders hunched. I didn't want to die at his hands in that hallway. He was terribly strong, you see.

And all those sirens four blocks south – police cruisers, fire trucks, ambulances – continued.

With unreasonable care I really can't explain, I placed the pistol – still warm to the touch – on the newel cap above Hake's body.

Somehow, I felt the German-made gun had killed him; it was the gun, obviously. I hadn't done it. And then I realized I was afraid of myself, not of the gun.

But everything was in order in the front hallway of our house.

I went out the front door, leaving it unlocked, and walked to my car. I drove the nine miles downtown to the paper.

On my way in the side door of our five-story building, Elkins the security guard asked me what I was doing arriving there at "lunchtime" – six p.m. on many morning papers – in that I was supposed to have early slot in Sports the next day. I told him I had to write "A" copy: argot for biographical background on a prominent person who had died. In this case, the prominent person was one of the two people I loved.

"Say what?" Elkins chirped.

* * * * *

I was well into my first-person sidebar slugged CHESTY when I took a moment to call the St. Louis Metropolitan Police Department. This case was no nine-one-one emergency.

I had perhaps twenty-eight or twenty-nine grafs stored in my computer when the police arrived on the fourth floor and arrested me.

"It's good, solid stuff," I told the officers as I pointed to my computer screen.

I have no idea who wound up writing the page one stories that night. I assume I wasn't given byline credit for my sidebar, but that's just an assumption. And, as we know from Journalism one-oh-one, never assume.

* * * * *

What happened at the end? Hell, I don't know. I know my head was upturned as I struggled at my computer terminal, as I wrote my sidebar that could've been slugged CONFESSION instead of CHESTY. I always seemed to tilt my head upward when I was concentrating.

I asked myself: What did the crime scene look like? No, when you left the house, what were you thinking? I remember the word "phantasmagorical" sprang to mind as Hake thudded down the fifteen steps toward me, and I told myself I never had used "phantasmagorical" in a sentence, written or spoken, and probably never would.

Before the four cops took me away – including one jolly guy who was a former copy boy at the paper and seemed reluctant to twist my arms behind me for handcuffing – I wanted to verbalize what had happened. I opted away from "phantasmagorical."

"He was face-down, but his – his neck was broken. I could tell. That big neck! The body was – his head was face-up! He was kinda looking at me. That's how I knew he was dead. Maybe not the shots. There wasn't that much blood, really. But with – with his head turned around, that's how I knew he was dead. I killed him; I knew I had. His neck was broken."

"Just come with us, Paul," said Marler, the copy boy cop. "We'll leave your story in the computer here, and somebody'll find it. Somebody else'll write the lead story after we turn in our report."

"Thanks, Officer Marler," I said, reading his nametag. "I remember. You have very small hands, Jimmy."

"You have the right to remain silent," Officer Jim Marler said.

Fifty-Two

Consider: I killed my best friend after he killed my ex-wife and current lover. That's a page one story, right?

What might've been a really sensational trial was a bust. Murder trials usually get full media treatment in St. Louis County, but mine was much too short, too cut and dried to suit the paper and radio and TV stations that assigned battalions of reporters, technicians and producers to cover it. The courtroom was full every morning, but it didn't need to be.

Even with the *vois dire* jousting, my trial lasted only eight days. Circuit Judge Milton Royal knew what had to be done.

I opted for a public defender. She was Julie Clear, a sharp and incisive young attorney who probably would become a private-practice lawyer making a couple of hundred billable dollars an hour. She got no cooperation from me. For that, I hated myself. But she wanted to bring out that my skin is somewhat red and my father's family came to the Midwest along the Trail of Tears. I wouldn't allow that.

Then she wanted to use as a defense the stress created by daily dead-
lines, strange working hours, the newspaper environment. I refused.

In chambers, Julie Clear told Judge Milton Royal of my reluctance
to defend myself.

"What can I do, Your Honor? This is a big case for me – lots of
media people – and I don't know how to handle this guy. He's like
Tonto: no facial expression, no emotion, no nothin'," she said to the
white-haired jurist. "He keeps telling me he deserves the maximum."

"Honey, I'll make it quick and painless," said Royal. "You don't
need this. You don't deserve this."

"Thank you, Judge."

"But tell me, Miss Clear, doesn't it bother you you're going to
face me, a jury of Tenkiller's peers, a bevy of newspaper and magazine people, a horde of radio and TV types armed with microphones,
and a bunch of people who read nothing but the banner headline in
the paper each morning? Doesn't that bother you?"

She looked at the older man across his desk.

"Your Honor, it scares the shit out of me."

He paused, the way a jurist should.

"Julie, you won't get him off, but I'll bet you do a fine job."

Σ * * * *

She slammed the judge's door on her way back to Circuit Court
No. Three in the St. Louis County Government Center. Hell yes, she
had every right to be pissed at the judge and me.

I had told detectives of the Clayton Police Department – on videotape – I had intentionally killed Chesty Hake at Ninety-nine-oh-nine
Kingsbury Boulevard, Clayton, Missouri, with his own gun, which I
believed to be a weapon he didn't legally own. I told both detectives,
quite emphatically, the crime was carefully thought out, that I want-

ed his stamp collection and all those wonderful antiques. I told the detectives, both really nice guys, I knew a good deal about early American antiques and a great deal about U.S. stamps in mint or near-mint condition.

They were impressed. I had planned for some time to kill Hake, I told them, for still more reasons, including his relationship with Sara, which meant, if it went to fruition, I no longer would be living at Ninety-nine-oh-nine Kingsbury Boulevard. I told the cops I was a serious gambler and needed my twenty percent of Chesty's estate to support my habit. They were very interested in names like Smooth Watkins because my knowledge of those names proved to the cops I wasn't fantasizing about my gambling. They knew.

And I told those two Clayton cops Hake occasionally threatened me when I wasn't a proper servant, his houseboy.

I hated myself for that. Chesty never belittled me, and I was disgusted with myself when I said those words. But I knew what I had to do. The detectives knew what I was doing in admitting to murder, but they couldn't alter my plot. Julie Clear, a novice, didn't work very hard at getting to the truth when she talked with me.

Because I was charged with murder, I was transferred from downtown to the St. Louis County Jail and placed in a quiet, maximum-security cell. Because of the heinous nature of my alleged crime, I actually was treated better than those grunts who had held up convenience stores. But celebrity doesn't become me, I'm afraid.

J. Billy Wingo sent me word Chesty's body had been cremated, as he had stipulated in his will, after completion of the autopsy. The autopsy had shown a gunshot to the brain was the cause of death, not the tumble down the staircase.

I missed my best friend. He never scored a touchdown in the pros, but that's okay. I guess he did a good job of improving the driving habits of St. Louis Countians.

In my early edition of the paper, I read with interest in a second sidebar that tickets issued and vehicular accidents had been considerably reduced in several St. Louis County municipalities in recent months. Perhaps Chesty's ability to pop a Michelin with a silenced piston accomplished something more than snarling traffic.

Σ * * * *

And I miss Sandi – Sandi when we were recent lovers, just good ol' Sandy when she was my wife.

She may have been a high-handed, imperious bitch who played on her beauty and her second husband's power, but she utilized that power in her work with the homeless and the illiterate. She told me all about that last summer, at a local charity golf tournament – while we were making love in some dense woods on the thirteenth hole at Fair Oaks. I loved her when her name was Sandy and when her name was Sandi.

Thirteen years ago, when I headed off to the University of Missouri, I vowed I never would embarrass my family. Hell, I fully intended to win a Pulitzer Prize. How much has changed!

She's dead, and so is he. I probably should be. But I don't need a Trail of Tears, believe me. Just leave me alone and let me get through the appeals process quickly so I can write my Chesty Hake story without interruption. How about this:

Death Here on Life Row

I receive virtually no mail – and all of that's screened. But I got an interesting postcard the week after I moved here to Cementville, Missouri. It contained a poignant, incisive four-word message:

Paulie:

Your loss and mine.

Sara

END